Shenandoah Summer

Also by John Jaffe

THIEF OF WORDS

Shenandoah Summer

JOHN JAFFE

WARNER BOOKS

NEW YORK   BOSTON

Warner Books

Time Warner Book Group
1271 Avenue of the Americas, New York, NY 10020
Visit our Web site at www.twbookmark.com.

Printed in the United States of America

First Printing: August 2004
10 9 8 7 6 5 4 3 2 1

Library of Congress Cataloging-in-Publication Data
Jaffe, John.
    Shenandoah summer / John Jaffe.
       p. cm.
    ISBN 0-446-53154-5
    1. Shenandoah River Valley (Va. and W. Va.)—Fiction. 2. Artist colonies—
Fiction. 3. Married women—Fiction. 4. Virginia—Fiction. 5. Artists—Fiction.
6. Summer—Fiction. I. Title.
    PS3610.A364S54 2004
    813'.6—dc22   2004001674

To Terry Miller and John Fuller,
who prove home is where your friends are.

We would like to thank the following people:

Carla Golembe. She taught us not only how to draw, but how to see like an artist. Her beautiful paintings and passion for art inspired us.

Natalie Wolf. Her exuberant love for teaching drama to kids was the foundation of this book. Thank you for letting us cannibalize parts of your life.

Suny Monk and the Virginia Center of the Creative Arts. Limespring is an arts colony of our imagination. Our fellowship to the VCCA allowed us to imagine it.

Don Schofield, for his expertise in Greek dance and for the long walks and even longer talks about love, life, and poetry.

Laura Judkins, for sharing her accident experiences.

Betsy Parker, for sharing her vast equine knowledge.

Phyllis Richman, for, once again, reading as many drafts as we gave her.

Dr. John Davidson, entomology professor emeritus at the University of Maryland, for his glowworm help.

Ben and Sam Shepard, for being two great young men.

Esther Newberg, whose support provides welcome comfort in the tough world of publishing. And her always helpful and cheerful assistants, Andrea Barzvi and Christine Bauch.

Jamie Raab, for her terrific editing.

Tina Adreadis, for her publicity help.

The booksellers and readers who supported *Thief of Words*.

Shenandoah Summer

"The iron tongue of midnight hath told twelve:
Lovers, to bed; 'tis almost fairy time."

—*A Midsummer Night's Dream*

PROLOGUE

(1991)

There are four things Alyssa Brown knows for sure:

She'd kill to protect her family. On the eighth day God created Shakespeare. No matter how little she ate, she'd never get below 131 pounds. And there is such a thing as love at first sight.

She didn't know the last one until an early July day in 1991 when she stood in an overgrown grassy field in Markham, Virginia.

"This is it!" Alyssa spun around, startling the real estate agent as she flung her arms in a wide arc and declared her love. "No need to go any further, B.J. I'm going to make your job simple. I love it, I love it, I love it."

Darryl Brown, who hadn't even gotten out of B.J. Goode's Land Rover yet, looked at the clapboard tenant house with the faded yellow paint, four tiny windows, and cockeyed front steps. "Am I missing something here, Lissy? What exactly do you love about this dump?"

Alyssa walked back to the car, opened the door, took his hand, and said, "Come here, you have to see the herb garden and the little barn out back and the creaky porch swing."

Darryl scanned the view in front of him. "Lissy, I don't see anything but weeds, and this place doesn't even have a porch, let alone a porch swing."

She tugged on his arm. "Oh come on, you sourpuss, where's your imagination? We can make this place anything we want. That's the beauty of it."

"Okay, okay, calm down," Darryl said. "I think we should take a look around before we buy it, don't you? B.J., what's the story here?"

B.J., a woman in her fifties who wore earthy tweeds and spoke with the chiseled diction of Katharine Hepburn, went into high sales-pitch gear.

"It's a lovely property, isn't it? I showed it just yesterday to another young couple from Washington like yourselves."

Darryl rolled his eyes at Alyssa. She squeezed his hand and shot him a warning look. B.J. continued: "The house was built right after the Civil War. I'm certain you could list it on Virginia's historic house registry. It might need a little updating, but that's part of the charm, don't you think? And that view—well, what can I say? This is simply the best-sited property I've seen in quite a while. You should see it in the fall. The foothills over there turn the most spectacular colors. It's breathtaking, just breathtaking. You won't find a more suitable property in your price range. I've been in this business for thirty years . . ."

Alyssa left Darryl to the particulars as B.J. continued talking. She walked to the crooked front steps and sat down. She'd let her husband listen to the numbers; she knew what she saw. Stretching before her were miles of varying shades of green, all curving in and out of each other like Florentine paper. Blue-green fescue hay-fields rolled up against deep green forests that gave way to bright green pasturelands. She counted three red barns of neighboring farms and nearly two dozen black dots that were cows or horses. At the very farthest reach of her view, the muted outlines of the Blue Ridge Mountains zigzagged against the horizon, making a smoky violet border against a cloudless sky.

It was the kind of view she'd been imagining since she was a little girl looking out her bedroom window. Then, there'd only been the backs of red-brick row houses and an alley to see, but in her imagination there were hills and trees and mountains and horses.

Always there were horses. Horses for horse-crazy Alyssa, who every Sunday became cowgirl, trick rider, and grand champion aboard the plodding horses that filed, nose to tail, along the cobblestone streets of West Philadelphia into Fairmount Park. She'd clean stalls all day Saturday at Mike's Stables on Girard Avenue, just to get a chance to ride on Sunday.

It wasn't until ninth grade, when she stole the show singing "America" in the Beeber Junior High School production of *West Side Story*, that horse fever gave way to the stronger urge to perform. But even later, after college, during her brief New York fling with Off-Off, cafés, callbacks, and waitressing, she never completely lost her longing for the country.

For a while, the possibilities of New York were enough. Then on a bad day, after a bad week, when a callback didn't come and the tips were terrible at Eddie's and the sky was so gray it blended into the buildings, she saw the yellow ponytail of a passing girl and it reminded her of the flaxen tails she used to brush at Mike's. She was at the bottom of a chilly concrete canyon on West 36th Street. No place for a horse; no rolling pastureland; no big skies with long, clean views; no smell of green or sweat or speed.

Two months later she left the City.

A small black bird with yellow wings made a ruckus overhead. The air hummed with newly hatched summer bugs. A cow mooed in the distance. Alyssa leaned back on the step, took a deep breath, and exhaled. Her shoulders sank down, her spine rounded, her muscles softened. She felt wrapped in the strong arms of the surrounding hills.

This was the place she'd always imagined.

She looked over at her husband and B.J., who was motioning vividly with her hands, pointing here and there to various attributes of the property. Darryl had that expression, the same one he got when salespeople read labels to him.

"Hey B.J.," Alyssa called out, "what's that tree you're standing under with the crazy pink plumes? It looks like something out of Dr. Seuss."

B.J. glanced up. "It's a mimosa," she said.

"Mim-*mo*-sah," Alyssa repeated, as if it were an introduction. "Well, Ms. Mim-*mo*-sah, you're so beautiful, I'd marry you if I were a tree."

That silenced the real estate agent for a moment. But only a moment. She smiled wide, forced a little laugh, and said to Darryl, "Marrying a tree, that's a new one. Your wife has a wonderful imagination."

"That's putting it mildly," Darryl said, walking to Alyssa and putting an arm around her waist. "She's an actress, if you haven't figured that out yet."

Alyssa dipped her head against his shoulder. "Was an actress," she said. "That was twenty pounds and ten years ago. Now I teach drama to high school kids."

B.J. clapped her hands. "So you're in the arts. How perfect! You'll never believe what's just down the road—Limespring, the famous arts colony. It's filled with people of your ilk."

As B.J. turned toward the house, Alyssa looked at Darryl, twisted her face into a goofy expression, and mouthed, "Ilk?"

"Let's go inside, shall we?" B.J. said, fumbling with the lockbox on the front door. "Now remember, it may need a little updating."

The house didn't have central heat or kitchen cabinets; there was a hole in the bathroom floor; a colony of ladybugs blackened the back windows. "I've always wanted to learn how to plumb," Alyssa said, after Darryl pushed down on the toilet lever and nothing happened. "Maybe I could get a pair of jeans that slide halfway down my butt."

B.J. pretended not to hear and directed the couple back to her car. "I think we should take a look from the top of the hill in back of the house. That way I can point out the property lines."

They drove up through the pasture and stopped where the forest began. From there they could see miles of Fauquier County, Virginia. "Right now we're halfway up what locals call Mount Buck," B.J. said.

Alyssa looked down to the house below. A couple hundred yards to its left, a pond nudged up against two small hills. She pointed that way and said, "Is that part of this property?"

"Yes, the owner put the pond in himself. Lowers the home-owner's insurance, you know. It was stocked—"

"No, I mean the hills next to it. Those are on the property, too?"

B.J. nodded, and before she had a chance to talk about the virtues of hills, Alyssa announced, "Well then, if this is Mount Buck, then that's Mount Roz and the—"

Darryl took his wife's arm and led her out of B.J.'s earshot. "Alyssa, let's take it one step at a time, okay? You're already naming the mountains and I'm not even sure I want to do this."

She shook her arm free. "Not sure? You've been promising for years we'd do this, now you're not sure? We're living in a city because that's where you want to live. All I'm asking for is weekends and summers in the country. This place is a steal and you know it. I think we both deserve to be happy, don't you?"

Forty-five minutes later, B.J.'s Land Rover was headed back out the dirt road that had led them to the farm; Alyssa in the front seat, Darryl in the back. The only one talking was B.J.

"Stop for a second, please, B.J.," Alyssa said. It wasn't clear whether she meant talking or driving, but B.J. did both. Alyssa rolled down the window and looked out at the small yellow house with the red tin roof nestled in the hills behind her.

Quietly she said, "This is what I've wanted since I was four. It looks like home. Finally, a farm."

Part 1

CHAPTER 1

(June 1, 2003)

One year at Limespring a packet of letters, stored for decades in a metal box, was turned into a novel. Another time, the winged seeds of a sugar maple became the feathers of a fantastical bird of prey. A father's forgetfulness, originally fashioned into a cycle of poems, was later refashioned there, against all convention, into an exultant movie script.

Some people say Limespring is a magical place. So do some of the participants. And if you search, you can find the word "magical" attached to it in several magazine articles. But magic is a lazy word for what happens there; it's too easy, too abracadabra. People agonize at Limespring. They work all night on a single page and fall asleep as the rising sun warms the nearby Blue Ridge Mountains and touches the tops of the Shenandoahs beyond; they cry in frustration over the gap between imagination and the shape of clay.

And yet—though no one can say for sure when or where or why it works—there is a force at Limespring, a transformational power. How does a corn beetle become an eye in a famous face? At what point do words of regret begin to dance? Maybe what happens at Limespring is alchemy. If so, it's an alchemy that brews up its potions using the most commonplace of ingredients: hard work and hope; experience and inspiration; luck, liquor, laughter, passion; and love.

In fact, love most of all.

Alvin Dwight Palifax Jr. (mercifully nicknamed Tug since he was six years old) was thinking about none of these things as he turned onto Limespring Hollow Road and followed the signs to the Commonwealth of Virginia Shenandoah Center for Creativity at Limespring Farm (mercifully nicknamed Limespring) on a June first that just happened to be prettier and brighter than a new daffodil.

He wasn't thinking about creativity or love or inspiration or even the beauty of the Virginia countryside as his battered black station wagon rattled down the tree-lined road.

Tug was thinking about basketball. In particular, about the Soft Palettes, a team of alums from the Pratt Institute and gym rats from the Prospect Park YMCA. The Palettes had come in second last season in Brooklyn's Summer Y League, Division II. The buzz was that Stacey Deal, power forward for the Hot Wires—the division champs—had gotten a job in Arizona. Stacey had once played college ball at Seton Hall. If he were gone, and if Tug stayed for the summer, the Soft Palettes had a chance.

Shooting around before the Palettes' first practice, Tug broached this idea to Joel Feinblom—video artist, waiter, carpenter, best friend, and shooting guard.

Joel looked at Tug as if he'd just announced he'd become a Republican. "Are you out of your fucking mind?" he said. "Turn down Limespring? Do you know how many of us would kill for a summer there? Don't be an idiot. Besides, I'm tired of hearing about Leonardo and your midlife crisis. Go listen to the crickets for a while. Go smell the corn, or whatever it is people do in the country. This is your chance and you're going there if I have to take you myself. Don't worry about the Palettes—I'll send you a picture of the trophy."

Tug passed the ball out to Joel, who nailed a fourth straight three-pointer.

"Besides," Joel said, "if I keep shooting like this, we won't need you."

Tug grabbed the ball and held it. "Yeah, and who's gonna get the ball to you? I'm the only point guard we've got—and don't start talking to me about Ed, he's never gone left in his life."

Joel put his thumbs in his armpits and started flapping his bent arms. *"Cluck-cluck-cluck-cluck!"* he squawked. "Come on, man, we both know what this is all about. Stop being a chicken. It's a hell of a lot easier worrying about being great than actually trying for it. You think Leonardo sat around and whined about whether he could be a great artist? Just go. Maybe you'll find what you're looking for, maybe you won't. Maybe you'll give up art and become a lawyer."

Joel finished his little speech by swatting the ball out of Tug's grasp and making a drive to the basket. But Tug, timing it perfectly, leaped up and knocked Joel's layup attempt out of bounds.

"Oh, yeah!!" Tug shouted. He chased down the ball and dribbled it back to midcourt. "So, you don't think I'm completely crazy to go to Limespring?"

Joel guarded him halfheartedly as Tug took a shot beyond the foul line. It clanked off the side of the rim. "I didn't say that at all. I think you *are* completely crazy. You're showing around here; you're selling. You just got into that Houston gallery, for Christ sakes. It all seems pretty good from my perspective. But maybe when I'm your age, old man, and maybe if I ever sell anything, I'll have time to worry about the 'transcendence and validity' of my work. Until then, I'll just worry about whether anyone other than my mother ever sees it."

"Hey, punk, I may be old but I can take you any day of the week," said Tug, who was exactly one month older than Joel. He turned, shot, and missed again.

"Better keep your Pratt job, gramps," Joel said. "By the way, have you told Margaux yet?"

"Sure. She knows I'll be gone this summer."

"No. I mean the other thing. The 'Let's take a few steps back' thing."

"Not exactly."

Joel repeated the flapping motion with his arms. *"Cluck-cluck-cluck!"*

*   *   *

The road ended in a sunny clearing and a large sign that declared, in plain black script, "Limespring Art Center, Markham, Virginia." Tug pulled up and got out. Ahead of him, forty yards away, was a long, low wooden building with a wide covered porch neatly punctuated by four green Adirondack chairs. To his left was a gravel path that led to an area of lawn, big maple trees, and some aging cabins. Behind him was New York City and a life he wasn't sure of anymore.

He walked up the steps of the porch and knocked on a door marked "Office."

CHAPTER 2

Tug ran his hand down the neck of the horse. He closed his eyes and tried to imagine the muscle, bone, and tendons under the skin. He tried to feel what Leonardo da Vinci must have felt, to know what he had known before he transformed the shapes of a fifteenth-century horse into contour lines and crosshatchings and revealed the living engine underneath.

Tug stroked the animal's chest. All he felt was horsehide.

He opened his eyes. His drawing pad was covered in pencil sketches of horses and horse parts, mostly heads and legs. They were recognizably equine—in the way that a bottle of Boone's Farm is recognizably wine.

The horse stood behind a board fence. Except for white patches on its forehead and back legs, it was the rich brown color of a polished mahogany desk. Tug hadn't thought of horses as so big, with such massive necks and curves. This one seemed practically prehistoric, like some kind of extinct creature that shared the Ice Age with mastodons. He couldn't imagine having something this big for a pet.

Still, it seemed friendly enough. Yesterday the horse had wandered up to the fence, sniffed a couple of times, and then wandered off. Today Tug had brought a handful of carrots that he'd liberated from the relish plate at last night's dinner, thinking it might make the horse hang around the fence longer. It had worked, and now the horse nuzzled his empty hand looking for more.

After six days at Limespring, he'd established a routine. In the mornings he was outside sketching; he spent middays in his studio reworking the sketches and roughing out scenes; in the late afternoon he was back outside with the sketchpad. After dinner he'd return, at least briefly, to the studio.

His first subjects were close by: torn cabin screens, tree roots in Limespring Creek, the broken wing of a cicada. Then he explored the surrounding countryside, adding wooden barns, tractors, rock walls, and horses to his portfolio.

As a kid, Tug had drawn constantly—spaceships, cartoon characters, portraits, but mostly comic books. He'd come up with his own series starring Poundo Man, a superhero who could turn his arms into giant sledgehammers and batter the bad guys. He'd based Poundo Man on his father, Alvin Sr., who worked at the Mack factory, pounding metal into trucks.

But as a student at the Pratt Institute he became captivated by the movement and energy of kinetic sculpture. They were like comic books come to life. He studied ready-mades and collage and was inspired by the works of Man Ray, Kurt Schwitters, and Ed Kienholz. For the past fifteen years he had confined his drawing to schematics for installations or to sketch out suggestions at the sculpture classes he taught at the institute.

He wanted to start over at Limespring, so he began like an art school freshman. First he practiced gestural drawings with charcoal, the roughest of techniques. Without even looking at the sketchpad, he would try with just a few quick strokes and scribbles to make his hand capture the essence of what he was seeing. After a couple of days he began using pencils for more detailed renderings.

It was frustrating at times. He was out of shape, a couch potato training for a marathon. But he liked the straightforward challenge of representational art: find the fundamental geometry in nature, turn three dimensions into two, make it live again.

He also liked the easy pace of things at Limespring, though at first the nights made him restless. He had to go cold turkey in a cabin with no phone, no TV, and no computer. The constant chirping of crickets made him jittery. But by the fourth evening he began to enjoy the calm. The streetlightless dark nights felt cool and soothing to his eyes; the air seemed thicker and softer here, cushioning him against his doubts, absorbing his worries. Maybe it was a Zen acceptance—not that he knew much about Zen—or maybe a synchronization with country rhythms. Whatever it was, the drawing came more easily and he was asleep by ten.

What extra time he had, he spent with Abbi Bondi, a longtime friend from the City and a Limespring veteran. She'd been encouraging him to apply to Limespring for years, but he'd never felt the need for it until the previous fall, when Leonardo da Vinci came to the Metropolitan Museum of Art.

The exhibit, called "Leonardo da Vinci, Master Draftsman," was huge, nearly two hundred drawings—the biggest ever assembled in the United States. There were scores of faces and figures, studies of light falling on drapery, fantastic machines, buildings, and riders on rearing horses.

Tug had gone to the show on a Tuesday morning. It was late in the run and the blockbuster crowds had diminished. For years he'd praised da Vinci's compositions to students and recommended they copy them as drawing exercises. In his own student days he'd aped the master's *Head of the Virgin in Three-Quarter View* using five different mediums.

But when he met the drawings face-to-face, his world changed. Some of them seemed to spring from the parchment with photographic realism; some swirled with suggestive pen strokes. All were filled with motion and life. More motion and life and breath than all the paintings in all the Chelsea galleries put together. More than anything he'd ever produced himself. He stood for ten minutes before a sketch of the head of a soldier, simply studying the vitality of his mouth.

His favorite drawing was the least significant. It appeared on a page covered with studies for a heroic statue. All of the figures depicted knights atop charging stallions, except for one. At the bottom of the parchment was the sketch of a little horse looking down at a barking dog. It was little more than a doodle, but in sixty-three lines—Tug counted them—da Vinci had completely captured the horse's dignity and befuddlement.

That drawing reached out over five hundred years and grabbed Tug by the throat. It was utterly simple and charming. It was funny. It was genius.

He stared at the little horse and wished his father were there.

Alvin Dwight Palifax Sr. had died the year before at age fifty-seven from liver cancer. He had taken his illness as he took other misfortunes life had dealt him: with a shrug, a homily, and a joke. "Well, Tug, the Lord works in mysterious ways," he said when he got the diagnosis. "But I wish he'd let me in on the secret."

The cancer took six months to run its course. A horrible time in every way except that it gave the two of them time to say good-bye. Tug spent more time with his father in that half year than he had in the previous fifteen, and his father treated each of Tug's visits like a special occasion, as if he'd been blessed with a month of Thanksgivings.

He would pump Tug for details of his latest art project, then shake his head in mock bewilderment. "People in New York have more money than brains," he'd say. Or, "You know, Tug, if you put a tuxedo on a pig, it's still a pig." But he was proud of his son. He'd lined the back wall of the den in corkboard and covered it with newspaper clippings and magazine articles about Tug—along with pages and pages of Poundo Man.

Alvin Dwight Palifax Sr. took hard work for granted. Before he could drive, he was working weekends and after school at a nearby dairy farm. Through high school he worked the loading docks at Mack Trucks, and two weeks after graduation he started on the line, making body parts. Twenty-three years later, when the factory closed down, he became a tool-and-die man. He filled his weekends with chores and projects. When he could no longer punch a clock or putter around in his garage workshop, the end came quickly.

On Tug's next-to-last visit, his father was propped up on the living room couch. A college football game played on the TV with the sound off. Alvin Dwight Palifax Sr. tried to act as if he were just fighting a bad flu.

"You know, son," he said, "I've gotten really smart in the last few months."

"It's about time, Pop," said Tug.

"No. I'm serious," he said. "I know that I don't know a damn thing about your crazy art. Truth be told, I understood your comic books a whole lot better than those sculpture things you make. But I know they're important to you."

Tug's father looked toward the hall to make sure they were alone.

"I never thought I'd be saying this—and I don't want to say it too loud, because your mother'll kill me. She's already mad because I got this cancer. But you were right to go to art school. I'm glad you didn't listen to us. You wouldn't have been happy at that college in Pennsylvania. I know that now. Cancer has a way of smartening you up. I also know I couldn't be any happier about how you turned out."

Two weeks after Alvin Dwight Palifax Sr. died, Tug placed a sculpture on his father's grave. It was a figure of a man made from old machine parts. The inscription on it read: "Poundo Man, 1944–2001."

Tug looked at da Vinci's horse in the bottom corner of the page. This is what it's all about, Pop. Reaching out and touching someone with something you've created. Making them laugh or see things in a different way. I wish I could've shown you this exhibition. It might have helped you understand what I'm trying to do. But even if it hadn't, you sure would have liked this little horse.

After spending nearly four hours at the exhibit, Tug went back to the studio he shared with two other Pratt teachers. Even before he walked inside he knew what he'd find—a room full of three-dimensional projects looking far flatter and more lifeless than what he'd seen earlier that day. He picked up one of his conglomerations. It was the beginning of a torso made out of Slinkies.

Twenty-four hours before it had seemed clever and mildly subversive. Now it just seemed phony. There was no technique, no essence, and there sure as hell wasn't any genius.

For a moment, he considered smashing it up. But the gesture seemed as phony as the art. He put it down and called Abbi. "Hey, sweets," he said when she answered. "Can I come over? I want to know more about that arts colony you've been trying to get me to go to."

In his fellowship application, he'd written that he wanted to "burn everything away until only the stroke of the pencil was left." It was more than a phrase to catch the selection committee's eye. He needed simplicity, he needed to start from the beginning. He needed sixty-three great lines.

The mahogany horse, bored with the carrotless artist, walked away, stopping now and then to crop tufts of grass. Tug leaned on the fence trying to capture the ovals that defined the horse's haunches. Later, on the same page, he drew the curves of the meadow and the shadows that bounded it.

He sketched until the shadows took over, then closed up the pad and walked hurriedly back to Limespring. Dinner was at seven and Jackie Burke, the director, had told everyone not to be late because they had a special guest.

CHAPTER 3

"Who's the blond?" Tug elbowed Abbi and nodded toward the dining room table where Jackie was sitting. Across from her was a woman with chin-length hair the color of butter. She was wearing blue shorts and a red T-shirt imprinted with the image of a windmill and the word "Oklahoma!" swooshing across in dramatic black letters.

"Down, boy," said Abbi. "That blond's married. Besides, you have a girlfriend, remember?"

Tug leaned back in his chair and held up his hands in surrender. "Just wondering who the new face is, that's all."

Abbi rolled her eyes. "Right. And I believe in the tooth fairy."

The butter blond was telling a story to the six others at Jackie's table. Her hands cut through the air as she talked, in a swooping, slicing language of their own, her face a gallery of expressions.

With his renewed sensitivity to shapes, Tug noted her combination of hard angles and soft curves. She had a short, sharp nose but rounded cheeks and full lips. Her jawline curved smoothly, while her chin was punctuated by a crooked dimple. Her thick, wavy hair bounced as she moved around.

As Tug watched, she got up halfway out of her chair, plopped back down, and made an extravagant wave with both arms. Her audience exploded with laughter.

"So, who did you say she was?" asked Tug. "And how do you know she's married?"

"Her name's Alyssa Brown," said Abbi. "She lives right down the road. I've known her for years. She's a drama teacher and every—"

Abbi stopped as Jackie rose from her chair and began clinking a fork against her glass to get the room's attention. It wasn't easy. The group was a rowdy one, full of noise. Almost half of the "Limeys," as the fellows were called, were returning veterans, and three of them, Abbi included, had been coming each June for years. As a result, mealtimes seemed more like summer camp than arts colony, stopping just short of food fights. When the twenty-seven painters, sculptors, writers, composers, fabric artists, and lone filmmaker realized what Jackie was trying to do they started chanting, "Jack-*ee*, Jack-*ee*, Jack-*ee* . . ."

Since the first day of the summer session, they'd chanted her name every time she stood to make an announcement during the dinner hour. As usual, she turned red, which contrasted sharply with the cloud of white hair that fluffed around her face and made her look like a peppermint candy stick. She coughed, cleared her throat, and waited for them to settle down.

The spring session Limeys had been completely different. They'd stuck to their cabins and studios, emerging only for meals—if that. They had been loners with little camaraderie. Even the nightly after-dinner get-togethers that Limespring was known for—where fellows read from that day's work or showed paintings in progress—were awkward sessions that ended quickly.

Not this group. And for that, Jackie was thankful. She looked forward to the summer Limeys all year. The central core was like a family, though they were generous enough to invite first-timers into the clan.

The social director of the little subset was thirty-eight-year-old Abbi, a writing teacher at City College in New York. She'd first come to Limespring nine years ago with twenty pages of a new novel that was a modernization of the *Arabian Nights*. Abbi had transformed poor fishermen into street vendors; her genies were

Armenian rug sellers; Scheherazade was a high-class prostitute in the thrall of a drug lord. She'd written 679 pages since her first summer at Limespring yet had hardly put a dent into the thousand and one nights.

Abbi was slender, with wispy brown hair, an assertive nose she'd inherited from the Levinsky side of her family, and eyes as dark as Kalamata olives. Her left eyebrow always seemed arched in a perpetual parenthesis of irony. That night, sitting next to Tug, she wore her usual outfit—a long skirt in the purple family, black tank top, flip-flops, and earrings with dangling stars and moons.

If Abbi was the social director, then Marius Rheiner was the group's court jester and mad scientist. In 1964, the twenty-year-old Marius had left his native Bohemia, in western Czechoslovakia, crossed the Iron Curtain, and eventually emigrated to the United States. He had Falstaffian dimensions and a voice that filled the room. "I'm the only real Bohemian artist in Limespring," he'd say to newcomers. Unruly tufts of faded blond hair stuck out from his temples like handles; a perpetual three-day stubble of coarse white hairs made his face seem dipped in sand.

Marius had studied engineering in East Germany but for thirty years had been a sculptor of kinetics, a molder of motion. The previous summer, he'd installed *Cohesive Particles of the Meanderer, No. 37* in the grassy field next to Limespring's dairy barn/art studio. For *No. 37*, he'd welded a motorized mixing blade inside a huge oil drum, then filled the tank with a concoction of liquid and metal flakes. When the mixing blade was turned on, it churned and spun everything so that it looked like a vat of molten fairy dust.

Marius was sitting at the table with Jackie Burke and the woman with the butter-colored hair. Next to him sat Nattie Gold, the third member of the summer regulars. Marius and Nattie were best friends, though some said there was more to it than that. Limespring's longtime housekeeper Cora Beeson told Abbi—and anyone else who'd listen—that she'd seen Nattie and Marius walk hand in hand into the maze of giant boxwoods the previous summer and not come out for forty-five minutes.

Regardless of the nature of their relationship—Marius was married, Nattie divorced—they looked like Mutt and Jeff walking around together. She was as short as he was tall, and as wiry as he was stout. At fifty-three, her long red hair had whitened at the temples, and the sprays of freckles across her arms, legs, and cheeks had fused into faint amber planes.

She'd been a newspaper reporter in North Carolina, but a weekend art project—laying a mosaic in the entryway of a friend's mountain cabin—had turned into a calling. Seven years before, she had given up ink for shattered tiles and become a professional mosaic artist. At first she filled in the financial gaps with her savings account. But in less than two years she'd laid so many floors that she was adding to rather than subtracting from her passbook.

"Okay, everybody," Jackie said as the chanting subsided. "I have a couple of announcements and then I want to introduce you to a very special guest. First, Limespring is proud to announce that Jeremy Ring, our very own photographer/choreographer, who was a fellow two years ago, has been awarded one of those MacArthur genius grants."

There was a brief swell of applause, during which Marius whispered to Nattie, "Ring's a genius for appearing to be a genius."

"And second," said Jackie, "we've been having a terrible problem with ants in the silo studio, so please, please, don't take food there while you're working. Let's confine our snacking to the dairy barn kitchen."

This announcement received a burst of boos and then laughter. Snacking and napping were considered inalienable rights in Limespring's studios.

"And finally, next to me is the real reason I'm standing up here making a fool of myself," said Jackie. "Those of you who are veterans, know her as Limespring's brilliant and beautiful adjunct professor of drama. To those of you who are new here, she's still Limespring's brilliant and beautiful adjunct professor of drama. In any event, and without further ado, here's Alyssa Brown."

This brought heartfelt applause, amplified by the Limespring veterans and led by Marius, who shouted out, "Hail, Penelope!"

The blond adjunct professor stood up and responded to the outburst by curtseying as if she were meeting the Queen, then blowing the big man a stage kiss across their table.

CHAPTER 4

Alyssa looked across the familiar dining room with its log-beamed ceiling, pine-paneled walls, worn green linoleum floors, and round tables covered in bright oilcloth. So little had changed in the nine years she'd been doing the Follies at Limespring, including many of the faces. She'd started coming the same year Jackie took over as director, which was Abbi's first year, too. Marius and Nattie had arrived the following summer.

They'd become her second family, and a lifeline of sorts. When she'd volunteered to come up with "a skit or something" for Limespring's annual solstice party, she had needed something to help blot out the pain. The Follies were born and it became a welcome distraction.

In the years that followed, her Limespring friendships had reached well beyond the summers. She and Abbi e-mailed and telephoned regularly, and there was an open invitation to any of them who came through Washington to stay at her house.

"Hello, everybody," she said. "I don't know about the 'brilliant and beautiful' part, but I am in fact Alyssa Brown, as many of you already know. And, also as many of you know, I live in D.C. during the school year, where I teach drama and direct productions at the Emerson School. Summers, however, I live here; just down the road in that little yellow house with the begging horses out front.

Let me warn you—if you feed them, they will follow you around forever.

"Anyway, for the past nine summers I've organized the play that caps off Limespring's annual summer solstice party. We call it the 'Limespring Follies.' And you," Alyssa said, sweeping her arm around the room, "are the stars."

She tilted her head, pausing just long enough for dramatic effect, but not enough for anyone to groan, and then added, "Don't worry, it's completely voluntary and it's completely silly. In fact, calling it a 'play' is probably making Shakespeare spin in his grave right now."

"Trust me," blurted Marius, "the Follies are to Shakespeare what a bar fight is to Gettysburg."

Marius's remark got a laugh from the crowd and Alyssa, too. "And Marius should know," she said. "He played Odysseus in last year's production of the *Odyssey*. To give you newcomers an idea of how the Follies work, we reduced Homer's entire epic—Cyclops, sirens, shipwrecks, angry gods, bloody revenge—into forty-seven ridiculous minutes. And I think everyone will agree that the highlight of the show was when the five evil suitors sang a chorus of 'I'm a Believer' with fake arrows through their heads."

This brought more applause and a refrain of "I'm a Believer" from one of the suitors, a balding composer from Michigan.

"This year," said Alyssa after the noise subsided, "we're doing a similar disservice to the *Arabian Nights* in honor of Limespring's own Abbi Bondi." She pointed toward Abbi's table.

"As some of you may know, Abbi has a novel, a work in progress that's based on *The Thousand and One Nights*, and she's graciously taken time out from it to write the script for this year's Follies. Thank you, Abbi."

More applause. Alyssa saw the man sitting next to Abbi whisper something in her ear. Abbi gave him a playful slap on the cheek; he returned a conspiratorial smile. New boyfriend? He didn't seem her type. Abbi went for intense intellectuals with pale skin and complicated faces. They were usually tall and reedy and looked like vampires. This one had bulky shoulders, wide planes on his face, and a big, easy smile. He didn't have dark circles under his eyes and he actually had a bit of a tan. The last time she'd talked to Abbi, she was seeing a novelist named William. This guy looked more rugby player than writer.

Alyssa continued to explain the project, listing the roles that needed to be filled—she offered to play Scheherazade if no one else wanted to—and the props that had to be made. Central to this summer's Follies was a giant genie bottle. She asked for volunteers to see her after dinner, then sat down to dessert.

It was banana pudding. Her favorite. Jackie had ordered it specially for her; she did it every year. She spooned up a big mouthful and moaned. "Okay, Jackie, this is the last time," she said. "I'm putting it in my contract, no more banana pudding when I'm here. I'm already deep into my fat clothes."

Across the table, Marius raised his wineglass. "I propose a toast. That Alyssa eat banana pudding the rest of her life and that all women should have curves like her."

There was a chorus of "hear, hear" and a hearty "amen" from Jackie, a perpetual dieter. Alyssa smiled and dug in. The last time she'd really cared enough about her weight to do something—the Atkins diet—was right before her audition for a *Little Shop of Horrors* at the Orpheum Theatre in 1982. She didn't get the part, but she lost seven pounds in ten days and her appetite for bacon.

Sure, she'd like to be fifteen pounds lighter, but she'd like to be fifteen years younger, too. The likelihood of either was about the same.

The conversations swirled around her and, parched for the sound of adults after the long school year, Alyssa drank them up. Jackie and Marius began planning a group canoe trip on the nearby Shenandoah River, then got off on a tangent about the Hudson River school of painters; a novelist and a collagist were talking about the rise of reality TV; Nattie wanted to discuss the *West Side Story* revival on Broadway. Nothing about grades, or dress codes, or the latest atrocity the new headmistress had committed. No teenage gossip about who's breaking up and who's "doing it." Another reason to love summer vacation.

Alyssa was happily starting to expound on Sondheim's lyrics when she glanced over at the adjacent table and saw Abbi huddled with the man she'd slapped on the cheek. Well, she thought, maybe a little Limespring gossip would be okay.

"Who's the jock with Abbi?" she asked Nattie. "Her latest? What happened to the guy who wrote novels about an elevator operator?"

"Oh, William's still in the picture," said Nattie. "I wouldn't be surprised if they actually get married someday. No, this guy's just a friend. At least now he is. I think they had something going years ago."

"Writer?" Alyssa said, taking the last spoonful of pudding.

Nattie looked over at Abbi and Tug. "Nope. Sculptor. Kind of. Urban art collages. You know, piles of toilet seats, empty window frames—that sort of stuff. He's pretty well-known in New York. The art magazines call him 'the Junkman.' He's kinda cute, in a jock sort of way. I bet he's terrific in the sack."

Alyssa laughed. "That's beyond my field of expertise. I always went for the brainy ones."

Nattie gave her a curious look. "Well . . ." she said and paused, "there's something to be said for smarts." Then she tipped back on her chair to get another look at Tug. "Wish I were ten years younger."

CHAPTER 5

Later that night, Alyssa leaned on the porch railing and looked out over the fields of Finally Farm. A three-quarters moon had turned them a silvery gray, and the opalescent light refracted through the slatted leaves of the big mimosa, dappling her like an Appaloosa's rump.

She was wearing just a T-shirt and even that was too much. The crimped cotton pressed damply into her underarms; a bead of sweat rolled down the channel of her back. It was too early in the summer to be this hot. When a timid breeze edged down the hollow, she turned and let it try to cool down her damp skin.

Mr. Ed, she'd said to him. *Mr. Ed!* The memory giggled up from the farcical lobe of her brain and she almost laughed out loud. He'd been pretty gracious about the insult, she had to give him that.

It had happened after dinner. Nearly half the Limeys came to her table to volunteer for the Follies and it turned out that Abbi's friend—what kind of a name was Tug?—had experience building sets for an experimental performance troupe in Brooklyn. "I'll build or design or act, whatever you need," he'd said.

She liked his enthusiasm. The Follies always went better when there was at least one dynamo fellow involved.

After Alyssa had handed out assignments and rehearsal sched-ules, she'd taken the building crew—Abbi and Nattie, Tug, and three other first-timers—over to the old hay barn to survey the props from previous productions.

"We take recycling to its most ridiculous extremes," she'd said. "One year we used hubcaps for shields in *Macbeth*, or, as we called it, 'Big Mac.'"

She watched Tug charge through the stacks and could see why he was called the Junkman. He rummaged quickly through piles of castoffs, seeing possibilities in pieces of broken sets that even she hadn't considered: half a stairway from *No Exit*, a rusted bedframe from *Metamorphosis*, the battered head of a papier-mâché snake from *Cleopatra*, and the back end of a rowboat from the *Odyssey*.

Looking up from his stack of reclaimed junk, he'd flashed a smile and said, "All I need now is twelve-gauge wire and I'll build you Arabia."

Alyssa knew that smile. She'd seen it a thousand times on the face of the charming smart-ass in the back of the class, the one who forced you to laugh in spite of yourself. It was a bad-boy grin that said, "We both know I'm clever and cute," and made you complicit in its sly conspiracy.

Alyssa smiled back at him. I know your type, Mr. Junkman, she thought. I bet you've got a girl in every gallery.

They added a few more items to Tug's stack, worked out a prop checklist, and then walked across the grassy courtyard to the studios. Nattie had seen some drop cloths there and thought they might work for backdrops.

The studios were empty that evening, so the group could ignore the strict no-talking-no-humming-not-even-any-loud-breathing rule that was usually in force. Most of the studios opened onto a central common area called the Square. Scattered about it were three bulletin boards on rollers and four long tables. Nattie stopped by one of the tables and pointed to an assemblage of red plastic straws melted into what looked like a human brain.

"This isn't yours, is it, Tug?" she said.

"Sorry, can't claim it," he said.

"That's a relief," said Nattie. "What do you suppose it's trying to be, anyway?"

"I know, I know," said one of the newcomers, an essayist from Wisconsin, waving his hand like a first-grader with the answer. "How about *This Is Your Brain on Slurpees?*"

"More like *Brain Drain*," Abbi said to the group's guilty laughter.

"Then maybe they should call these *They Shoot Horses, Don't They?*" Alyssa had wandered over to one of the bulletin boards and was examining a series of sketches. "I'll bet the closest this person's ever been to a horse is watching *Mr. Ed.*"

Abbi burst out laughing. "Well, why don't we ask him? Oh Tuuuug, been watching *Mr. Ed* reruns lately?"

Alyssa looked from Tug to Abbi and back to Tug. Her face flashed red, but she kept her composure. "How about if I open my mouth wider for the other foot?" she said. "Sorry, I thought you were a sculptor."

Tug put his hand on Alyssa's shoulder. "Don't worry about it. I've had worse reviews than that—and a lot less accurate. You're right, they're pretty terrible. I've been sketching these damn horses for days and they still look like big dogs."

Nattie had walked over to look at the drawings. "What's with the horses, Tug? I thought you did that assembled stuff."

"I did. I do, but I've been a little dissatisfied lately."

"A *little* dissatisfied?" said Abbi in a mocking voice.

"Okay, okay, 'a little dissatisfied' might be an understatement. So I had a major breakdown and almost threw myself into the East River after I saw the da Vinci show at the Met last fall. I needed to get away from what I was doing. Away from New York, the galleries, the assemblages, everything. I needed to go back to the beginning—drawing."

He beamed that smile, this time straight at Alyssa. "I'm like a caveman and Limespring is my Lascaux."

It was straight flirtation, no chaser. She stared right back at him and said, "So you started with horses because there weren't any mammoths around?"

"Not exactly." He hoisted himself onto a table and told them about his epiphany at the Metropolitan Museum of Art, leaving out nothing except the part about his father.

"Da Vinci was so much more than a master draftsman. He captured their souls, their essence, their, their . . . utter horsiness."

"Is that a technical art term you learned at Pratt?" said Abbi.

The laughter that followed didn't diminish Tug's fervor. He continued talking about the drawings with the passion of an environmentalist defending the giant redwoods. Then he shrugged his shoulders and said, "Anyway, that's what led me here—chasing the ghost of Leonardo da Vinci and massacring it. I've spent hours watching those damn horses, but I just can't see them."

That's when Abbi had sprung her plan. She slipped an arm through Tug's and nodded toward Alyssa. "The answer to your problem's standing right there. You want to really *see* horses? Spend a few hours with Lissy. By the time you're finished, you'll be drawing them from the inside out. She knows more about them than anybody could possibly care. And this way, she'll actually have an interested audience when she warps off into equine land."

Alyssa had to admit it was true. She'd watched many of her friends' eyes glaze over when she started talking about horses. She loved everything about them. Their briny smell, the way her arms fit into the small dip between their chest and neck when she hugged them, the metronomic grinding of their teeth as they pulverized hay and grain into liquid. Some days she sat outside their stalls and listened as they ate.

Tug tilted his head. "What do you think?"

Alyssa smiled and said, "Sure."

And so it was set, Tug's first horse lesson at Finally Farm. The next morning at nine.

The breeze had died down. Alyssa flapped her T-shirt a few times, but that only moved a few beads of sweat down her body. She didn't care. After nine months of occasional farm weekends, she was here for good. Or so it seemed from the vantage point of the first week of summer vacation.

She closed her eyes and slowly inhaled. The farm's June smell was as layered as a Middle Eastern spice market. The pungent fragrance of first-cut hay floated atop the insistent smell of manure and damp ground. There were grace notes of something sweet, maybe honeysuckle or maybe even the last spring hyacinth that hadn't shed its frilly blossoms yet.

She opened her eyes just in time to see the lights of Dr. Holland's truck as it turned off Limespring Hollow Road into his driveway. In a few seconds the lights disappeared and she was left alone with the moon and the smells and the nightly chorus of cicadas, peepers peeping by the pond, the occasional nicker of horses, a cow grunting.

She scratched the soles of her bare feet against the edge of a porch plank, then turned and walked into the dark bedroom. She pulled back the sheet and lay on her back; an overhead fan stirred the air and cooled her face. Already she could feel the change coming. The rest of the world was beginning to drain away. She closed her eyes. I'm back, she thought.

Then she laughed, out loud this time. "Mr. Ed."

CHAPTER 6

The next morning, Alyssa was in the kitchen making coffee when the phone rang. For a second she thought it might be Roz calling from Chicago. Her daughter was interning there, at her uncle's architectural firm.

Though Roz had left less than a week ago, Alyssa already missed her and wanted to hear her voice. But she had promised that she wouldn't keep calling as if Roz were still a kid. "I'm grown, Mom. Face it," Roz had said.

But Roz never called until after nine at night when it was free on her cell phone. And it was too early to be Darryl. He was in California. He'd been there nearly a week preparing for a project at a sister facility. He was coming home in a few days, but would go back for most of July and August. They'd discussed her going out with him. But they both knew she wouldn't give up a summer at the farm.

"Hi, it's me, any cuties I should start losing weight for?" the voice on the other end of the phone said. It was Carol Richman, a friend and fellow teacher at Emerson. She always called the morning after Alyssa met the new crop of summer fellows. Carol was Emerson's art teacher and designed the sets for Alyssa's school productions. She wanted to know who the Limespring artists were, what they were working on, and if any of them were single, cute, and straight.

In the four years Alyssa had known her, Carol had talked many times about applying for a fellowship. But she could never bring enough order into her life to complete the application.

"Hey there, Carol," Alyssa said. "There's a couple new ones mixed in with the usual returnees. You know—Nattie, Abbi, Marius . . ." Carol had met them all before at Alyssa and Darryl's annual July Fourth party.

"As for the cuties, hmm, let's see, there's a painter from Florida who does tropical landscapes. But if I had to guess, I'd say he was gay. There's also a sculptor who does assemblages but really wants to draw. I'm sure he's straight. His name's Tug, of all things. He's been drawing—well, that's a generous word for it—he's been trying to draw my horses and wants to come here for 'horse lessons.' Funny, huh?"

They continued to talk about the fellows and the Follies until Carol interrupted. "So how about this Tug guy, anyway? Is he someone I might want to meet on the Fourth of July? What's he look like?"

"A rugby player. Maybe a little like Jeff Bridges—not as handsome, but hearty in that midwestern 'Yes, ma'am' kind of way. Like he stepped off the stage from *Oklahoma!* Nattie told me he and Abbi had a thing going years back. I'd be happy to vet him out for you, but if you ask me, he looks like trouble. He's got one of those Sam Isaac smiles."

They laughed. Sam Isaac was the teen heartthrob at Emerson. According to the gossip, he'd already sampled the delights of half the girls in the eleventh and twelfth grades and was working through the tenth grade.

"That's the last thing I need after Nick," Carol said.

Alyssa knew all about Nick and all the other Nicks who'd preceded him. Carol had been through at least five boyfriends in the time Alyssa had known her. When Alyssa and Carol talked, their conversation usually bounced between two topics: Carol's love life and the latest controversy involving Emerson's new headmistress, Justine Shriker.

The Shrike, as everyone called her behind her back, was an autocrat with a tight Texas accent and a closet full of angular black-and-red blazers. She prefaced all criticisms (and there were plenty) with a pinched face and the words, "Thank you for your comment," and then went on to filibuster for forty minutes, disregarding the question.

Alyssa didn't like her any better than Carol did. She'd already been through five headmasters during her twelve years at Emerson and was hoping the Shrike would have an even briefer shelf life than the others. But she was afraid that even two years under the new regime would change Emerson into a place she didn't know or like. The school had always been one of Washington's more progressive, filled with creative kids and edgy parents. She'd taken the job as drama director for that reason. She could stretch as far as she wanted at Emerson, and the kids, parents, and administration would be right there with her, pushing her even further outside the box.

But the Shrike liked to stay inside the box. Under her rigid new rules, Emerson was becoming more and more like a military school. In January, Alyssa had been told she couldn't stage *The Runner Stumbles* because of its "risqué" content. "I'm sorry," the Shrike had said, "but a play about a priest's affair is not the kind of message we want to be sending to the Emerson community." Alyssa almost quit on the spot, but Roz still had another six months to go there and they could never afford the tuition without the faculty price break.

"So has she declared herself empress yet?" Alyssa asked. Both of them knew who she was referring to. "Or let me guess, she's going to make the kids wear uniforms?"

Carol screamed into the phone. "Oh my God, are you psychic or what?" And she launched into a tirade. For the next five minutes, she revisited all the horrible things the woman from Texas had done to their school—censored the valedictorian's graduation speech, expelled four students for posting a letter protesting the graduation speech censorship, abolished the students' right to call teachers by their first names, caused the resignation of four administrators and nine teachers, one of whom was the county's teacher of the year. She'd created such turmoil that the kindergarten and elementary teachers had boycotted her Christmas party.

"I mean, think what you have to do to piss off *kindergarten teachers*," Carol said. "They're, like, the nicest people in the world."

Hearing about the new regime made Alyssa feel sad. Justine Shriker had spent her first year dismantling the old, quirky Emerson and rebuilding it into a place she hardly recognized. And not just figuratively. The campus was a fourteen-acre oasis of green in the middle of dense subdivisions. Yet by May it was lined with new and formidable fencing. The lot where parents and students had parked was cordoned off and peppered with crisp black, white, and red signs announcing, "Tow-away zone. School Administration only."

In the middle of rehearsals for the spring musical, *Cinderella*, Alyssa had found half her prop room emptied, caged off, and locked—to be used to store 15,000 granola bars in case of emergency. The prince and one of the ugly stepsisters had climbed into the cage and laid out a dummy on the floor next to a sign that read, "This is where we put bad children."

The headmistress had summoned Alyssa to her office and demanded to know who'd broken into the new storage area. Alyssa had lied. "I have no idea," she'd said. A lecture about the need for more discipline followed, and when Alyssa tried to tell the Shrike about Emerson's traditionally liberal background, where such pranks would have been laughed at in the past, she'd been cut off in midsentence.

"You are never to use that word again," Justine Shriker had said. "There is no more 'traditionally' at Emerson. We are all starting from scratch, including you."

Alyssa was ready to send out résumés, but Carol had talked her out of it. "She'll be gone in a year. Besides, you can't leave me there alone with her."

Teaching at Emerson had been the only good thing about living in Washington. Now that was in jeopardy, thanks to the

Shrike. Alyssa was tired of thinking about it. There was nothing she could do to stop the woman. And she refused to let the new headmistress invade her summer anymore.

It was a few minutes before nine. Abbi's sculptor friend would be there soon to learn about horses. A knock on the door would be the perfect excuse to get off the phone.

CHAPTER 7

Though he'd been wandering around Limespring for almost a week, he'd never noticed the little yellow farmhouse tucked up against the hills at the end of the dirt drive. It was painted a sunny gold and had a red tin roof; the trim was the kind of green you sometimes see in mountain lakes. Tug liked it from a distance and even more up close.

The night before, after the *Mr. Ed* comedy, Abbi had told him Alyssa's farm had "serious charm" but refused to say more so as not to "ruin the surprise." By the time Tug reached the front door he knew what she meant. The walkway to the house was an amalgam of stepping-stones, sunken pool balls with their numbers facing up, odd bits of hardware—spigot tops, rivets, barn-door hinges—and a frieze of plastic action figurines set into silly poses. G.I. Joe held hands with Barbie; Gumby rode Raphael the Teenage Mutant Ninja Turtle; Trigger took a bow. Near the front door, a centaur whirligig kicked out in the breeze.

In her usual talkative mood, Abbi had told him much more about the owner than her farm. He'd heard all about Alyssa's acting days in New York. She'd made it to the final cut for *Les Misérables*; she was the Jergens "take me away" woman in the television commercial; she'd been a prostitute on *NYPD Blue*; she'd been a singer on *Sesame Street*. Abbi had also told him about

Alyssa's passion for teaching. "She's the only person in the world who actually likes teenagers."

Tug had already seen for himself that Alyssa was bright and funny and attractive. Plus he liked her convex lines. The women he knew in New York were as hard-edged and angular as Italian eyeglass frames; Alyssa curled and curved.

Abbi also filled in the details about Alyssa's split life between Washington, D.C., and Virginia, how she'd been trying for years to get her husband to move to their farm full-time, but he wouldn't budge.

"A smart guy," said Abbi about Alyssa's husband. "But a joyless twit. And boooooring. This guy could put an insurance salesman to sleep."

He was, according to Abbi, a scientist of some kind who disliked the country. "Every time I see Darryl at the farm," she said, "he's vacuuming up the ladybugs. As far as I can tell, that's all he does there."

Tug was thinking about ladybugs, wondering whether there were such things as gentlemanbugs, when he reached for the door knocker absentmindedly. Then he realized it was a kid's toolbox hammer tied to a hook. When Alyssa answered the door, Tug had a grin on his face and an orange plastic handle in his hand.

She was wearing a purple shirt, blue shorts, and red clogs. Between that and her yellow hair, Tug hadn't seen so much color on a female since he'd left home and moved to the land of women in black.

She took the hammer from him and hung it back on the door. "My daughter's idea," she said and smiled back at him. "So, you're here to learn about horses. Want to start with *Mr. Ed* reruns?" She didn't wait for an answer, just shook her head and rolled her eyes. "I can't believe I actually said that. Sure there's no hard feelings?"

"Well, maybe a few," Tug said. "But show me around and I'll forgive you. Abbi told me your farm had 'serious charm.' I see what she means."

He was flashing that bad-boy smile again. She found herself smiling right back—and enjoying it more than she'd expected. It was a lot more fun volleying smiles with someone who looked like Tug than a gawky teenager who thought he was hot.

"I don't know about charm, serious or otherwise," Alyssa said. "But I do know that I love everything about this place. Even the bugs. Follow me."

She ushered him in and started the tour. The walkway, it turned out, was only a prelude to the eccentricities inside. To his immediate right was a small bathroom tucked under a flight of stairs. The walls were the color of sweet potatoes, the trim edged in deep ruby. On the floor was a tile mosaic of a horse's head encircled by a horseshoe made from flattened copper tubing and marbles for the nails. Underneath it said, "Finally Farm, 1991."

Tug reached down and ran his fingers over the marbles.

"I know," Alyssa said. "Floors are supposed to be flat. But think of it as reflexology. Come in here barefoot and get a treatment. Nattie did the floor; the marbles were my idea."

"A three-dimensional floor," Tug said. "I like the concept."

"Well, that makes you the first person, then. I had to force Nattie to put them in, and my husband complains every time he walks over them. He says they're dangerous."

"Let's see." Tug slipped off his sandals and walked around the small bathroom while Alyssa watched him from the hall. "I'm still alive *and* my kidney points have been stimulated. Seems safe and therapeutic to me. I like it. Floor as shiatsu. You might be on to something."

Alyssa eyed him skeptically. This guy was good. In less than five minutes he'd zeroed in on her soft spot—anything to do with her farm.

For the next ten minutes, she gave Tug a room-by-room tour of her farmhouse-as-funhouse. There was a Mardi Gras of colors and artifacts and props and stage sets from Alyssa's various school and Limespring productions. On the living room wall hung a painted backdrop of ancient Rome from *A Funny Thing Happened on the Way to the Forum*. Near that were several sawed-off Corinthian columns holding up long steel grates—*West Side Story*—for stereo equipment. On the other end of the room, a huge papier-mâché head of the Trojan horse—the *Iliad*—loomed over the fireplace mantel. Heavy stainless steel pots and a selection of sabers, hatchets, crossbows—*Macbeth*—dangled from a ladder—*Oklahoma!*—that was suspended over the kitchen counter.

Tug pointed to a life-sized stuffed gorilla. It was sitting on a turquoise slatted swing hung from the ceiling near a large set of barn slider doors opening to the porch. The gorilla wore a Santa Claus cap and red-striped socks.

"What play's that from?" he asked.

Alyssa walked to the swing and sat next to the gorilla. She put her arm around it and said, "No play. He's just old Mr. Monkeysocks. I made him for my daughter's eleventh birthday party."

Upstairs, Tug saw a purpley-blue bedroom papered with playbills from school productions and a poster of Shakespeare with these words underneath him: "Take my word that time will bring on summer when briars will have leaves as well as thorns and be as sweet as sharp."

What surprised Tug most about the house was the second bedroom—stark white walls, two twin beds covered with steel gray blankets, a plain black chest of drawers, and three black-and-white Ansel Adams photographs of ghostly aspen trees.

"That's Roz's room," Alyssa said. "My daughter. She's in her Bauhaus-be-anything-your-mother-isn't stage."

Alyssa led Tug back downstairs, stopping here and there to explain which walls had been knocked out, what the place had looked like when they bought it twelve years ago, and how they had fixed it up on their modest salaries.

"We hired out for the tricky stuff like electrical and plumbing and did the rest ourselves. I've gotten pretty friendly with a power saw. The roof still leaks in the kitchen when it rains, but otherwise everything works."

They were standing in the main room, which was all of the first floor minus the little bathroom with the mosaic floor. It functioned as living room/kitchen/dining room/office.

Tug did a 360 turn. "For once, Abbi understated something," he said. "'Serious charm' doesn't begin to describe this place. Now I know what the inside of Stephen Sondheim's mind looks like."

"Ha!" she said. "Don't insult the master."

"I think he'd consider it a compliment," Tug said. "Hey, got a spare cup of that for me?" He motioned to the coffeemaker on the kitchen counter.

"You bet," she said and poured him a cup. "This is how I bribe all my Limespring artists. A few pots of coffee and before you know it I've got a mosaic floor, a mural on the barn wall, a crazy-quilt walkway, a whirligig, and an installation from Marius that I'm still not sure how it works."

She handed him the coffee. This time it was Alyssa who flashed "the smile." "Your contribution remains to be seen."

CHAPTER 8

The horse was the color of wet copper paint. Alyssa ran her hand over his haunch, stopping halfway down his rear leg to a cord of muscles as carved and defined as a weightlifter's triceps.

"Here, feel this." She took Tug's hand and pressed it onto the copper hide. Her palms were rougher than he'd expected. Against his skin, he could feel a washboard of light calluses.

"That's the engine," she said as together their hands retraced the path she'd just made. "Everything comes from the back end."

The big copper horse didn't move.

"You'll see what I mean in a second," she said. "Keep your hand there."

Alyssa pressed in close to the horse's hind end; wisps of yellow hair clung briefly to the sorrel coat as she bent down. Using her thumb and index finger as a pincer, she lightly squeezed the back of the horse's leg a few inches above the hoof. He raised his leg and Tug jumped back.

Tug laughed nervously; Alyssa, crouched by the raised leg, looked as calm as if she were picking daisies. "He won't kick," she said. "He's just lifting his leg because he's trained to do that when you touch him there. He thinks I want to clean out his hoof. Do it again, put your hand back where it was. But this time close your eyes. It's magic, I swear."

She stood up and pushed her weight into the horse's rear leg, signaling him to put his foot down flat on the ground.

"Eyes closed?" she asked. Tug, with his hand back on the horse, complied. He could feel the animal's heat radiating against his face. The air smelled of sweat and earth and hay.

Still leaning into the horse, Alyssa slid down his leg again and crouched by his hoof. Again she pressed her fingers into the tendons. The horse lifted his leg. This time Tug stayed where he was, feeling the muscles contract, coil, and lift.

"Holy shit!" he blurted. "That's amazing. I never really understood the meaning of horsepower till now. This thing could kick me into July if it wanted."

Alyssa walked to the horse's head and rubbed her face against his muzzle. "It's more likely he'd curl up into your lap if he could. They don't come any sweeter than Roy."

Roy moved his face up and down against Alyssa's cheek. "See what I mean?"

Tug's first horse lesson had come after the house tour and begun with a change of shoes. "Forget the sandals," Alyssa had told him. She'd pulled a pair of worn work boots from a closet. "Horses don't know about personal space. Your space is their space. Put these on even if you have to curl up your toes. Believe me, you'll thank me after we lead the boys into the barn."

The boys, it turned out, were Alyssa's two favorite horses. Theo was the mahogany horse that Tug had been bribing with carrots the past few days. Roy was all copper except for the white on his legs—he looked like he was wearing knee socks—and a matching blaze that ran down his face. Both horses, she said, were refugees from the track.

They'd caught Theo and Roy at the edge of a pasture along the dirt road to the farm. Actually, Alyssa had done the catching while Tug stood anxiously by, waiting for one of them to buck or rear or bolt. But nothing dramatic happened. Both docilely accepted halters and began plodding after Alyssa as she led them to the barn. It seemed to Tug like a kind of circus act—Pretty Blond

Woman Wearing Clothes the Color of a Flower Market Makes Horses Behave Like Cocker Spaniels.

Tug followed as Alyssa walked through the grass. He admired her grace of purpose; she seemed oblivious to the two behemoths behind her. Her stride was easy and loose. She ambled. Nobody ambled in New York City.

"Here, take Theo," she said, handing him a rope. "You lead him in. If he gets bossy, like trying to walk ahead of you, whack him right here above the shoulder. That's where they bite each other to show who's boss." She made a fist and tapped the horse at the base of its neck, above the front leg.

"You just have to show him you're the alpha horse," she said.

Tug gave the huge mahogany neck what he hoped was a manly, alpha sort of pat. "Good boy, Theo," he said, lowering his voice to a deep, manly alpha baritone. Theo leaned down and sniffed Tug's arm. Theo was not fooled, of that Tug was certain. As they walked to the barn, with Tug doing a kind of gingerly two-step to keep clear of Theo's huge hooves, it wasn't at all clear who was leading who.

"Roy and Theo were racehorses?" asked Tug. "Real racehorses? Like Secretariat?"

"Not like Secretariat—that's the problem," she said. "If they had been, they wouldn't be here. These guys broke down. Don't get me started on the racing industry and its greed, taking two-year-old babies and racing them into the ground. Their bones aren't even completely formed and they're pounded into the track. The ones that don't break down early run their hearts out until they can't go fast enough to win. Then they're shipped to junkier and junkier racetracks until the Thoroughbred Rescue League finds them half-starved. I take in some of the league's horses and rehabilitate them and then find homes for them. At least that's the theory. But every once in a while, one of them gets stuck in my heart. These two are lifers here. I could never get rid of them."

After the hands-on anatomy lesson, Alyssa attached Theo's halter to a long green webbed line. As Tug waited by the fence, she led the horse into the open pasture.

"I'm going to lunge him—that means make him walk, trot, and canter around me—so you can see how he moves," Alyssa said. "You can't draw them if you don't know how their bodies work."

Alyssa began to slowly pivot and Theo, on the other end of the green line, started circling around her. For three revolutions he lumbered along like a fifty-cent-a-ride pony with his ears lopped back and his head hung low.

"Hard to believe he was on the track," said Tug, leaning, chin on hands, against the top board of the fence.

Alyssa smiled. "Just watch."

Holding the line with her left hand, she called out, "Trrrot." Theo's ears pricked forward, his head snapped to attention, and he immediately launched into a kind of sprightly jog.

"Wow," Tug said. "Do the kids at school obey you like that?"

"I wish," said Alyssa, as she and Theo continued turning, the green line tracing out the area of a circle. "That's the beauty of horses. They listen and don't talk back. Watch his shoulders move, see how long and sweepy they are? That way he can cover a lot of ground fast."

The sound of her voice waxed and waned, as she turned and Theo circled, churning up clods of dirt as he passed Tug's spot by the fence. "You're seeing three hundred years of breeding at work here. It all started when the hotbloods—the Byerly Turk, Darley Arabian, and the Godolphin Barb—were brought to England to breed with carriage horses for speed. Watch this."

In the same firm tone as she'd said, "Trot," she called out, "Caaan-*ter*." The horse pushed back on his haunches and rocked forward into a gentle lope. "Count the beats as his legs strike the ground. It's one-two-three, one-two-three, up and down like a sine wave. Feels just like a rocking horse. You'll see."

Tug forced a casual smile and nodded. *You'll see?* What did she mean by that? He'd rather wrestle a bear than get on a horse, especially this one, which had moved from amiable lope to serious gallop as he raced around Alyssa, squealing and kicking up his hind legs every few seconds.

"He's just having fun," she said, laughing. Then she gave the line three sharp pulls and singsonged in a low, soothing voice: "Easy, boy. Easy. Easy. Settle down, now. Settle down . . ."

It wasn't until Theo slowed to a walk and then stopped that Tug realized the exhibition had been wasted on him. He hadn't been studying the horse, he'd been studying the blond woman with the wild colors and dirty boots make a 1,200-pound creature do her bidding using just her voice. She had held on to the green line with one hand and animated her lesson with the other, occasionally glancing over her shoulder at him as she turned. She seemed happy there, as if the pivot point were the center of the world. Her smile narrowed her slightly downturned eyes; her cheeks blushed red from the exertion and the sun.

Alyssa's command impressed Tug. But not nearly as much as the joy and energy she brought to the simple job of running a horse around in a circle. It reminded him of his art school days when even the simplest assignment was new and fun and everyone was powered by possibilities. He wondered if he could learn to capture that feeling with a 2B pencil.

When the lesson was over, Alyssa took the horses back to the pasture, gave them a handful of carrots, and shooed them away. Theo took off at a gallop, once again squealing and bucking. Roy followed, without the shenanigans.

"Aren't they beautiful?" Alyssa sounded like a thirteen-year-old girl with a crush on a boy band. "I could watch them all day. I can see why you want to draw them."

Tug hesitated. Beauty had nothing to do with it. He needed an exercise in movement and musculature, a way to sharpen his eye, tone his technique, enforce discipline. He wanted to train his hands so that they, like Leonardo's, would obey his vision. Horses were an artist's way of practicing scales. They weren't the actual music.

But he couldn't ruin Alyssa's enthusiasm. "Extraordinary," he said.

"You'll be riding one in no time."

"I don't—I don't think," Tug stammered.

"Don't worry. I've taught all kinds of Limeys to ride, even Marius, though he swears he rode in the 'old country.' Abbi rides with me all the time now, didn't she tell you? And she'd never been on a horse either when she first got here. It's easy."

"Easy?" Tug said. "There's no way you're getting me on that brown monster. Maybe . . . maybe Roy. We'll see. But one step at a time. First let me draw them."

He was about to suggest another meeting, but Alyssa beat him to it. "Then you'll have to come tomorrow. How's nine o'clock? I'll supply the coffee. You supply the pencils and paper."

It was afternoon when Tug, once more in sandals, headed down the dirt drive. As he turned onto Limespring Hollow Road, he looked back toward Finally Farm. Against the hills, a side of the yellow farmhouse peeked out from behind the trees. In the mid-distance was his new friend, Roy, looking even shinier against the light green pasture grass. Overhead, a little herd of puffy clouds trotted across the wide acreage of blue sky.

He ran his fingers back through his hair, wondering if he'd gotten everything reversed. Maybe Leonardo hadn't created beauty through technique; maybe technique simply allowed him to be a conduit for the beauty that was already there. What if Leonardo thought of horses the same way Alyssa did? What if his sketches were little acts of appreciation?

Maybe I'm wrong about beauty having nothing to do with it, Tug thought. Maybe beauty has everything to do with it.

CHAPTER 9

"I'm giving horse lessons now." Alyssa was talking to Darryl on the phone. He was calling from San Diego.

"So what's new about riding lessons?" Darryl said.

"No, not riding lessons. *Horse* lessons. There's this new artist at Limespring who wants to learn to draw them." She could hear Darryl shuffling papers on the other end.

"Let me guess, you're not charging her anything, right? Another part of the Brown family Limespring charity?"

"It's a him and let's not start this again, okay? We get a lot from Limespring. This is the least I can do."

"*We?*"

"Yes, 'we.' What about the mural in the barn and the mosaic floor and the whirligig? Do I need to go on?"

She could still hear the papers rustling.

"No," he said. "Spare me. You're right, let's not get into it again. I've got to meet someone for dinner in a few minutes. By the way, did the Amerigas guy come to check for the leak?"

For the next few minutes they went over Darryl's to-do list of maintenance chores at the farm.

"Oh, one more thing," he said. "I had to change my flight to the red-eye. I won't be in till early Saturday morning. I'm going to go home and sleep and I'll probably be too tired to come out there later."

"Fine," Alyssa said. Then they bid good-bye so quickly, she forgot to wish him a safe flight. She almost called him back, but then she thought about the rustling papers. She turned and headed for the front door instead of reaching for the phone.

A slight glow remained in the sky as she walked up the dirt drive to Limespring Hollow Road. It was her summer evening ritual, her good-night to the pastures and trees, her prayer before bedtime.

She liked the crunch of dirt and gravel beneath her clogs and she loved the little bursts of green light left behind by the starbugs as they scurried from her path. They weren't really called starbugs. Alyssa had coined the name their first summer at Finally Farm and it had stuck.

As she'd walked along the drive that evening twelve years ago, a glimpse of chartreuse light caught her eye. She looked down, but the light was gone. She continued on and the same thing happened. She stopped again, squinting in the darkness at the ground around her feet. No light. She thought her eyes were playing tricks on her. She started off; another green flicker. This time, she bent down and rubbed her hand against the gravel. A small bug hustled away in a huff, flashing its little green warning light as it went.

She stood up and made another tentative step forward. More flashes. Three more steps, quickly, one-two-three. Lots more flashes.

She ran back to the house to tell Darryl about her discovery. "Come outside, I have to show you these starbugs," she'd said. "When you walk down the road, they light up. Whole constellations of them! It's like being sandwiched between Milky Ways."

She'd grabbed his hand and led him to the driveway. "Oh, I know what they are," he said as bugs flashed around them, "they're glowworms, *Phengodes plumosa*."

Alyssa loved that Darryl could identify and classify, that he knew the Latin names for things. It made her feel as if she were part of a secret order: the Society of Phylum and Genus.

"Say it again," she said and threw her arms around his neck.

"*Phengodes plumosa*," he said and she pushed him down onto the

grass, where they made love by the light of the stars and the glow
of the starbugs.

Alyssa couldn't recall the last time she and Darryl had gone
starbug gazing. Still, each time she returned for the summer and
caught the first glimpse of green light, it brought back that night
of discovery. And for a moment—in the dash of time it took for
the bug to issue its phosphorescent warning—everything was as it
had been. For a moment, the gap inside her wasn't there.

Over the years, Alyssa had shown the starbugs to many of the
Limespring fellows. Invariably, they were a big hit. Starbugs found
their way into a cycle of hexameter sonnets called "Illuminations
of the Third Desire" by a Seattle poet who was so intrigued he
camped out in her driveway. They inspired the use of phosphorescent pigments in a series of experimental paintings, called *Starbugs
1–13*, that showed at the Corcoran Museum in Washington, D.C.
And Marius, the Falstaffian Czech artist, swore that starbugs were
the idea behind his *Cohesive Particles of the Meanderer, No. 37*, the
quirky installation he'd put up next to the Limespring studios.

But Alyssa's favorite starbug creation was something else. One
night when Roz was seven, she'd gone outside with a flashlight
and an empty pickle jar. She had refused to tell her mother what
she was doing. "Let her go," Darryl had said, "she's got an important job." And he winked at his daughter.

Ten minutes passed and Roz was still outside in the dark by herself. "I think I better check on her," Alyssa had said, but Darryl
said no. "Quit worrying, she's fine. It could be a while."

Finally, after nearly a half hour, Roz returned wearing a big
smile, her left hand hidden behind her back. She edged around to
the stairs so Alyssa couldn't see. Then she bounded up to her
room, calling out, "Mommy, I have a surprise for you. I'll be down
in a while."

She soon returned, still hiding something behind her back.
"Come outside," she said and with her free hand pulled Alyssa out
the screen door.

After a few steps into the darkness, Roz stopped and held out
her hand. "Here, Mommy, starbug earrings. I made them for you."

There in her palm, a little place no bigger than a hummingbird's nest, were two silver-dollar-sized pieces of paper, each with a safety pin attached.

Alyssa bent close to Roz's gift. In the light from the open door behind them, she could see that her daughter had glued a single bug to the middle of each piece of paper and surrounded it with a few sprigs of something.

"Oh, I love them, sweetie," she said. "What are these other decorations?"

"It's grass, so the starbugs don't get hungry," Roz said. "Get close so I can show you how they work."

Alyssa knelt down and Roz attached the safety pins to the gold hoops Alyssa was wearing.

"Now shake your head so they light up."

Roz placed her fingers on Alyssa's cheeks—her touch was feathery and a little bit sticky from Elmer's glue—and guided her head back and forth. As much as Alyssa's head shook, the bugs stayed dark. Roz started to cry and Alyssa almost joined her. Finally she gathered her daughter in her arms and told her in ten different ways how much she loved her new earrings. Then, because she couldn't possibly tell Roz the earrings had died, she explained how starbugs often got tired after a long night of flashing and needed a comfortable place to rest before they could flash again.

In a drawer upstairs they found a white jewelry box that Alyssa insisted was the perfect place for starbugs to sleep. Together she and Roz removed the slender gold chain inside and replaced it with the earrings.

Roz's starbug earrings were still inside the white box, still inside the top drawer. The white paper circles had yellowed over the years like a set of tea-stained teeth. Little parts of the bugs had fallen off—one was missing its hind legs, the other its head. Their food, the blades of bright green grass, had turned to straw.

As Alyssa walked down the drive, she saw Theo and Roy, nibbling tufts of grass on the pasture side of the fence. "Hey, fellas," she said. Both their heads went up and Theo walked up to her to have his face scratched.

Horses always made Alyssa feel better, and she needed a lift. This evening, she'd pulled out the starbug earrings. They only made her feel worse. Roz wouldn't be at the farm at all this summer. Her internship was going to last three months. Alyssa hadn't wanted to agree to it, but Darryl and Roz had ganged up on her.

"Time to cut the umbilical cord, Mom," Roz had said. "Besides, this could help my career."

"What career? You're seventeen years old," Alyssa had said.

"Eighteen in three weeks, and I've told you a million times, if I intern with Uncle Ron, I'll be the only freshman with real architectural experience."

Alyssa knew she'd lose. And most of her knew it was the right decision. A summer working with Darryl's brother would be the best thing for Roz. She mostly knew that.

Alyssa reached the pavement of Limespring Hollow Road and turned back. Only her bedroom light was on at the farmhouse. She'd braced herself for great tsunamis of sadness to overwhelm her this summer. Little wavelets started coming during Roz's junior year in high school, when she got a brochure in the mail from Johns Hopkins University. A year later, Alyssa found herself crying at the stupidest things—walking past the college dorm-room displays at Target, reading about a Mr. Rogers exhibit at the Smithsonian, tripping over Roz's ridiculous platform shoes.

But as the school year and Roz's childhood came to an end, Alyssa found herself settling into the inevitability of her daughter's leaving home. The loneliness she felt walking through the farm's empty spaces was balanced by a profound gratitude that, this time, the natural order was running its course.

And now there was a different natural order to consider. This wasn't only Roz's first summer away from the farm, this was the first summer Alyssa would be there by herself.

It hadn't surprised her when Darryl said he wouldn't be coming out the next weekend. He'd already told her he'd only show up occasionally before he left for California again in July. She'd just said, "Okay, do what you have to do."

She knew he'd been coming to the Follies the past few years just for Roz, to keep up the charade of a unified Brown family. With Roz in Chicago, there was no reason for Darryl's show of family alliance and forced half-smiles at the Follies foolishness.

Secretly, Alyssa was happy he wouldn't be around much. She wouldn't have to put up with his complaints about the swarms of ladybugs or bad wiring or sluggish plumbing. She knew her love for the farm made him feel like an outsider, a jilted suitor. And, in a way, he was. Over the years, she'd found more comfort in the four walls and fifty acres than in his arms.

In her most desperate times, when she didn't think she could hurt any harder, she'd tried to turn to Darryl. But he told her he couldn't handle her "big Broadway emotions."

"They don't leave any room for me, Alyssa," he'd said. "You're not the only one who's having a hard time."

Each time she drove up Limespring Hollow Road and saw the little yellow house, she felt the same way as the first time she'd seen it: like she'd returned from a long journey. Even before they'd signed the mortgage papers, she was telling friends the only way she'd leave it was horizontally, in a pine box.

But Darryl had never felt that way about the farm. A mild interest became indifference, then dislike. Once when they'd turned onto Limespring Hollow Road and he'd made another sarcastic remark about entering "the Redneck Nation," Alyssa had made him stop the car and let her out. She'd walked to the house alone and wouldn't talk to him for the rest of the day.

She'd tried to find projects and activities they could do together—gardening, hiking, building the barn. But he didn't like the outdoors. He preferred reading his journals or playing tennis, and the nearest tennis courts were thirty minutes away.

She'd also tried to get him involved in Limespring, but he didn't like the fellows and the fellows found him irrelevant. His disdain for them turned seating arrangements at farmhouse dinner parties into a kind of chess game. Inevitably, whoever Alyssa sat next to him would chat until politeness had been served, then turn for the rest of the evening to a friendlier, livelier guest.

She couldn't make him like the farm. It was as much a chore for him to be in Markham as it was for her to be in Washington. At least in Washington she had her job. In Markham, Darryl—as he'd told her many times—had nothing.

She wished he could care more.

She wished she could care more.

She looked down and scraped her clogs against the gravel. No flashing lights, but she knew the starbugs were there, somewhere around her feet.

CHAPTER 10

Alyssa woke earlier than usual the next morning. In the bathroom, she stood in front of the mirror wondering how old she looked. Someone once told her she could pass for thirty. But that had been three years ago, at her fortieth birthday party.

She stuck her tongue out at the face in the mirror. "Take that, you old bag."

Nonetheless, she knelt down and rummaged through the cabinet below the sink. Next to half a bottle of nail polish remover, she found an old tube of concealer.

By the time Tug got to the barn, Alyssa was there waiting, her dark circles erased and a curry comb in her hand.

"Here." She handed him something that resembled a gear made out of black rubber. "This is a curry comb. For the horse, it knocks off the dirt. For you, it'll show you how the muscles are connected. Do it in a circular motion. Start here."

She pointed to Theo's mud-caked rump and watched as Tug began to make tentative circles on top of the muddy crust.

"Tug, the object is to get the mud off. Do it harder. He won't mind. In fact, he likes it. Didn't they teach you currying in art school?"

"That was an elective," he said. "I opted for sculpture. How's this?" He pressed the comb harder against Theo's back end and rubbed, sending a cloud of brown dust between them.

"Much better," Alyssa said. "This should help you feel the density of his haunch muscles. Just imagine the thick bands underneath."

He did as instructed. "I see what you mean. Now all I have to do is figure out how to draw that feeling. But this is good, I'm starting to get the muscle memory in my hands of what it should look like."

Alyssa grabbed a brush and ran it across the star on Theo's forehead. "Have you always wanted to be artist?" she asked.

"Yeah, I was one of those kids who couldn't stop doodling." Tug continued to curry Theo as he talked. "But I'd have probably wound up a poli-sci major if it hadn't been for Mrs. Miller, my third-grade teacher. One day she lugged out a big roll of brown paper, plopped it on my desk, and told me to put my doodling to good use. She needed a mural for the holiday pageant. So I drew three wise men. They looked more like Santa Clauses, but she loved it. Every Christmas for years she rolled out my mural and hung it across the front of her room."

Tug banged the curry comb against the wall to dislodge the dirt and hair. "God bless Mrs. Miller. She was the first person, other than my mother, to tell me I was good at something. And I believed her. I branched out from Christmas murals and doodling to comic books. I was hooked from my first *Spider-Man*. I even started my own series. I kept drawing straight through high school. I taught myself to do those fifteen-minute portraits and worked street fairs in Ithaca and Syracuse. That's what paid for Pratt, mostly."

He paused. "I'm finished with this side. Can I walk around to the other? Does he kick or anything?"

"Not so far," Alyssa said. Tug froze.

"I was just kidding," she said. "Theo doesn't kick. But it never hurts to be cautious with horses. Good luck, his other side's even dirtier. He was a pig in his last life. Weren't you, boy?" Alyssa buried her face into the slight dish between the horse's eyes.

Tug attacked the mud on the other side. "Your turn. How'd you get into *the theater*." He gave the last two words a portentous, PBS-documentary-style pronunciation.

"That's easy. I was never not into it. I've been singing and dancing since before I could even remember, according to my parents. You were the kid who was always doodling? I was the one always staging talent shows. I've been forcing people to watch me perform since I could barely walk. And not just people. My dog was my first paying audience, except I had to pay him. I'd dress up in my grandmother's nightgowns, high heels, and all the costume jewelry I could load on. Then I'd line the hearth with Milk Bones and whistle. He'd come running, and while he ate the bribe I'd sing 'People' into a hairbrush. If I went fast enough, I could just about make it through the whole song with an audience."

After Theo was decaked of his muddy veneer, Alyssa took Tug on another tour of Finally Farm.

They walked to the pond by the two hills and then to the creek that flowed down from Limespring. He had lots of questions and she had lots of answers. Alyssa loved talking about her farm. Tug occasionally jotted down notes in his sketchpad to remind him of things he wanted to draw.

Alyssa started with a tale about the camouflaged snapping turtle that burrowed into the mud by the creek to lay her eggs. "Right about there." She pointed to the stream's bank. "I used to walk barefoot down that creek until Odie showed her to me."

Odie was Odie Watkins, the farmer who ran his cows on her front pasture. "Odie's so skinny his wife says if he stood sideways and stuck out his tongue, he'd pass for a zipper."

That led to a story about Odie wearing his only suit to help bury a neighbor's dead dog, which led to a story about that dog chasing a coyote into old Mrs. Tomkins's front yard. "She's eighty-five years old and chased it away with a broom," Alyssa said. "Imagine that."

Stories and stories, layered like millefiore glass. To Tug, it was like getting a private seating to a one-woman show.

"What's that?" he said as they walked by a piece of bright purple farm machinery with a row of lethal-looking blades jutting out the back. "It looks like a torture device from a drag show."

"That there," she said in a thick low-country accent, "is a shit kicker, son. A man-*yooooor* spreader."

It turned out that Marius had found the manure spreader while trolling the countryside for parts for his next installation called *The Gates of Hell*. The farmer didn't even know if it still worked, but Marius gave him $75 on the spot and asked Alyssa to pick it up for him.

"Up till then, I'd been hauling out manure one wheelbarrow at a time to the front pasture. So when I saw it, I begged Marius to sell it to me. And Marius will do anything for a woman. He not only fixed it, but painted it purple."

Back at the barn, Tug gathered his drawing materials. "Thanks for the horse lesson and the tour. There's a million things here I'd love to draw."

"Then do it," she said. "Anytime you want."

They walked outside and Tug stopped for a moment. "You know, this place is like a mirror image of you."

Alyssa cocked her head. "Is that a compliment or an insult? I've been compared to Bette Midler and Meg Ryan, but never fifty acres and a manure spreader."

"Neither," Tug said. "Just an observation. When I do a sculpture, it becomes part of me and I become part of it. That's what you've done here. You and your farm are like this."

He laced his fingers together, and when he did, Alyssa clapped her hands.

"Hallelujah," she sang and fluttered her fingers in the air like a gospel singer.

Tug was taken aback by her exuberance. But he liked it; he liked her unabashed glee. It was a welcome change from the oppressive irony of his New York friends. And there was something contagious about her excitement.

"See you tomorrow?" He was surprised by the eagerness in his voice.

"No," she answered, "I'll see you tonight. Practice, remember? Our first Follies rehearsal. Aren't you glad Abbi volunteered you to be the Sultan?"

CHAPTER 11

Rehearsal was held in the Limespring dining room. Alyssa had invited both performers and crew members so that everybody could see how the show would come together.

They sat at the tables, discussing staging and sets for a while, then Alyssa handed out scripts to the would-be actors, with each one's role individually marked in a different-colored highlighter pen.

The first read-through was horrible. Marius declaimed his lines as if he were on a high school debating team; a writer from Boston sounded like Elmer Fudd; and a painter named Stephanie kept reading the wrong parts.

"You're the one in red marker," Alyssa reminded her.

Tug tried so hard to enunciate clearly that he ended up sounding like a robot. By the time it was over, his tongue felt like it was the size of a salami.

Alyssa stood up and faced the group. "Wow," she said. "Amazing." She had a look of awe on her face, as if she'd entered Notre Dame cathedral for the first time. "That may have been the worst Follies reading I've ever heard.

"Don't worry," she said after the nervous laughter died down. "You'll be fine. You'll be better than fine—you'll be great. By Follies night, you'll be funny and clever and sophisticated. Look, here's the thing to realize: An actor's most important gift is brains.

There are no dumb actors. Everyone here is smart and creative. All I'm going to do is unleash the actor that's already inside you.

"Now let's read through one more time and I'll show you how it might appear on stage."

This time, as the actors read their lines, Alyssa acted out some of the parts. She ran back and forth in front of the tables doffing imaginary hats, swordfighting with invisible opponents, and dancing to unheard music. In the middle of a series of pirouettes she started singing Motown, "Papa Was a Rolling Stone." Toward the end she lost track of the action and, panting and sweaty, collapsed, laughing, on the linoleum.

Like all the other newcomers, Tug was amazed. In the middle of her performance, he nudged Abbi, who was sitting next to him. "Jesus," he whispered. "It's like I'm going to be playing opposite Lily Tomlin."

"No way," Abbi whispered back. "Alyssa's a lot better."

Afterward, as they walked back to their cabins, Tug groaned. "I can't believe you roped me into this. She's great and I'm an idiot."

"Oh, relax," Abbi said. "You're going to be fine. Just remember what Alyssa said: 'There are no dumb actors.'"

"Not until now."

CHAPTER 12

The next morning Tug arrived at Finally Farm as scheduled. Alyssa met him at the barn carrying two mugs of coffee and a plate of oatmeal cookies. She was wearing a huge orange turban that tilted over her forehead and covered one eye.

"This is for you, O Grand Master." She nodded forward and sent the turban into Tug's lap. "I found it in my closet. It was either a Halloween costume for Roz or something from *The King and I*. Oh, and by the way, don't worry about last night, everyone's always terrible the first rehearsal. In Marius's first year, he froze solid during the actual performance. I had to keep saying things like, 'So, Hamlet, have you reached a decision yet?' just to get him to utter a word. You'll be fine. It's a farce."

Tug tried on the turban. "Just don't let me turn it into a tragedy," he said.

Over the coffee, he pumped Alyssa for acting tips and she kept reassuring him that the audience wasn't expecting Sir Laurence Olivier. When their mugs were empty, she hitched her horse trailer to her truck and drove to Marshall, the closest town.

"Hang around and draw if you want," she said before she left.

Tug strolled up and down the center aisle of the barn looking into stalls and rooms hung with horse gear. Eventually he placed a folding chair in the middle of the aisle and laid the sketchpad across his knees. He began to draw a line of shovels and rakes hanging on the wall.

Usually, drawing focused him completely, but this time his attention drifted between the shapes before him and thoughts about his first week at Limespring. Now he understood why Abbi kept raving about the place. "It's like a battery recharger for the soul," she'd said. "You can't not be creative there."

Tug didn't know where the summer would lead him, but after only a week he was certain that by the time fall came his eye would be sharper and his way clearer. He hadn't figured his Limespring fellowship would be this inspirational. And now there was this crazy farm with all its doodads and horses to draw.

And there was Alyssa.

He began packing up his drawing things around noon, just as she returned with a new orphan from the Rescue League.

"Jesus!" Tug said when he saw the gray horse step off the trailer. "That thing's as big as an elephant."

The horse limped behind her. "He's a big boy, all right. Nearly eighteen hands. As big as War Admiral. Unfortunately, that's where the similarity stops. He was a dud on the track. He's farsighted and couldn't see the other horses closing in on him."

"You can test a horse's eyesight? That's amazing. How do you get them to read the chart?"

She pushed Tug's shoulder. "Don't be ridiculous. You can't give a horse an eye test. I heard it from a friend of mine who's a horse communicator. She said the horse told her he couldn't see the other horses closing in and it made him very anxious."

Tug burst into a laugh. "You're kidding, right?"

"No, not entirely," Alyssa said. "It's all part of the fever, horse fever. It burns out the rational side of your brain."

She led the limping horse into the wash stall.

"Need some help with him?" Tug asked. "I'm receiving a message that he wants to be curried, it makes him anxious to be dirty."

Tug hadn't planned to spend his afternoon at Finally Farm, but after they'd groomed Poli—short for Poltergeist for his gray, ghostly color—Alyssa invited him in for a sandwich.

While she rummaged around her refrigerator, Tug studied the knickknacks, mementos, and art pieces that covered the walls and cabinet tops. Among them was a series of black frames, each containing a little three-dimensional cartoon person and an accompanying block of text glued to a piece of eight-by-ten canvas board.

"These are great," he said. "Sculpey?"

"You got it," Alyssa said. "My friend Carol made them. She calls them her 'ladies.' You'll meet her at our Fourth of July party. She teaches art at Emerson, and more importantly, to me at least, she designs the sets and runs tech for all the plays. Grilled cheese okay?"

"Sure," Tug said. He leaned closer to Carol's ladies to read the copy. "Who are they, anyway?"

"People we know. Friends, mostly."

"I don't think this one's a friend." Tug was examining the figure of a severe looking woman in a red power suit with snakes coming from the top of her head.

Alyssa laughed. "Oh, you must be looking at the Shrike. No, she's definitely not a friend. In fact, she's ruining my life."

Over sandwiches and iced tea, she told Tug all about Emerson's new headmistress.

"I can probably stand it for two years," she concluded, "but any longer and I'm shipping out—to another school, that is. I can't imagine not teaching. It's about twenty times more rewarding than performing. There's a nobility to it. Sure, you give your audience a gift in performing, but in teaching you go so far beyond that. Your legacy continues and the creativity lives on in so many different ways and . . ."

She covered her face with her hands. "Oh my God. I sound like I'm giving a career night speech. Stop me, I'm babbling."

Tug, who had a hunk of grilled cheese in his mouth, waved his hand in front of his face and a garbled "No, no I want to hear more" came out.

He held his index finger up, swallowed, and continued: "You lis-

tened to me bellyache about Leonardo. This is a lot more interesting than that. Go on. Please."

"Okay." She said it so quickly it made him laugh. She cleared
her throat. "Career night 101. Teaching and Its Many Gifts.
Where was I?"

"Legacy," Tug said between bites.

"Rachel Levine, Jarret Colby, Mandy Rosenfelt, Alex Crafton,"
Alyssa said. "I could go on and on. They're my legacy. Them and
many others. They all went through my drama program. I don't
know whether they'll ever act again, but I do know they'll enjoy
and appreciate theater for the rest of their lives. And that's my job,
to perpetuate a love for theater and get these kids thinking."

She got up and walked to the refrigerator to get a pitcher of tea
and returned by way of the bookshelf. She pulled out a slim blue
volume, which she put on the table. It was the Emerson yearbook,
class of 1999.

She leafed through the pages, stopping near the middle. "See
this kid?" Alyssa pointed to a picture of a gangly teenager who
bore a slight resemblance to Christian Slater. The page was enti-
tled, "Emerson Drama, *All My Sons*."

"That's Alex Crafton. He'd never acted in his life. But in his
senior year, he showed up to audition for one of the toughest
shows we've ever put on. His reading was brilliant. Who knew
Alex had such talent? I cast him in the lead as the son who has to
confront his father about selling defective plane parts during
World War II.

"Then came rehearsals. His first one was pretty bad. Nothing
like his audition. Right after the second rehearsal, which was even
worse, he came into my office and asked if we could talk. He
looked like an old man worried about funeral arrangements for his
dead wife. I thought, 'Uh-oh, he's going to quit.'"

She lightly brushed her fingers across Alex's picture. "I couldn't
have been more wrong. 'I'm confused by Chris,' he said, so
earnestly I almost hugged him. 'If he feels so guilty about going
into his father's business, why doesn't he do something else? And
he knows his brother's dead, why doesn't he tell his mother to stop

pretending?' Alex wasn't quitting, he was just wrestling with his character like all actors do! We talked for so long about guilt, duty, loyalty, and forgiveness that the night janitors had to clean around us.

"Sure, bows are exhilarating, but they're nothing compared to watching a student's breakthrough performance. Alex got a standing ovation. After the show, he thanked me, not just for teaching him about acting, but for helping him understand the nature of human flaws. I still get teary thinking about it."

Alyssa closed the yearbook and placed it back in the shelf with great care, as if it were a rare and valuable first edition.

"You're a lucky woman," Tug said. "You've got three grand passions—your farm, horses, and theater. I'd be happy if I had one."

A slight frown creased her forehead. She looked out the open porch doors, nodding slowly. "Lucky," she said without inflection.

Lucky was the last thing she ever considered herself.

CHAPTER 13

Alyssa had expected Tug at nine the next morning, but he sneaked to Finally Farm a half hour earlier. "Yes!" he said under his breath as he peeked around a corner of the barn and saw that she wasn't there yet. He'd come up with the plan the night before and could hardly wait to see how she would react.

He walked quickly to the third stall on the left. Big gray Poli was inside, head down, eyes closed, bottom lip drooping. One of his back legs was cocked under him; he made a slight snoring noise.

Tug reached over the stall door and patted the horse's side. Poli started awake. "Sorry for the early wake-up call, buddy," Tug said. He held out a couple of carrots. Poli ate them slowly, as if he were savoring the flavor.

Tug rubbed the horse's neck and ears for a while. When Poli seemed to enjoy it, or at least tolerate it, Tug decided that it was safe.

"This'll just take a minute," he said and slid open the stall door.

A few minutes later, when he was done, he gave Poli a pat on the neck. "Thanks, big fella," he said. Then he turned on the barn lights, set up the folding chair, and started drawing.

"You're early," Alyssa said when she walked into the barn twenty minutes later and set down two cups of coffee.

"I had to fix Poli," Tug said.

"What?" Alyssa shook her head. "What are you talking about? His limp?"

"No, not that problem." Tug grabbed Alyssa's hand and led her to Poli's stall. "His running problem. Remember what the animal communicator said? Well, voilà!" With a flourish, he slid open the stall door for the second time that morning.

Poli looked up from the hay he'd been eating and Alyssa nearly collapsed with laughter. The big gray horse had a pair of eyeglasses drawn on his face.

From that morning on, their routine was set. Tug would walk from Limespring to Finally Farm carrying his sketchpad, pencils, charcoals, and gum erasers in a purple plastic portfolio. Alyssa would greet him with coffee, conversation, and carefully brushed hair.

They traded gossip—Tug told Alyssa about the tintypes photographer hitting on the memoirist from Atlanta (she said no), and Alyssa told Tug about the Warrenton weapons heiress who killed her South American polo player boyfriend (she got two weeks in jail)—and they frequently discussed the progress of the Follies.

They also traded life histories, like kids trading baseball cards. Alyssa matched Tug's tale of Mrs. Miller's Christmas mural with her own elementary school memory of Mrs. Wentzel's fourth-grade fingernail check. Bit by bit they got to know each other. And bit by bit, they found themselves surprised by how much they looked forward to the next morning.

Of course, Alyssa asked about Tug's nickname. "My mother tells the story to anyone who'll listen. Apparently I used to follow her around all the time—at home, in the grocery store—tugging on the hem of her skirt. She called me her 'Little Tugster.' Eventually that became 'Tugger,' then 'Tug.' But I don't mind. Anything's better than Alvin Dwight Palifax Jr."

"I have to agree with you there," Alyssa said.

Tug talked a good bit about his family. He called his father, Alvin Dwight Sr., the most decent man he'd ever met. "I saw him run across a rocky beach at Lake Oswego, breaking every one of his toes, to save a little girl who was screaming for help."

In turn, Alyssa told Tug about her family. "I was genetically destined to teach," she said. "Mom teaches music, Dad teaches chemistry." She told him about her obsession with horses. Though she left out the part about how she and Shelley Bush used to play mare and stallion in the sixth grade, she did tell him about her shelves of plastic horses, her plan to win a pony by selling the most cans of Salvo, and that she'd read *Misty* so many times she knew it by heart.

She told him of her transformation into the mini-diva of Beeber Junior High who planned to star on Broadway; the New York City waitress/bicycle courier who worked nights with an experimental theater troupe; the drama teacher facing the daily dramatics of teenagers; and the woman whose dream of living on a farm finally came true.

"So you see," she said a little too brightly, "I have everything I've ever wanted." Alyssa Brown could act, of that there was no doubt. But even she couldn't pull off that line. She quickly changed the subject. "So tell me more about the adventures of 'the little Tugster.'"

And he did.

After their morning coffee, which usually stretched close to lunch, Alyssa would turn from horse instructor to farmhand, leaving Tug to his sketching. Most days he left by one o'clock, though sometimes he returned in the late afternoon after the day had cooled.

One early evening, after mowing the fields, she'd come back to the barn to find Tug sitting in the middle of the center aisle on a folding chair, staring through the open tack-room door at a confusing tangle of leather, rope, and metal hanging from the wall. From a stall behind him, Poli looked over his shoulder like a ghostly art critic.

"You're here kind of late, aren't you?" she said.

"I'm going to get these leather things right if it kills me," Tug said.

Alyssa looked at the sketchpad on Tug's knees. He'd drawn a row of bridles. Somehow he'd given the same straps of leather and bits of metal she'd been around for years a kind of life she'd never noticed. They had shadows and dimensions and a slightly coiled, helical energy.

Tug tipped his head back and looked up at Alyssa. "I'm trying a kind of Toulouse-Lautrec/*Bal du Moulin Rouge* perspective. What do you think?"

"I don't know how you do it," she said. "It looks so real. Beyond real."

Tug started drawing again. He worked quickly, the charcoal tip making numerous short strokes and a delicate scratching noise. Soon, an old horse show ribbon and a faded, curled photograph appeared. She liked watching him draw. It was like watching a photograph develop.

By now, she'd seen him working many times. Each time the process was the same, each time the results were surprising. At first, the marks seemed extraneous and vaguely geometric—wobbly triangles, unparallel parallelograms—but as the charcoal sped its way across the paper familiar shapes began to materialize. Sometimes it seemed as if the figures had been there all along and the pencil or pen or charcoal just picked away at the white paper covering them up.

Suddenly in the middle of a downstroke, Tug stopped. "It's not actually how I *do* it," he said. "It's more how I *see* it. When I look at all that stuff on the wall, I don't see strips of leather. I see blocks of light and shades of dark that define the depth. Abbi says she writes to think. I draw to see."

He leaned back and put the piece of charcoal behind his ear. "But you'd be surprised how hard it is to see. My old drawing teacher at Pratt, Harold Reifman, insisted you couldn't draw the human body unless you knew what was underneath the skin. He'd say things like, 'One cannot represent the pelvic region faithfully without knowing the fascia lata.' That's why my horses look like dogs. I don't know a damned thing about their structure. I can't *see* how they're built from the inside."

Alyssa put her hand on his shoulder. She'd been finding reasons to touch him a lot lately. "That's why you're here."

He went back to his drawing and she went back to her chores.

Over the years, lots of Limeys had come to Finally Farm for one project or another, but none had worked as hard as Tug. He sketched for hours at a time. While he joked about his own competence (every day he teased her about the *Mr. Ed* comment), his skill surprised Alyssa. She hadn't expected someone who could draw that well, based on the horse sketches she'd seen at Limespring. And though his horses were still awkward, his other work was remarkable. Some offered the thrill of recognition, and some, like the bridle drawing, made her see the farm in a new way. One showed the manure spreader casting a hulking shadow against the barn in the late-afternoon light. She'd never noticed the shadow before. When she offered to buy the sketch from him, Tug tore the page out of his book and handed it to her.

"It's yours," he said. "Keep it safe—someday an original Palifax will be worth millions."

"I'll guard it with my life," she said. She tucked it under her arm and started to walk outside. "Oh, I forgot to tell you. It'd probably be better if you didn't come tomorrow or Sunday. Darryl's coming out and he's a little bit touchy about Limespring fellows."

Touchy. It seemed an odd word for her to use, and though she smiled when she said it, there was something in her voice that told Tug not to pursue the issue.

CHAPTER 14

Alyssa drummed her fingers to the beat of the "Jet Song" from *West Side Story* as she waited for the images on the computer screen to fill in.

"Alyssa, I'm trying to read," Darryl said.

He was sitting on the sofa on the opposite side of the room. She'd set up the computer on an old laundry table and her assault against the enamel sounded like Chita Rivera tap-dancing on a garbage can.

"Oh, sorry," she said. "I was daydreaming. It takes forever for this thing to unload. But thanks for getting it fixed. An old computer's better than no computer. "

"It's the connection, not the computer," Darryl said without looking up from his magazine. "Someday this county will move into the twenty-first century."

Alyssa stared at the screen. Slowly a page of party hats appeared. She clicked on the white plastic boater with the red, white, and blue band around it.

"Darryl, I found it! Come here, look. They're just like the ones at Judy's party. If we order more than fifty, we'll get a pretty big price break."

"Liss," he said. "I know you've got to have a July Fourth party, but do we have to make such a big deal of it? Let's scale back this year, okay? Forget the hats."

"You wore a boater just like that the first time I met you," Alyssa said. "At Judy's July Fourth party. Remember, everyone was wearing them?"

"I can barely remember Judy, let alone what I was wearing to her party."

Darryl turned back to his reading and Alyssa back to the computer screen. She was still waiting for the order sheet to pop up.

"Judy was your sister's friend from college. She was an actor, she worked at Eddie's with me. Short, dark hair, Liza Minelli eyes?"

Darryl nodded and turned the page. "Right," he said.

Alyssa had almost skipped Judy's Fourth of July party for a trip to the shore with a friend. But her friend's car broke down so she went to Judy's instead. There'd been a pile of those boaters by the front door. Everyone inside was wearing one, including the tall, slim, dark-haired man flipping burgers on a little hibachi in the backyard.

She'd asked him for a burger, rare, and they'd introduced themselves. Judy had already told Alyssa about "the brainiac from Washington" and had even tried to fix them up once. "He's a nice guy and he's straight, which puts him way ahead of everyone we know," she'd said. But Alyssa refused. "What could I say to a scientist that would be interesting, or vice versa?"

Plenty, as it turned out. He loved her backstage stories and was enthralled by the life of a struggling actor. "I could never do that," he said several times in an awed voice. At one point he asked her to recite a passage from *Private Lives* she'd memorized for a reading early the next morning. In turn, he made his research sound like a treasure hunt. The way he told it, all his professors were characters out of Dickens. He monopolized her evening and made her laugh, as if he were auditioning for the role of boyfriend.

Returning home after the call the next day, she found a page torn from the *Daily News* slipped under her front door with two horoscopes circled and a note that read: "It's in the stars—Darryl."

Her horoscope was Aquarius: "Venus, your ruler, aligned with the sun means there's a surprise in store. Capricorn, Libra, or Sagittarius individuals could play role."

His was Capricorn: "The moon is in a harmonious angle. Dichotomies and contradictions are cleared up. Dogged determination gives you the advantage over those who only have speed going for them."

For six months Darryl pursued Alyssa with the dogged determination of the most tenacious Capricorn. He called her nearly every night and took the train up every weekend to see her in New York. He stood in line with her at cattle calls and a couple of times helped her with the courier job. By the next July Fourth, they were married and living in Washington.

Over the past few years, Alyssa had often wondered how different her life would have been if her friend's car hadn't broken down and she'd gone to Beach Haven that July Fourth, nineteen years ago.

Darryl stood and stretched. "It's late," he said. "I'm heading to bed. Are you coming?"

"In a little bit. There's a couple more things I want to look for."

She ordered seventy-five party hats, then clicked to another page featuring patriotic bunting. As she waited for it to electronically unfold, her fingers began to pick up where they'd left off: "When you're a Jet, you're a Jet all the way . . ." But they stopped when the sound of whinnying came drifting through the open windows.

She sat for a while, listening for horses. Then she turned back to the computer and interrupted the search for bunting. She called up the Google box again. Her fingers hesitated over the keys momentarily. She typed in, "Tug Palifax."

CHAPTER 15

On the morning after Darryl's departure, Tug walked over to Finally Farm and Alyssa met him in the barn with coffee and muffins.

There was a sly look on his face as he took his first sip. "So, where are the humping horses?"

"I see you've been talking to Jackie," Alyssa said.

"She told me about all your erotic etchings. Come on, you've got to show me."

Alyssa led him to the north end of the barn, where she pushed a large wooden trunk away from a corner of the center aisle. There, drawn in the concrete, was a cartoon of a stallion mounting a mare. Both horses were looking up with wide eyes and oversized grins. Above the drawing were the words, "Finally, a barn for Finally Farm." The stallion's rump was branded with the name "Darryl." The mare's flank read, "Alyssa."

"A Limey did it, of course," said Alyssa. "I can't remember his name, except that it was a mouthful, something like—Dagomar Petrosian. He was a composer who cartooned as a hobby. He drew it in the wet concrete with a nail. We didn't realize he'd done it until the next day when the concrete was already set."

"Well, it's . . . uh . . . cute," said Tug.

"It was funny for about a day. Then Roz saw it and refused to walk in the barn until I covered it up. It's really the only thing I'd change about this place."

They sat on a hay bale, their coffee mugs in hand. Alyssa looked down the center aisle. After seven years, everything about the barn still thrilled her: the thick wood boards of the stalls with their knuckle-sized knots; the wisps of hay that drifted down from the loft and rode the currents of the fan-swirled air; the pine shavings that looked like twists of lemon taffy; the pitchforks with their metal tines aligned as straight as soldiers; the orange wheelbarrow that Roz had painted with flowers before her Bauhaus phase; the big plastic trash cans filled with sticky-sweet corn and oats; the voodoo mural of devil horses painted by a (strange) fellow from Miami.

"This is my favorite place on the farm," she said. "Possibly even the Earth. This is where I am—pardon the hippie talk—the most centered. I could be happy living right here in this barn, even if I were alone."

"Alone?" said Tug. "No stage, no lights, no Shakespeare?"

"I meant alone except for the annual theater festival in the front pasture and weekly visits to Limespring."

"Jackie also told me you guys built the barn in just a day."

"Mostly. Did Jackie also tell you that she was behind it all?"

"No."

"She's being modest. If it hadn't been for her, we'd be in the middle of a field right now. She got tired of hearing me bellyache about standing in the rain with my refugees. You know, doctoring their legs and cleaning out their cuts. She told me to do the prep work and she'd organize the rest. So Darryl and I poured the footers and bought the lumber, barbecue, and beer. Jackie got all the Limeys and some of the farmers to come over. She organized teams—blue armbands hammered, red armbands sawed, that kind of thing—and the barn went up in one day. It was just like *Witness*, except the men weren't wearing turquoise shirts and we clearly didn't have God on our side because as soon as we'd gotten half of it raised, the sky turned black and it started to rain. And I mean *rain*, like God opened a fire hydrant. Or as Odie says, 'Like a cow pissing on a flat rock.'"

Tug laughed hard at this description, a reaction that gave Alyssa a little jolt of triumph.

"Then everybody started running like crazy, grabbing power tools and food from the barbecue. We all crammed into the living room smelling like wet dogs and ended up having a picnic on the floor. The rain turned the barn site into a mudpit, but afterward we went out and finished it up. It was the most fun I've ever had in my life."

"Well then," said Tug, lifting up his coffee mug. "Here's to cow piss."

CHAPTER 16

Two picnic tables had been pushed end-to-end under a big elm in front of Limespring's old dairy buildings. It was a fine spot with long views of soft green hills, and it often caught a breeze. Over the years the tables had become the Limeys' unofficial summer commons.

At night, the more social fellows would gather in the lodge, either for poker games or readings or just to talk. But during the day it was those two picnic tables that they went to. The place to escape the rigors of the creative process or creative procrastination. The place to break bread or, in the case of Limespring lunches, ham salad sandwiches. At noon, Cora would drive her station wagon up the dirt road from the kitchen and deliver the black lunch pails to an alcove in the dairy barn kitchen. From around noon to about one-thirty, poets and painters, novelists and composers, photographers and memoirists emerged from the studios, blinking in the sun, and walked to the tables carrying their pails and their preoccupations.

Tug's preoccupation that noon was food. He'd missed breakfast because he'd gone to Finally Farm right after sunrise. Alyssa had told him her barn was a different place in the early morning, and she'd been right. At that hour, the sun angled through cracks in the siding, catching dust particles in midair and making the narrow rays of light almost palpable.

Alyssa had come by around eight with coffee and a present. She had handed him a large folio book tied up in a bow of orange baling twine. "This is exactly what you need," she'd said. "It'll help you see horses from the inside out. But don't get carried away. This artist got so caught up drawing horses, he started dissecting them."

The book, *The Anatomy of the Horse* by George Stubbs, was a cross between veterinary text and art. The first eighty-three pages were filled with impenetrable medical terms such as "infra-pinatus scapulae." But they were followed by thirty-six exquisitely detailed drawings of horses and their skeletons. Tug could almost hear his old Pratt figure drawing teacher saying, "Bones, it's all in the bones."

"Harold Reifman thanks you, and so do I," Tug had said.

Alyssa had left to go grocery shopping in Marshall and Tug had turned back to the separation of light. The next time he looked at his watch it was after eleven. He hadn't eaten anything since last night's dinner.

He power-walked back to Limespring and intercepted Cora as she drove up to the dairy complex with the day's lunches. He grabbed his pail—it had his studio number, C4, painted on one end and a panel of stick-figure horses, which he'd recently added, on the other—and headed to the tables.

For a change, he was the first one there. This rare moment of lunchtime solitude gave him the chance to admire the view and assess future sketching possibilities.

Just down the hill from the tables were the rustic cabins where Tug and eight others lived; next to them was a small red-brick dorm that housed eighteen others. Farther on was the lodge, where breakfast and dinner were served. Hidden from Tug's view was the small white clapboard tenant house that served as the director's residence. Jackie Burke's home for the past nine years.

The "Little House," as it was called, was the only remaining building from the original farm. The main farmhouse had burned down in the 1940s. Grainy black-and-white photos of the old four-columned building hung in the lodge near a haunting sculpture, called *The Cold People*, depicting three shadowy, elongated figures with pointy fingers and balls for legs. The lodge was filled with art made at Limespring. A mobile dangled from the ceiling in the dining room, paintings lined the walls, and the shelves were filled with books written by Limeys.

The cabins and lodge were leftovers from Limestone's merit badge period. For twenty-five years, after it ceased to be a dairy farm and before it became a "Center for Creativity," the property housed a Boy Scout camp. Then, in 1975, the 280-acre property was deeded over to the state. With help from wealthy benefactors in Washington and nearby Warrenton and Middleburg, it re-opened five years later as Virginia's first official arts colony.

Limespring hadn't changed greatly from its Boy Scout days. It was a shoestring operation, a stepchild of the state bureaucracy with a lot more cachet than cash. A previous administration had been so worried about money that it had added the name "Shenandoah" to the colony's title, ignoring geography. Lime-spring actually sits closer to the foothills of the Blue Ridge Mountains, but it was thought the word "Shenandoah"—with its melodic sound and ability to conjure up visions of majestic American mountains—would attract more donors than "Blue Ridge."

The name change might have accounted for a few more patrons, but it wasn't enough to support the operation. As an additional source of income, much of Limestone's acreage was leased to local farmers. Ten acres of feed corn grew not far from the Little House. Cattle grazed within twenty yards of the studios. A favorite Limespring activity was watching Ferdinand the bull have his way with the cows, and just as Tug opened his lunch pail that noon, a black-and-white Holstein heifer began scratching her rump against the nearby pasture fence.

He hadn't gotten far into his ham salad sandwich when Marius and Nattie joined him, followed by Don Schofield, an expat American poet living in Greece, and Charisse McDowell, an Atlanta writer. "My father was a leg man," she'd said her first day at Limespring, "and a great fan of Cyd Charisse."

By the time Abbi showed up, the tables were covered in open pails, sandwich wrappers, and juice bottles.

"I'd skip these if I were you," said Don, holding up a Baggie containing something that looked like fat orange worms. "I think they were made before the Parthenon."

Tug took a cheese puff from his own bag and bit down. "Yowza," he said. "Like eating a sponge. Nice color, though. It's peppy."

"We used to have something like these in Czechoslovakia before glasnost," said Marius, "but they were brown and heavy and tasted like potatoes."

"In other words, they were nothing like cheese puffs," said Nattie.

"They were, in our imagination," said Marius. "Czechoslovakia had much more imagination before glasnost."

"Speaking of imagination," said Charisse, who, unlike her namesake, was a short, plump woman with a ribbon of glossy dark hair running halfway down her back, "it's only four days to the Follies and I don't have a clue what to wear. Alyssa says be exotic and the closest I have is a pair of black running tights."

"Not to worry," said Abbi. "I've got a whole closet of exotic. Come by tonight after dinner. Cabin seven. You'll look like Cleopatra by the time I'm through."

"Does that mean you'll miss our walk?" said Don. He was an avid hiker who'd started a group stroll on his first evening at Limespring and hadn't missed one since.

"Don't wait for us," said Abbi. "We'll be busy playing Barbie doll."

"Count me out, too," said Tug. "I'm going back to Finally Farm this evening. Alyssa said the light on her pond is amazing as the sun goes down. It's a good chance to do some light and shadow studies."

"No, no, no, Tug my friend," said Marius, shaking his head. "You've got it all wrong. It's a good chance for you to study the delicious Alyssa Brown."

"Oh, Marius, stop drooling," said Nattie.

"Besides, Alyssa's married," said Charisse, who leaned across the table toward Tug and batted her eyelashes overdramatically. "Unlike some lonely Limespring writers I know. By the way, have I ever told you about the light in my room? The shadows in my cabin are amazing around ten o'clock at night."

"Very funny," said Tug amid the laughter. "But, unlike you, Marius, my mind's on art, not women. Finally Farm's a dream. Hills, horses, barns, all that crazy stuff in the house. And what about those starbugs, Marius? They even inspired you. I feel like I'm back in art school. Anyway, Charisse is right. Alyssa's married and I have a girlfriend . . . Sort of."

"Good God, Tug!" said Abbi. "You're not still stringing Margaux along, are you?"

"Who's Margaux?" Don and Charisse said together.

Marius pointed at the red-faced Tug. "There seems to be more to our Mr. Tug than we know."

"Or less," said Abbi sarcastically.

"Enough, enough," said Tug. "I'm trying to have a serious discussion about art."

"And," said Marius, "we're trying to have a serious discussion about sex."

Tug started packing the remains of his meal into his lunchbox. "Then there's nothing to discuss."

Marius looked up at the elm branches. "Forgive him, God. He's a madman," he said. Then he held out a hand like a tour guide making note of the late spring landscape. "Women are like flowers. Each one should be handled carefully; each one should be savored; and each one should be pollinated."

This brought howls of friendly outrage from Nattie and Charisse and the utter annihilation of any serious discussion about art. New lunch recruits arrived and, under the cover of greetings and updates about artistic progress, Tug said his good-byes and walked back to the dairy building and his studio.

The dairy, built in 1917 of ash gray cinder block, had been gutted of its stanchions and milking apparatus. The cavernous rooms that remained were partitioned to create the studios, which surrounded the Square, where visual artists often moved their work for different light or longer views.

Tug's studio was a large white room that contained several

workbenches, a couch, a sink, and a block-and-board bookshelf. A grid of iron piping hung from the ceiling; eight adjustable spot-lights were clipped to it. Dried paint drips and splatters gave the bare concrete floor a Jackson Pollock motif. For the past few years, occupants had written or painted their names and dates on the door frame so that from a distance it resembled a column of col-orful hieroglyphics. Tug had tacked up dozens of sketchpad pages around the room. Horse heads and haunches filled some; others contained partial landscapes or barnscapes. None were completed.

A series of vertical shapes in black, gray, and white covered a page that lay on one of the workbenches. Tug tore the sketch off the pad and sat down in front of the blank page. He thought about that morning's trip to Finally Farm. The light had been inspiring, but what had struck him more was the calm. An overlay of barn noises only amplified it. From his first day at Limespring he'd begun slowing down. But that morning was different. Its peaceful-ness had reminded him of a seventeenth-century Delft landscape. At that moment in the barn, he would have traded all the video installations in the world to be able to capture the feeling. And then Alyssa had come with the book and coffee.

He knew what his daily trips to Finally Farm might seem like to the other Limeys. And he knew what he'd told them at lunch wasn't the complete truth. It wasn't only about art. If it had been, why hadn't he ever mentioned Margaux's name to Alyssa?

Absentmindedly, he picked up a Sharpie and began making crosshatching patterns in the lower right-hand corner of the paper.

After a while he stopped doodling and began to draw an oval shape near the center of the page and, next to it, a faint triangle. In a few minutes the oval became a cheek, the triangle a nose. Somewhat later an eye, with the slightly downturned lids he'd been looking at for the past few weeks, took shape and began to look back at its creator.

CHAPTER 17

Two days after Tug missed the evening hike to see Finally Farm at sundown, Nattie leaned over to Abbi and whispered, "Still think they're not doing it?"

She didn't need to whisper—the Limespring theater was as noisy as a construction zone. Fifteen yards away, three Limeys were knocking together fake storefronts of Baghdad with a nail gun. Near them, another three were testing out spotlights and cursing creatively. A few yards in the other direction, Marius was practicing line readings in a booming voice. "Your wish is my *command!*" "Your *wish* is my command!" "Your wish is *my* command!"

Nattie and Abbi were on the scenery crew, painting a Herez design on a piece of plywood that was to be a magic carpet. They had stopped to watch Tug play the Sultan to Alyssa's Scheherazade on the small stage below them.

The theater, or "Follies Coliseum" as it was called this time of year, was a rustic amphitheater carved into an opening in the woods behind the barn. The stage was just a circle of concrete that backed up to a bank of Limespring Creek. It faced two sections of split-log benches stepping up the grassy slope that Nattie and Abbi were using as a studio. The theater dated from Limespring's Boy Scout era. Some kids from New Jersey, bused down for a month's stay in the country, had built it as a summer project. The

Boy Scout fleur-de-lis and the inscription "Fort Lee Troop 6" could still be seen etched in one corner of the concrete. Not to be outdone by a bunch of Jersey teenagers, some Limeys had added multicolored tiles and a removable bronze gnomon to turn the circle into a huge sundial.

Preparations for the performance had sputtered along for ten days, but now, with the summer solstice party and Limespring Follies only four days away, Alyssa had forced the pace, getting the volunteers to work an extra two hours after dinner. Things were in a shambles. Confused actors tripped over tools and smeared themselves on half-painted backdrops; a bank of lights had fallen over with a frightening crash. But old hands knew that, somehow, Alyssa would pull it together. It helped that she not only oversaw everything but was also the lead actress. Unlike her amateur cast, she could turn a corny script into delicious ham.

"All right, you sorceress. Live another night," Tug was saying in an accent that sounded more like something from a Tijuana sombrero shop than a Middle Eastern palace. "Once again, you have left me hungry for more."

Tug took Alyssa's arm and started to chew it up and down as if it were an ear of corn. She spun into him, wrapped her free arm around his neck, and threw her head back.

"Oh, Master, I thank you a thousand times," she said, sounding suspiciously like Barbara Eden in *I Dream of Jeannie*. "You will not regret this. I will satisfy *all* your hungers."

Nattie nodded down at the stage. "That looks like a lot more than acting to me. I'll bet you ten bucks they're . . ." She finished the sentence by sliding her index finger in and out of a tunnel she'd made with the fingers of her other hand.

Abbi put down her paintbrush and peered over her glasses at the diminutive redhead on the other side of the plywood. "You are, as usual, your wonderfully eloquent self. But, not to put too fine a point on it, I don't think they are . . ." Abbi made the same hand gesture, then added, "Yet."

Nattie shook her head. "Wrong."

"I'm not wrong," Abbi said. "Tug told me so himself. He said they were just really good friends."

"Ha! Good friends," Nattie said. "Maybe three weeks ago. Just look at her now. Watch the way her hands move and her face lights up. Yeah, I know she's always animated, but now she's . . . she's . . ." Nattie searched for a word. "She's . . ."

"Carbonated?"

"Exactly," Nattie said. "So you've seen it, too. And what about Tug? He's been at her place every morning since they met. Have you seen his sketches? What happened to the horse project? Now he's drawing everything there. Even the shit spreader. And catch the way he looks at her."

"I didn't say they don't have the hots for each other. I simply said I don't think it's gone beyond their imagination. At this point, yes, I do believe they're just really good friends. Kind of like you and Marius." Abbi cocked her head and arched her left eyebrow. "Right?"

"Here we go again. Marius and I *are* just good friends. I don't care what Cora says about the boxwoods. He was just showing me where he wanted to put his next installation. That's it, end of story. No married men for me. The sad truth is it's been so long, I don't even remember what a penis looks like anymore."

"Sure, Nattie. Whatever you say. But for your information, Marius looks at you the way Tug looks at Lissy."

"Marius looks at every woman that way. Even Mrs. Tomkins, and she's eighty-five."

As other cast members joined Scheherazade and the Sultan, Abbi turned back to the magic carpet. But Nattie kept watching the stage.

"Back to this Tug-Alyssa thing," Nattie said. "Maybe Tug's just being discreet. Ask him again. Or better yet, ask Alyssa, you guys are close. Next time you go riding, ask her then."

Abbi's tongue was pressed to her upper lip in concentration as she tried to paint a series of minute orange zigzags inside some tiny green rectangles that Nattie had outlined. "Nattie,

ease up on these designs, would you? I'm a writer, not a calligrapher. And I can't just come out and ask her if she's you-know-
whating Tug."

She continued painting zigzags and wiping off the orange over-
flow with a rag. "Lissy's pretty private about her personal life. It
took her eight years to open up to me *once*. And that's only because we were both drunk. Remember last year when she made me
dinner for my birthday? After you guys left, we finished the last
bottle of wine and I started complaining about men in general and
William in particular. Then I asked her what she thought about
the notion of great love. 'Luxury of youth,' she said—she was
even drunker than I was. She started talking about Darryl, how
they'd separated, but got back together for their daughter's sake.
Then she said the saddest thing—I went back to my cabin to write
it down to use it in a book. She said she and Darryl had found a
way to stop hurting each other and sometimes that's the best you
can hope for in a marriage."

"Ouch, I've been there," said Nattie, "except Henry and I never
found a way to stop hurting each other."

For a moment Nattie was silent. "I know why she stays," she
said, breaking her reverie.

Abbi put down her paintbrush. "Okay, Dr. Freud, lay it on me."

"Because after a while you stop seeing the bars and start thinking your jail is your safe house. It's like the way our brains flip
everything over, so we don't have to stand on our heads to make
things seem right side up. Then if you stand on your head, everything looks upside down, for a while. And you know something's
wrong.

"But here's the catch: You don't have that long to fix the problem, because before you realize it, your brain will flip things over
so everything seems right, even though you're standing on your
head. And after a while you don't even know you're standing on
your head. That's what happened to me. I was standing on my
head for eighteen years, but everything looked fine. If it hadn't
been for Henry wanting to go to MBA school, I'd still be standing
on my head. He actually asked me for a divorce because he

thought I'd make fun of his fellow MBA classmates. Which I would have. If you ask me, Darryl's been making Alyssa do head-stands. The real question is, has Tug flipped her back over and will she do something about it?"

CHAPTER 18

The next morning, Alyssa was in the wash stall, soaking the foot of an uncooperative horse that was trying to muscle his way out of the bucket, when Abbi walked in. "Hey Liss," she said. "Does this mean we're not going for a ride?"

Alyssa shoved her weight into the side of the horse, shifting him enough so his foot landed in the bucket of hot water and Epsom salts. "No," she said, wrestling with him as he tried to remove his foot again. "This one's not ready for trails yet, anyway. He still thinks he's on the track. Plus he's dead lame. You should see the poor guy walk. It's just a stone bruise, but he acts like he broke his leg. Give me a few minutes to finish up, then we'll get Roy and Theo, okay?"

"No problem," Abbi said. "I'll go talk to Tug, unless you need an extra hand."

Alyssa waved Abbi on and as Abbi walked away she heard a loud, "God bless it, Rascal," and a bucket of water spilling down the wash stall drain.

Tug was sitting on a folding chair outside the barn, his back to the sun. He was facing Mount Buck, the hill that formed the back of the property. He was trying to capture planes of light shifting over the long grasses.

"Hey, Tug, how's it going?" Abbi said, looking over his shoulder.

"My, how representational we're getting. Very Andrew Wyeth. Want me to lie in the grass and play Christina?"

"Ha-ha, very funny," Tug said and then began an earnest explanation of this new phase in his art, how he was finding inspiration, even comfort, in the discipline of realism. When he got to the part about fundamental shapes and line, Abbi interrupted. "Yeah, yeah, yeah," she said, "this creativity talk is all very interesting, but before Alyssa comes out, I'm supposed to deliver a message from Nattie. A question, actually. Look up at me. She told me to do it exactly this way."

Tug turned his head. "Are you and Alyssa . . . ?" She finished by making the finger-sliding-in-the-tunnel gesture.

Tug shook his head and laughed. "Leave it to Nattie to put it that way. She and Marius are perfect for one another, two knuckleheads. Alyssa and I are friends, that's all." Then he gave her a smile. "Besides, you know me better than that."

Now it was Abbi's turn to laugh. She certainly did know him. She herself had been felled by his contagious smile and country-boy charm. She'd met him fifteen years ago at a Guggenheim show of Donald Judd's boxes. He'd graduated from Pratt and was welding at an auto body shop to pay the rent. She'd just graduated from Barnard and was waitressing at a coffee shop. The two months that followed had been intense, but Abbi knew from the start it wasn't serious. He wasn't ready to settle into anything resembling monogamy and neither was she.

When the romance wore off, she found that she wanted to keep him as a friend. She hadn't been in love with him, so there was no deep hurt when he told her he'd met someone else. And she liked him. She liked his energy and his concern. He was as passionate about people as his art.

A few weeks before they became "just friends," they were walking down West Fourteenth Street. It was bitterly cold and they saw a straggly-haired homeless man standing by a corner. He was carrying a cardboard sign that read: "Please help. Please. Vietnam veteran. Cold and homeless. Need work or money for food and shelter." As the light turned green, a hand reached out from a car and dumped coffee into the homeless man's donation cup. Then the car sped off.

They were both outraged, but Tug turned his anger into art. He and some Pratt buddies scoured the boroughs for homeless people and paid each one $5 for their signs. Then, using old ornate wood frames they'd decorated with gilt paint, they matted and mounted the signs and, with the arm-twisting of some of the Pratt faculty, got them hung at a Chelsea gallery that specialized in outsider and folk art. Tug called the show "Please Help Please." He had the gallery charge a $1 entrance fee and donated everything, including money from sales, to a homeless shelter in Brooklyn.

Abbi went to the opening, which attracted a surprisingly large crowd, including a local TV station. Tug and his crew were there, wearing secondhand tux jackets and jeans; so was the homeless man whose plight had started it all. That night she and Tug went back to her apartment and never got to sleep.

But over the years, they'd turned out to be far better friends than lovers. Abbi became the big sister Tug had never known he needed. She'd helped extricate him from several unsatisfactory relationships that the Smile had gotten him into. He had a weakness for the thin, the dark, and the dour. Of which Margaux was one of the thinnest, darkest, and least likely to chuckle.

Abbi's armchair psychoanalysis was that Tug was trying to prove to himself, by conquest, that he belonged to New York's art crowd. She'd never told him flat out: "Okay, you've proven it, now grow up and move on." But in the past few years she'd tried to fix him up with friends who had more effervescence and fewer black outfits. She was certain that Tug would find a way out of his crisis of art if he found someone who helped him be happier, looser, and goofier.

Someone like Alyssa Brown?

That possibility had never occurred to Abbi when she was arm-twisting Tug into a Limespring summer. But suddenly he was happier, looser, and goofier than she'd seen him in years.

"Well, maybe Alyssa will have more to say on the subject," she said. To her delight, this wiped the Smile from Tug's face.

He narrowed his eyes and pointed a finger at her. "Abbi, if you say or hint or suggest anything to Alyssa about anything like this, I'll kill you. Slowly and painfully."

She rolled her eyes and pretended to swoon. "Oooh, Tug, I love it when you get rough. Quit worrying, I'm on your side. Discretion is my middle name."

CHAPTER 19

"Tug's great, isn't he? I mean he's funny and serious at the same time. And he's a really good person, too. You know he helps coach a boys' basketball team, and did I ever tell you about his homeless art project . . ."

Abbi's words drifted up to Alyssa from behind. She caught most of them, but as the horses' hooves rustled the leaves and crunched twigs, some of them were lost. It didn't matter, she got the picture. They were all about Tug and what a great, generous, handsome, sweet, Mother Teresa kind of guy Tug was.

It seemed odd for Abbi to go on like this. Gush didn't suit her. Irony, yes, but not adulation. It reminded Alyssa of Roz talking about her latest boyfriend. She'd met him during spring break at a used bookstore and couldn't stop talking about him. Alyssa met him once; his name was Jackson, he was a wiry philosophy major at Georgetown with bold blue eyes and frizzy hair. She'd found him pompous; Roz found him intense and charismatic. She'd wondered at the time if Roz had lost her virginity to him. She started to wonder about it now, but chased away the thought.

She didn't want to think about that. She didn't want to think, period. That was the beauty of trail rides. She could just melt into the sway of Theo's body. She'd sink herself into his rhythm until she didn't know where she stopped and he began. Every move of his felt like a move of hers. Even when he coiled his muscles and sprang to the side, she did the same, riding the spook as if it had been choreographed. She'd always imagined figure skaters stitched together with invisible elastic threads that kept them bound through every spin and curve. When she was on a horse, she felt tied with the same invisible threads.

While Abbi continued to talk, Alyssa nodded her head every so often and tried to fall into Theo's rhythm. But the no-think magic of trail rides wasn't working. Every time she settled in, Abbi's words yanked her back to the surface.

Abbi couldn't stop talking about Tug, just like Roz couldn't stop talking about Jackson. Alyssa didn't know what she found more annoying: that Abbi had the hots for Tug, or that she cared that Abbi had the hots for Tug. Thinking about it only made her more irritated. She tried to drive away the irritation with rationality. Abbi was single, she could do whatever she wanted. She'd had a thing in the past with Tug, there was no law she couldn't rekindle it. And who am I to feel . . . whatever it is I'm feeling? I barely know the guy. We're just friends.

". . . and I know he downplays his work," Abbi was saying, "but I'd kill for the kind of reviews he gets—of course, that's assuming I ever get published. He's the whole package, don't you think?"

They'd gotten to a wider part of the trail and Abbi had trotted her horse up beside Alyssa's.

When Theo started prancing at the other horse's approach, Alyssa patted his neck and cooed, "Settle down now, boy. It's just Roy." As she continued to stroke his neck, he relaxed, dropped his head, and picked up Roy's easygoing pace.

She forced herself to sound casual and light. "Abbi, what's with all this talk about Tug? Things heating up between you two again?"

Abbi's mouth opened and for a moment nothing came out. Then she let out a loud, startled laugh that sent Theo skittering to the side. "Oh, sorry about that, Liss. Me and Tug? Are you out of your mind? Been there, done that. And yes, while it was an exemplary experience, I have no need to revisit my past. I just thought you might want to talk about Tug, that's all."

Alyssa recognized the arched eyebrow. It was Abbi's I-know-what-you're-really-thinking look.

"Now you're the one being ridiculous," she said. "I'll talk about Tug if you want to talk about Tug, but I've got no reason to. He's a terrific artist, he's curious, he's funny, he seems like a great guy, what else is there to say?"

There were a lot more things Alyssa could have said. Like how many different outfits she tried on every morning before he came over or how much she thought of him on her nightly walks or how she'd spied on him from the hayloft just the other day to watch his hands at work.

They were big hands, with broad, square palms. Nothing about them seemed delicate until they touched down onto a piece of paper. It was the delicacy of his movements that intrigued her. She'd noticed it the first time she'd watched him draw nearly three weeks before.

"I'm hunting for some extra halters," she'd called down to him from the hayloft. As usual, he was sitting on a folding chair in the center aisle of the barn. "Watch out, I may throw a few down."

She had plenty of halters in the tack room, but she couldn't think of another ruse. She stomped around for a while, moving buckets and rattling things. Then she quietly unzipped her paddock boots and tiptoed across the hay-covered floor to the edge of the loft. She wedged herself between two hay bales and peered down.

He didn't seem to notice that the loft noises had stopped. He had a stick of charcoal in his right hand and a dark glob of kneaded eraser in his left; his drawing pad was propped against his knees. As best as Alyssa could tell from above, he was sketching a water bucket that hung against the horizontal planking inside the stall.

As she watched, he looked down at the drawing pad, back up to the stall, then back down again. His hand made a series of quick, light strokes and the bucket part of the image began to fill in. Then he stopped for a moment and squinted his eyes at the scene before him. He rubbed the wad of eraser against some errant lines and slowly began to work an area to the lower right of the page, coaxing a shadow to life.

She didn't know how much longer she could keep up the halter charade. But she didn't want to leave. It wasn't just that Tug's hands were fascinating, there was also something seductive about hiding in the loft and spying like a thirteen-year-old. Something sexy. And it had been years since Alyssa had felt sexy.

She and Darryl had never been exuberant lovers. The first time they made love—on the couch in her apartment—she'd been on top of him. He'd been surprised by how noisy she was. Right in the middle, he looked up and said, "Oh my. I hope your neighbors aren't home."

From then on, she toned it down. By the time Roz was born, their sex life was routine at best. Occasionally she'd try to spice things up with a slinky nightgown or bottle of massage oil. Once she even suggested he tie her up. He'd laughed uncomfortably and said, "I don't think that's my style."

After a while, months began to pass before either of them made an advance. She couldn't even remember the last time they'd made love. There might have been snow on the ground.

That day in the hayloft, as she watched Tug's hands moving across the drawing board, she wondered how they'd feel moving across her.

The trail narrowed again and Alyssa pressed Theo ahead, ducking under some branches. "Seems like a great guy," was just the beginning of what she could have said to Abbi about Tug. But beyond it were things she could barely admit to herself, let alone to another person.

What she did say was this: "You know me, Abbi. I'll support Limespring any way I can, and if opening my farm to an artist helps, then my farm is open to Tug or any other fellow."

The arch in Abbi's eyebrow returned. "Right," she said.

CHAPTER 20

On solstice day the sun stands still. It hesitates at the horizon, as if it's wondering, Should I head farther north tomorrow? It never does. The next day, it turns back and, evening by evening, ever south, it heads to winter. But on the day of hesitation anything's possible. Put vervain, trefoil, rue, and roses under a girl's pillow and she'll dream of unknown lovers. Send Puck around the world and he'll find that flower, purple with love's wound. Mix an arts colony with midsummer and you'll get revelry and rococo.

Limespring's famous stone arch had been dressed with votive candles and long streamers of ribbon. Around sunset, the ribbons' bright colors matched the sky's magentas and marigold yellows. As darkness settled in, the candles, winking away in stained-glass cups, outlined the arch's lintel and the path that curved under it.

The arch was a massive thing, made of three granite slabs. The artist who created it claimed to be a druid and signed his works with the play on words, "Beodog." He had seen the stones bulldozed aside at a highway road cut. With Jackie pulling some strings, he got a county crew to haul them to a field near the main Limespring office. Two of the slabs were pushed upright and the third, a smaller, flatter piece, was rested on top. Astronomically sited, the arch faced the Shenandoahs, and, like the monoliths of Stonehenge, it exactly framed the sun as it dipped behind the mountains on solstice day.

Everyone gathered at Beodog's imitation Stonehenge for the sun-dipping moment. Afterward, there was a reading by a poet about his tortured childhood and three of the visual artists held open studios. One of them specialized in "captured" pieces of "information"—amebic shapes in varying shades of blue—with Sharpie pens, another drew miniature patterns in boisterous colors and planned to blow them up on wall-sized canvases, the third projected unsettling images (Robert Downey Jr. as Jesus splayed across the artist's lap) on a wall washed in red paint. In the room where Alyssa had first seen Tug's horse sketches, a composer played his composition of sounds he'd recorded in empty studios.

Afterward, the crowd made its way to the amphitheater, through the beribboned arch and down a path lit by flaming tiki torches. There were around seventy people at Limespring that night—fellows, staffers, locals, and a few family members, Darryl Brown among them.

Darryl walked along the path alone—a tall, thin man, with thinning dark hair and a salt-and-pepper beard. Alyssa had gone ahead to make final stage adjustments with her friend from New York who dressed like a gypsy and some artist named Bug or Tug or Doug. Bursts of laughter and conversation came from groups walking ahead and behind him. He hadn't minded the poems, they were actually kind of sad; and if he was forced to choose, there was an orange splash of watercolor bearing some resemblance to a hummingbird that he'd consider hanging on his walls.

But that was it. The video Pietà's self-conscious irony made him want to yank the projector plug out of the wall. Those splats of paint outlined in Magic Marker? Who was the artist kidding with her "capture" and "fill" and "information" talk? They were doodles. He had notebooks full of them in high school. And the sounds of an empty room? At first he'd thought it was parody, another Limespringer being ironic. Then he realized the composer was serious. Talk about the emperor; every last one of them had no clothes. Darryl was convinced that, deep down, they knew how phony it all was, but couldn't admit it because it would make their lives irrelevant.

When he and Alyssa first purchased the farm, the Limespring connection had been amusing. "People of your ilk," the real estate agent had said. They'd laughed at the lockjawed way she'd said "ilk," and imitated her for weeks afterward. Alyssa was excited about being near "all that creativity," and she came up with a theory, which Darryl found charming at the time, that the molecules in the air were bigger at Limespring and bombarded you with the urge to make something. In the beginning, he'd bragged to friends and co-workers that his new farm was just down the road from the arts colony where Benjamin Shepard had written the notorious avant-garde musical *Another Teen Pageant*.

And after the accident, he was even grateful to the place. Alyssa had become so withdrawn that he thought she might disappear into herself. He couldn't reach her—not that he'd tried so hard. In his most painful moments of reflection he might admit he was glad she'd closed herself off from him. The magnitude of her grief scared him; he felt like he'd be swallowed up by it if he got close. So he stayed away.

When, little by little, Alyssa began to open up, it wasn't to Darryl. She turned more and more to Limespring and the farm. At first, he was relieved she had something that gave him the space to heal. But over the years, he had felt more and more the outsider. Limespring and the farm became like pieces of grit in his eye that he couldn't wash out.

Last summer, he'd had it. Packing up on Fridays and fighting the I-66 traffic to Markham was bad enough. Some nights it took him two hours to make the fifty-five miles. But when he got to the farm, either Lissy would be at Limespring, or, worse, Limespring would be there. The farm would be overrun with *artistes*, eating dinner or drinking coffee on his porch. They were loud and disruptive, particularly Nattie, the small redhead, and her fat, obnoxious boyfriend who created "installations." By mid-August, Darryl had stopped coming.

He had come to the Follies this year only because he'd promised Roz. "You have to take pictures for me since I won't be there," she'd said. "Promise you'll go?" He knew the pictures were a ruse.

She really wanted him to go because she was trying to keep her mother and father together.

The candle-lined path took Darryl under the stone arch. As he pushed aside the ribbons dangling from the imperious granite, he wanted to tell the whole effete Limespring crowd what he really thought of their solstice party. But that would have given them something else to be ironic about. Besides, he didn't want to have it out again with Lissy about the farm.

He followed the path into the woods, ending at the top of the amphitheater. In another lifetime, he'd helped repair those benches. Down below on the stage he saw a backdrop of Baghdad storefronts, a four-foot-tall papier-mâché genie bottle that he knew would wind up in the farm's living room, a bed, and a piece of plywood painted to look like an oriental carpet. On the left side of the stage stood an oversized hat rack, its arms covered with outlandish headgear: four turbans, a fez, a fedora with peacock feathers, a sailor's cap, a bonnet with plastic fruit, and several wigs. Stage lights hung from two portable scaffolds and were powered by a portable generator, which hummed like an irritating insect just out of view.

Darryl sat down at the end of a row and was immediately joined by three Limeys, all women and all writers, judging by their conversation. "Yeah, but she got a $150,000 advance for it from Random House," one of them was saying as she squeezed in next to him. "God, I'll be glad when this whole memoir thing goes out of fashion," said another. "I don't believe them, anyway. Why don't they just write novels?"

He noticed that the one next to him was wearing miniature typewriter earrings. Why didn't she just wear a sign saying "I'm a writer"? He looked away.

Soon Alyssa appeared on stage to the chants of the crowd, "Al-lis-sa, Al-lis-sa . . ." She was wearing diaphanous purple harem pants, a pink midriff top crisscrossed with chains of glass baubles and yellow pop-beads, jingle bells around her ankles, and a cone of turquoise posterboard on her head, its tip erupting in a long stream of polka-dot silk that fell halfway down her back.

She held her hands up in front of her as Darryl had seen her do at the start of every production; smiling, nodding, waiting for the noise to stop. When it did, she thanked the crowd, the Limeys, the farmers, everyone for making this night possible. Darryl had heard it all before.

He noticed that his wife had grown even prettier over the years as her face hollowed out, accentuating her bones. She was poised and gracious on the stage, as if she were standing in her living room, greeting friends for dinner. Her talent was undeniable. Even after watching so many of her productions, it still surprised him to see her transform bits and pieces of junk into exotic stage sets.

He felt a small swell of pride as he looked at the stage. But the very things Darryl had found so alluring in Alyssa twenty years ago now rubbed against him like an itchy wool sweater. She was all flourish and curlicues. Why couldn't she have some straight lines?

The lights went out and when they came back on Alyssa was kneeling by the side of the bed, looking up beseechingly at a man in a sultan's outfit and a ridiculously large orange turban. "Please sire, no more," she said. "I am so very tired. Can I not satisfy your desires with a back rub this time? I'm well versed in the arts of shiatsu, Swedish, Reiki, reflexology, and the Barbara Brennan Hands of Light school of massage."

The Sultan crossed his arms imperiously and an exaggerated frown spread across his face. Darryl recognized him as the artist Alyssa had accompanied earlier in the evening. He boomed out, in the worst fake accent Darryl had ever heard, "No, I want to know what happened to Ali Baba. Finish his story or off with your head."

"Okay, okay, keep your pantaloons on," said Alyssa. "Get comfy, O great and munificent Sultan. Ready? The story begins like this: Once upon a time, in a town in Persia, there lived a poor woodcutter named Ali Baba . . ."

With that, Alyssa and the man—Doug? Tug?—jumped off the bed and bounded to the hat rack, where they joined four other actors wrapping their heads in turbans.

For the next forty minutes, the Follies troupe zoomed through

The Thousand and One Nights, telling stories at breakneck speed, flinging costumes to the audience as they changed from character to character. In the Aladdin segment, a bare-chested Marius sprang up from the big bottle to the gasps of the crowd and nearly stole the show with a Jewish genie routine. The actors read their lines from large posterboard cue cards set on two artist's easels, one facing the stage, the other facing the audience. Jackie turned the cards for the actors, and Abbi, wearing her usual gypsy clothes, which for once looked in place, turned the cards for the audience. When someone forgot or flubbed a line, Abbi rapped a pointer against the cue card and the audience—Darryl excluded—shouted out the correct line. For the finale, four Limeys in sheets tied up as harem pants ran across the stage with the plywood magic carpet and dumped Alyssa, who was riding on top of it like a surfer, back onto the bed and into the waiting arms of the now softhearted Sultan.

There was a boisterous standing ovation. Even Darryl applauded for a while. The cast and crew, hands linked, took some collective bows. After calls of "author, author," Abbi joined the line and more bows were made. And still the crowd wouldn't quit. As the applause continued, the curtain call choreography began to break down. Company members stood around, unsure of what to do. Finally, at Alyssa's urging, they lined up again for one final collective bow. But not before Darryl realized that the only two who hadn't let go of each other's hands were Alyssa and Tug.

CHAPTER 21

It was 2 A.M.; the solstice day was done. When the sun returned in four hours, it would make a different arc over the Limespring silos, it would miss the center of Beodog's arch.

The revelry and rococo was over, too. The Follies stage, stripped of its Arabian clothes, had become just a bare circle of concrete again. The storefronts of Baghdad, the giant genie bottle, the magic carpet—all were gone, turned back into wood, wire, and cloth and stored away until next year, when Alyssa's incantations would rematerialize them into something new.

As usual, the crew, the cast, and half the audience had stayed long past the standing ovation to strike the set and keep the midsummer spell from breaking. Guided by votive candles and lights from Limespring buildings, helpers walked back and forth between amphitheater and barn, pieces of disassembled sets and scaffolding balanced on their heads or tucked under their arms.

Outside the storeroom, a table was laid with reception food. Someone had brought a boom box and CDs of Beethoven, Björk, R&B, and the Dixie Chicks. Trips to the amphitheater were interrupted by glasses of wine and Texas two-steps. Somebody put on the peacock-feather fedora and soon costume hats were everywhere. Around midnight Don, the expat Greek poet, a shot glass of tequila balanced on his head, his arms outstretched, stepped off a slow *zembekiko* to the rhythmic clapping of the crowd. The June air, night-sweet and mild, danced a little, too, energized by the charge of performance electricity and James Brown wailing, "Please, please, please."

At one o'clock, Jackie Burke walked up from the amphitheater, blowing out the candles and putting the glass holders in a bag. At two o'clock, the only flame left was on a tiki torch burning by the barn entrance, a primeval memory of midsummer bonfires and Celtic fire festivals. The torchlight revealed only five people—Alyssa, Tug, Marius, Abbi, and Nattie—and one of them was about to break the spell.

"It's late, guys," said Alyssa, who was still wearing her Scheherazade hat. "I really have to go home."

"What happened to Darryl?" Abbi asked.

"He left hours ago," Alyssa said. "Now it's my turn."

"Not without us," said Tug, who was still wearing the orange turban with the glass ruby dangling to his forehead. He grabbed Alyssa's hand and, holding on to her, made a low bow to the others. "Citizens of Baghdad," he announced in his Mexican-Arab accent, "thee night eeess foooll of theeeves. We must eeesscort Scheherazade back to her palace."

Alyssa shook her hands free and pressed her palms together before her face. She turned to Marius and knelt on one knee. "O great and benevolent Genie," she said, "you must grant me one last wish, please."

Marius crossed his arms in front of him, each hand locked on the other elbow. He swelled his chest and lowered his voice. "Your wish is my command," he said, accenting the "command" this time. "What is it, Princess?"

"Restore Tug's New York accent," she said.

"With my deepest pleasure," Marius said and thumped Tug on the head.

Soon after, the little band of Baghdaders headed off to Finally Farm with Tug sounding like Tug again. Still, there must have been some lingering midsummer magic in the air or midsummer liquor in their heads. What else could explain why Nattie spun around like a dervish every so often, or why Alyssa and Tug spontaneously broke into a James Brown–inspired duet of, "Huh! I feel good! I knew that I would, now!"

The moon was low in the sky, and when they turned off the pavement, Alyssa's dirt road wound ahead of them, a gray stripe in a charcoal landscape. The little band fell silent for a moment.

"Where the hell are the starbugs when you need them?" said Nattie. "I can't see a damn thing."

"What'd you do, Lissy," said Abbi, "run them over with your tractor?"

Alyssa rubbed her foot against the gravel, searching for the familiar green glow. "Not a one of them," she said. "Well, don't blame me. I happen to be very careful with my tractor. I'm practically a Jain."

She went a few paces ahead, and in the gloom the group could just make out that she was facing them, walking backwards, the top of her pointed hat nodding back and forth like a conductor's baton. "Blame it on Tug. They all fled to Loudoun County because they thought he made them look fat in his drawings."

"Ah-ah, girl starbugs, vanity is thy name," Marius said. He paused, then singsonged, "Starbug, so bright. First bug I see tonight. Wish I may, wish I might, tell the starbug she looks skinny tonight."

This bit of doggerel brought a round of applause and cries of "Brilliant!" and "Bravo!"

"Next time you apply for a Limespring fellowship, I think it should be as a poet," said Nattie. "Give us another."

Marius made some humming noises for nearly a minute and then said:

> There once was an artist named Tuggy,
> Whose art was driving him buggy,
> He said, "Dear Miss Brown,
> Can I hang around,
> And draw while the weather stays muggy?"

If the group had been sitting down they'd have risen for a standing ovation. As it was, they whooped and cheered. "Marius, you're a genius!" exclaimed Abbi. "While the weather is muggy?" laughed Tug, who tried, futilely in the darkness, to high-five their newfound laureate.

Marius declared that the limerick was even funnier in his native language, and on the spot he translated it, though the words "Tuggy," "buggy," and "muggy" could still be heard among the formidable Slavic consonants.

But the ensuing hilarity was cut short when Alyssa gave the group a loud and dramatic "Shhhh!"

She gestured toward the house. "Uh-oh," she said. "We're almost there and I don't see any lights. Darryl must be asleep. Let's try to be quiet, okay?"

"Yeah, you guys," said Marius, "try to be quiet. Shhhhhhh." He said this at the decibel level of a chainsaw, prompting the rest of them to say "Shh!" as loud as they could.

"Okay, knock it off you guys," said Alyssa, trying to sound severe and failing completely. "You got me home safe, now off you go, shoo."

There were hugs and good-nights, and Tug, slipping back into character—and bad accent—said, "I have geeeven you back your life, Scheherazade, now use it well." Then the four revelers turned back toward Limespring Hollow Road and disappeared into the remains of the midsummer night.

CHAPTER 22

Alyssa leaned against the wall and tried to take off her tap shoes—there'd been a tap number in the Follies, "Oh Abdullah," to the tune of "Oh Susannah." But she'd had too much wine to balance with one hand and undo the straps with the other. So she sat down on the front steps, clicking her soles against the planks.

She hadn't wanted the evening to end. She'd almost suggested they make a campfire by the stage and tell ghost stories or roast marshmallows or sing "Kumbaya," anything to keep the night alive. But Darryl had come for the show and she couldn't leave him at the farm alone too long.

She knew she should go inside. Instead she sat on the steps, her feet softly tapping the wood, and replayed the night, humming the songs and remembering the moment of exhilaration as she slid off the plywood magic carpet onto the old bed. She'd missed her mark and fallen on top of Tug instead of next to him. The crowd loved it, erupting in applause. The cast loved it, too, especially Tug. Thinking about it now, she could almost feel his chest heaving up and down as he laughed.

Finally, she stood up, shoes in hand. Slowly she eased the screen door open, trying to keep the hinges from squeaking. As quiet as a tipsy woman wearing baubles and carrying tap shoes could, she made her way through the dark house and upstairs to the bedroom.

The French doors to the balcony were open, letting in a small breeze but little light. By then the moon was down. Alyssa could barely make out Darryl's shape on the bed. She took a step closer to see that he was on his side, his back to her. She watched the ghostly outline of the sheet rise and fall with his breathing as she slipped off her costume and put on a T-shirt. Then she lifted the sheet and, with exaggerated care, slid her legs down the cotton, trying to make as few ripples as possible in the still waters of their bed. She laid her head on the pillow.

"Nice of you to come home." Darryl's voice stabbed the darkness.

"Oh," she said. "You're awake. I thought you were asleep."

"Little chance of that with you and your friends outside shouting like a bunch of four-year-olds."

Alyssa didn't respond for a moment. She was caught between guilt and anger. Anger because she knew Darryl was about to launch into a Limespring rant, and guilt for waking him up, for wishing the Follies hadn't ended, for not wanting to come inside, for not wanting to join him in their bed.

"I'm sorry," she said, her voice as neutral as she could make it. "You're right, we were idiots. It's just that, well, you know how it is after we close a show. It's hard to stop the energy. Once it takes over it—"

Darryl cut her off. "Spare me the theatrical energy speech," he said, his back still to her. "I've heard it before. I'm sick of it. Sick of Limespring. Sick of the Follies and all those pretentious assholes. Tell me, Liss, does 'theatrical energy' explain why you and your co-star were so goddamned chummy on stage? Just how much 'theatrical energy' is there between you two? Are you sleeping with him?"

Alyssa felt like a cartoon character, her heart pounding right out through her chest. All she could hear was the blood rushing in her ears; her face felt like it was on fire. She was grateful for the darkness, so Darryl couldn't see her flush.

She sat up, hugging her knees to steady herself. "Sleeping with him? Sleeping with who? Marius? What are you talking about, Darryl? This goes way beyond your normal Limespring bullshit."

"You know exactly who I'm talking about. Tug or Bug or whatever phony name he goes by. The one you were holding hands with through the whole fucking curtain call. Everyone else dropped their hands, but no, not you. Not *my* wife. You were up there smiling and holding hands with that guy like you've been fucking him for months."

Alyssa tore the sheet back and jumped out of bed. "Jesus Christ, Darryl, this is crazy." She walked to the open balcony, searching for oxygen. "Just more of your crazy Limespring talk. I'm not fucking anyone. Not Tug and certainly not you. You made that pretty damn clear when you said you were staying in D.C. all summer."

"I have work there, and a life," Darryl said.

"Yeah, well I have work here, and a life," Alyssa said.

"So I see," Darryl said. He got out of bed and stepped to the wall where Tug's farm drawings were tacked up. "These his?" he asked.

Alyssa faced him, but in the darkness it was like trying to look up from the bottom of a murky pond. She could only make out the pale shapes of Darryl's T-shirt and jockey shorts against the dark wall.

"So what if they are?" she said. "They're just sketches. He's from the City and wants to learn to draw nature. I told him he could hang around here. Is that a crime?"

"Just sketches, huh?" Darryl said. "Then I guess you won't mind this."

The pale shapes lunged back and forth along the wall. Alyssa could hear the sound of paper being ripped off thumbtacks and torn to pieces.

"Stop it, stop it!" she yelled. "That's someone's work!"

"I thought you said they were just sketches," he said and ripped up another.

"Fuck you!" Alyssa said. "Fuck you!"

She started toward the bedroom stairs but Darryl chased after her. He grabbed for her arm and caught her wrist, digging his fingers into her.

"Don't you walk out of this room." His voice was low and stran-gled; the words came spitting out as if they'd been squeezed through a tube. She'd never heard him talk to her, or anyone, this way. They stood at the head of the stairs for a moment, facing each other, both paralyzed by the intensity of his tone.

Then he said, "You've been walking out of this relationship for years."

Alyssa jerked her arm away. "Oh really? Is that how you see it? You know I wasn't the first one out the door. Even before every-thing happened you were so cold and remote I'd have been better off alone."

"Better off alone? You think so? Okay then, you can kiss your Limespring buddies good-bye. My grandmother's money bought this farm, remember? It's not yours. You have zero claim to it. If you don't believe me, talk to the lawyer who told me so. And you know damn well this place would sell in a heartbeat to any one of those developers who've been sniffing around."

Alyssa stared at him, mouth open. "You talked to a lawyer?"

"You bet your ass I did. You go, the farm goes."

CHAPTER 23

Alyssa lay on her side, legs and arms tucked into her chest, listening to Darryl move around the room gathering his things to take back to Washington. He was trying to be quiet; she was pretending to be asleep.

Carrying his shoes in his hands, he walked down the stairs. He didn't stop in the kitchen for his usual morning cup of coffee. Instead, she heard the front door close and, a moment later, his car door open. She listened as the sound of tires crunching against the gravel grew fainter and fainter until all she heard was the mooing of a cow. Still she lay there, eyes closed.

She tried to replay the recent good scenes in her life: phone calls from Roz, the Follies, riding the horses, evening walks down Limespring Hollow Road, dinners with the Limeys, mornings with Tug. But last night's fight with Darryl kept intruding.

Usually she could push away the bad; she'd been doing it for years. It was like Lamaze breathing, a fancy form of distraction. Except Lamaze only worked to a point. No matter how hard you breathed or how focused you stayed, the transition phase of labor came bearing down and nothing could distract you from the pain of an eight-pound baby squeezing through a ten-centimeter tunnel.

And now she was beyond distraction. She kept seeing white shapes lunging demonically back and forth against a dark wall. No matter how hard she tried, she couldn't turn off the sound of tearing paper and of Darryl's voice, strangled in anger.

She exhaled heavily and opened her eyes. Why did Darryl ask if she'd been sleeping with Tug? He'd never paid any attention before to what she did at Limespring or whom she did it with. Why now?

She swung her legs over to the side of the bed and sat up. The answers were obvious, because she'd been so obvious.

For the last few weeks, she'd been acting like a teenager on her first date. Two days ago, she'd spent twenty-five minutes getting dressed before Tug came over. She'd tried on a pile of T-shirts before finally settling on a turquoise one that made her eyes look bluer. A week before she had splurged on a $17 jar of "Youth Revitalizing Crème" she'd found at the CVS in Warrenton. It was sitting on the bathroom sink, next to the $2.69 tube of Lubriderm she normally smeared on her face at night. On her way out of the store, she'd walked through the hair care aisle, and actually considered buying a home highlighting kit.

Then came the curtain call.

Of course Darryl had noticed something. He wasn't blind.

Alyssa got up and walked toward the balcony. What an idiot she'd been. Somehow, she'd gotten so swept up by Limespring and the Follies and Tug, she'd forgotten she had a husband. Even worse: a husband in the audience.

The cheeky morning sun and the shimmering green hayfields didn't brighten her dark mood. "Shit!" She slapped her hand so hard against the screen door that it slammed open against the siding. She stepped outside and leaned over the railing. The air was damp and felt cool to her skin.

Okay, so Tug and I held hands, Alyssa thought, but that's no reason to end up in divorce court. And, yes, I've imagined a kiss or two. But thinking about adultery doesn't make me an adulteress. People imagine lots of things. Even Jimmy Carter, the Nobel Peace laureate, committed adultery in his mind.

She closed her eyes and turned her face to the sun. In the red darkness behind her eyelids, she couldn't stop her favorite Tug fantasy from playing out. It always took place in his studio; always on a hot summer night. They've just come back from a walk. He tells her he wants to draw her, with her face flushed and the glow of sweat on her arms. He turns to get his sketch paper. She lets her dress fall to the floor. He turns around, she's standing there, naked. He doesn't say anything. He picks up his pad and begins to draw. She can feel his eyes tracing her, caressing the lines of her body. She listens to the scratch of the pencil against the paper. She hears Tug place the pad on the floor and walk to her. The next thing she feels are his lips on hers.

Her eyes popped open. "Enough," she said aloud and waved her hand across her face, like a windshield wiper erasing her thoughts.

She propped herself against the railing. It's just a fantasy, she rationalized, a fantasy, no big deal. The only thing I'm really guilty of is bad taste. *"Her face flushed; the glow of sweat on her arms."* If the cliché police patrolled daydreams, I'd be in jail. Thinking about Tug doesn't make me unfaithful. Hell, Darryl probably commits mental adultery every time he sees a Victoria's Secret catalog.

But then she pictured herself on stage with Tug as Darryl watched. She knew exactly the hollow look Darryl's eyes got when he was hurt. He didn't deserve deceit. He wasn't a bad man. They'd turned out to be a bad match. Neither of them could help the other when they had needed it the most. Even the best of couples would have had a difficult time. She and Darryl just didn't have the foundation to make it through.

Alyssa walked to the bathroom and ran a stinging hot shower. As the needles sprayed against her body, she tried to sort out her feelings. By the time the water ran cold, the only thing she knew for sure was that she'd managed to turn her skin a bright red.

She started her morning chores of mucking stalls, washing out water buckets, and feeding horses, but she couldn't focus. Finally, she let the horses out into the pasture, promised them she'd feed them later, and walked down the road to Limespring.

CHAPTER 24

"Busy?" Alyssa stood on the narrow porch of cabin 7 trying to sound nonchalant.

"Not particularly," said Abbi, on the other side of the screen door, trying to sound as if she hadn't just woken up. "Come on in." She was wearing a purple chenille bathrobe and the distracted look of a writer before the day's first cup of coffee.

"Sorry, I know it's early," said Alyssa as she stepped inside. "But I wanted to catch you before you went to your studio."

The cabin was just big enough to fit a twin bed, dresser, nightstand, and a frayed green corduroy club chair. Its original walk-in closet had been remodeled into a compact bathroom. In the corner opposite the chair was a tower of books and notebooks.

Abbi motioned Alyssa to the club chair and sat against a heap of pillows by the head of the unmade bed. "Something wrong?"

"You could say that," said Alyssa. "Darryl and I had a fight last night and we didn't leave it on the best of terms. I just wanted to talk it through. You know, figure out how to fix things. You mind?"

"Of course not. What are friends for?" Abbi said with a sympathetic tone that covered up her confusion. In all the years they'd known each other, they'd had only one conversation about Alyssa's marriage, and she'd been drunk. Abbi had seen Alyssa and Darryl squabble before, but this one must have been a doozy.

What else would bring her here this early? Then something clicked in the uncaffeinated fog of her brain.

"Oh," she said. "Does this have something to do with Tug?"

Alyssa winced. "Ouch. That obvious, huh?"

"To everyone but you," Abbi said. "I was trying to be subtle last week when we went riding. I should've just come right out and said it. He talks about you all the time and you're, you're . . . what was the word Nattie used to describe you? Oh yeah, 'carbonated.' You're *carbonated* when he's around. And you'll be happy to know it's driving Charisse crazy. Not that he's noticed. I wouldn't be surprised if he lights incense under that sketch of you."

Alyssa stopped twirling the green threads on the corduroy chair. "What sketch of me? He's just been drawing farm things."

"Then I guess you're just one of his favorite farm things. You didn't really think he was showing up every day just for the sake of art, did you?"

"Well, I've been teaching him about horses. He—"

"Oh please," Abbi said, interrupting her. "It's me you're talking to. Come on, Liss, I'm on your side. And Tug's. He's a great guy. Or I guess we already covered that on our trail ride."

Alyssa continued to twirl the frayed cords. "Okay, so it's not only about drawing. But we're just friends. Besides, he's only here for the summer and I'm married, what else could it be? If anything, I'm a diversion for him. And with Roz not being here I am kind of lonely, I admit it."

Abbi got up, walked over to the chair, and put her hand on top of Alyssa's fingers. "I don't think it's just that you're lonely. Or that you're just a summer diversion."

Alyssa hadn't expected this. She'd wanted the flippant, sarcastic Abbi, the Abbi who couldn't say, "How's the weather?" without an ironic twist. She'd wanted the Abbi who would arch her eyebrows, wave her hands, and tell her not to take any of Tug's attentions seriously. But instead she got an Abbi of care and gentle concern. It was almost as disarming as Darryl's rage.

"Abbi, you're making this worse. I was counting on you to be the voice of reality."

"I am. You just don't like that reality."

"Well the reality is I'm married."

"So you're married," said Abbi. "That doesn't mean you're happy; that doesn't mean you have to stay married."

Alyssa shook her head. "It's not that simple."

"How about something to drink? I've got a coffeemaker here and a couple of mugs."

Alyssa nodded and Abbi began puttering around with a little coffee machine on top of her dresser. "You're right," she said over her shoulder. "Nothing's ever simple. If it were, Shakespeare wouldn't have had anything to write about, now would he?"

Alyssa tried to laugh, but it came out like a sigh.

"So let's talk about the complications. You're married. That's a fairly large complication. But not insurmountable. It's not like you and Darryl are happy together. Or even mildly comfortable. Every time I see him he looks peeved."

"That's because he doesn't like Limespring fellows."

That brought out the arched-eyebrow Abbi. "Oh? So you mean he's not like that when we're not around?"

"All right, we have some problems. And it is true, everything I do irritates him—but it's also vice versa . . ."

"Now, there's a really good reason to stay together—mutual irritation. That's ridiculous. What else could possibly be keeping you two together besides inertia?"

For the next few minutes, Alyssa went down her list of reasons, starting with Roz and ending with Darryl. She invoked loyalty, commitment, perseverance, and was about to add responsibility when Abbi waved her hands like a traffic cop trying to stop a runaway truck.

"Liss, stop," Abbi said. "Roz is eighteen. She's old enough to deal with her parents splitting up. The rest is just crap. You told me last year Darryl wouldn't even notice if you never went back to Washington. What's this really about? What the hell happened last night, anyway?"

This was more like the Abbi that Alyssa had expected. Someone to cut through the emotion and force her to focus. She told

Abbi about the fight, how Darryl accused her of sleeping with Tug, how he ripped up Tug's drawings and then threatened to sell the farm.

"He's actually talked to a lawyer, can you believe it?" Alyssa said. "Talk about betrayal. He consulted a fucking lawyer . . ."

"Why does this surprise you?" Abbi said. "He's hurt. He's lashing back. And—I've never said this to you before—he's an asshole. What'd you expect him to do? Write you a nice note and ask you to stop making googley eyes with Tug? So he sells the farm, big deal. It's just dirt. There's a lot of that in the world."

Alyssa got up and walked to door. "It's not just dirt."

"Okay, so it's dirt and a lot of great art. But you can take that with you. Your farm is spectacular, no question about it. But Lissy, you made it that way, the spectacular part comes from you. You created it, you can re-create it, anywhere. You can't keep putting your life on hold for fifty acres. Things couldn't be any more rotten in Denmark. Darryl's talking to a lawyer, for Christ sakes! It's time to do something. Maybe Tug's your happy ending."

Alyssa turned back to her and said, "Happy endings are in fairy tales."

Abbi stifled the urge to shake her and say, "How could you have a happy ending married to that jerk?" But she figured calling Darryl an asshole was enough for one morning. Instead, she poured out a cup of coffee and handed it to Alyssa. "So, what are you going to do?"

"I don't know. But I do know I'm not losing my farm. I just can't lose the farm." She slapped her hips with her open palms at each one of the last six words.

The gesture caught Abbi by surprise. This was not the Alyssa she thought she knew. That Alyssa was in control, even of her own theatricality.

"What am I going to do?" Alyssa repeated. "The only thing I can do. Make it work with Darryl. And you can't say anything to Tug about this conversation. Nothing. You can't even tell him I was here, promise?"

Abbi nodded. "Of course I won't say anything. But that doesn't mean I agree with you. That doesn't mean I don't think you're making a big mistake. I don't want to sound like a Pollyanna, but you and Tug belong together."

"No we don't," Alyssa said. "I'm married. I'm a grown woman. I'm forty-three years old, I can control whatever this thing with Tug is. I can control my feelings. I am not a teenager. Besides Tug and I want different things, he's . . . Forget it, everything about it's hopeless."

Before Abbi could pounce on the word "hopeless," Alyssa walked over and hugged her. "Thanks for putting up with me and my babbling. I've got to feed the horses and I'm sure you've got plenty of work yourself."

The screen door slapped shut and Abbi watched Alyssa stride off down the pathway, a woman full of purpose and resolve. A woman playing a part.

CHAPTER 25

Two days after the Follies, the morning was overcast and smelled of early summer, an astringent tang of decayed leaves and new green. Limespring had presented Tug with a whole spectrum of new odors: the wooden siding of his cabin baking in the afternoon heat, pines, moss, wild mint that grew by a slow eddy of the creek. Almost everything about the countryside was new to him. It wasn't a simple patchwork of fields and woods. There were vast interlocking systems he'd never thought about before.

Wildflowers grew along wire fences, red foxes ran past black cows, low clouds left tree-topped hills dripping in fog, tractors disked under thistles and dug up rocks. The countryside unfolded like a fractalscape. The closer he looked, the more complex it became. It was probably all the sketching that had brought him this happy intimacy with nature. Whatever the reason, the area around Limespring now seemed teeming with as much wonder and change as Bleecker Street.

He walked down Limespring Hollow Road chewing on the slender stem of a weed, wondering about the people who can tell how long winter will be by the flight of geese or see a good harvest coming in the coat of a fuzzy caterpillar. He wished he could tell his own future that well.

Tug turned onto the dirt road to Finally Farm. He spotted the yellow house tucked between the hills. Had the sun suddenly peeked out from behind the clouds? Okay, maybe it wasn't all about nature and complexity. He pictured Scheherazade falling from the sky into his arms and onto his chest.

No one answered his knock at the farmhouse door so he walked to the barn. Alyssa's blue pickup was parked outside and she was standing on the bed, dumping hay bales off the end. She wore red cowboy boots, jeans splotched with green paint, and a faded yellow T-shirt with printing on the back. Her face was flushed; her hair flounced around her head as she struggled with the bales. She looked like a centerfold in a cowgirl magazine. The morning was definitely brightening.

"Shhhhhhit!" she grunted as a bale went flying to the ground.

"Hey, Scheherazade," Tug said, walking to the pickup. "Don't princesses get a break from this kind of work?"

"Oh, hi, Tug," she said. "I'm back to being a farmhand today."

"Need some help, my lady?" he asked.

"Nope," she answered matter-of-factly. "I'm fine. You go on."

Her brusqueness took him aback. "I was hoping to explore the big hill behind the house," he said, his smile fading. "You said you might show me the trail to the top."

"Did I?" she said as she turned her back to grab another bale. "Well, not today. I've got a lot to do here. Maybe another time."

Tug looked at her, puzzled. "You okay?"

The answer came at him from over her shoulder. "Sure. Just busy."

She turned to face him, a hay bale braced against her thighs, the orange baling twine pulling against her fingers. "Sorry, no coffee today. Ran out of it yesterday and haven't had time to buy more."

Tug gave her another puzzled look, then brought back the smile. "No big deal, I already tanked up at Limespring. Follies night was fantastic, wasn't it?"

"Yeah. It was a good show," Alyssa said. "The audience liked it. Next year I'm thinking about doing a mystery. Maybe some Sherlock Holmes thing. What do you think?"

Tug didn't know what to think. He was the Sultan, she was

Scheherazade, and she was talking to him as if he were a Safeway checkout clerk. "Sounds promising," was all he could come up with, and by the time he did, Alyssa had gone back to manhandling hay bales.

There was an uncomfortable silence. "Well," he said finally, "I guess I'll work out in the pastures today. You can't have too many horse drawings."

"All right," Alyssa said over her shoulder. "See you later."

Tug watched her push another bale off the end of the truck. "Did we wake up Darryl on Follies night?" he asked.

"No. No problem," she said. "He was sound asleep."

Tug turned away. Had he done something wrong? Had he insulted her? Or worse: Was he just another Limespring artist to her? He didn't have any answers. All he knew, as he opened the pasture gate, sketchpad under his arm, was that the magic of Follies night had disappeared in a puff of hay and dust.

But if he had turned around just then, he might have understood. He would have seen Alyssa standing in the back of the truck watching him walk away, trying to focus on the baling twine cutting into her fingers, to stop herself from calling out after him.

CHAPTER 26

For the next few days, Alyssa welcomed Tug each morning with the brusque reserve of a motor vehicle department clerk. She never made coffee. She never sat down next to him as he drew. Twice her blue truck was gone by the time he arrived.

He'd almost gone up to her and asked what caused the change. Had he imagined that there'd been something between them? But she came in and out of the barn so quickly, she made it clear that "hello" and "good-bye" were the only words she wanted to exchange.

Unbeknownst to Tug, there was a whole drama being played out behind his back. For once, Abbi kept her mouth shut and told Tug nothing about the blowup between Alyssa and Darryl, or Alyssa's conversation with her the day after, or her vow to do whatever it took to keep the farm.

Tug couldn't have known that Alyssa had called Darryl at their D.C. home, leaving an apology on the answering machine. Nor could he have known that she'd called Darryl again, later that night, to apologize a second time.

"Did you get my message?" she said. "I said I was sorry for making so much noise when I got back from the Follies. It was inconsiderate. And I should've come home sooner. I'm sorry. I'm sorry we fought. It was pretty horrible, wasn't it?"

If she expected a return apology, she didn't get one. After a brief silence Darryl merely grunted, "Uh-huh." She waited for him to say something more. Finally she asked, "Isn't there anything else you want to say?"

"Not really," he said, sounding like Roz in her most petulant teen years.

"Look, Darryl. We've got problems, and I think we need to deal with them."

"We've got problems all right."

"Maybe we should go to Dr. Levinson."

"We did that before."

"He might be able to help us talk things out."

"I doubt it. He took your side the whole time."

"Stop acting this way," she said, struggling to keep her voice from rising. She knew his tone was meant to hurt her but she refused to take the bait. "At the very least, do it for Roz's sake. She's had enough in her life to deal with."

"Only for Roz's sake?"

Alyssa could picture Darryl's face at that moment. The look of feigned nonchalance, the slight sneer playing about the lips. She knew it well, and knew that, at least for this afternoon, real communication was hopeless.

"Okay, Darryl, I'll call you in a day or so. Maybe then we can have an adult conversation."

She did call, the next day, and on Sunday, too. Each time they talked a little longer and a little more politely. Each time Alyssa fought to stay calm, but it wasn't easy. On Monday morning she woke with the metallic taste of panic in her mouth.

Then, that night, Darryl called her. After a while, the word "overreaction" was mentioned. Eventually, both agreed on the need for civility toward one another. It was a first step. The conversation lasted fifteen minutes. They talked about their upcoming July Fourth party, Roz's internship with her uncle, the possibility of a new furnace for their D.C. home. They avoided the subject of lawyers and real estate agents. The names "Tug," "Bug," or "Doug" never came up.

By Wednesday morning, Alyssa's feelings of panic had begun to subside. Then Tug knocked on the farmhouse door, and, for the first time, he wasn't carrying a sketchpad.

CHAPTER 27

"Hello, Alyssa," he said. It was far too formal a greeting. Tug usually said, "Hey, Princess," or "Blondie, can you come out and play?" She knew immediately he was there to say good-bye. And why not? She'd all but pushed him out the door.

"Look," he said, "I just came by to tell you that I'm pretty much done here. At least for a while. There are a bunch of tumbledown farms along the Shenandoah River that Charisse told me about. You remember her, the writer from Atlanta? She wanted to explore them for possible essays and thought they'd be good subjects for a series of drawings. Anyway, we're going to check them out today. So I probably won't be by in the mornings anymore."

He hesitated, waiting for Alyssa to say something, but all she could get out was a strangled, "Oh."

"Anyway," he continued, "I just wanted to stop by and tell you thanks. Thanks for everything. Showing me the horses, the farm, the cow piss story. Everything."

Alyssa could only manage a weak joke. "So you're trading me in for another farm because I ran out of coffee? If that's the case, you should know I bought a new can yesterday."

"No, no," said Tug, forcing a smile. "But thanks for doing that every morning. It was great. Really, everything here was great."

There was another awkward silence. Each hoped the other

would fill it. Neither did. "Well, anyway," said Tug. "Thanks again. I'm sure I'll see you around Limespring."

For the second time in a week, she watched him turn and walk away.

She bit down hard into the fleshy pad of her lower lip and stared at his back as he became smaller and smaller. She felt incapable of moving or saying anything. She just stood there, holding open the porch door, watching Tug walk out of her life and into the horizon.

Who knows what broke the spell. The sharp pain in her lip? The nearby squawking of an angry cardinal? Whatever it was, suddenly the porch door slammed behind her and she was running out to the barn. She grabbed two saddles from the tack room and threw them on Roy and Theo.

"Sorry guys, no time to brush you down," she said.

Tug was walking along Limespring Hollow Road when he heard the rapid clopping of hooves behind him. He turned to see Alyssa atop Theo. She had the reins in one hand and a rope tied to Roy's halter in the other.

"Hey there, I just happened to be out for a trail ride and I just happened to have a spare horse along . . ." She nodded Roy's way. "So what do you think? Time for your first riding lesson? Couldn't have a more beautiful day."

Tug felt like doing a victory dance. Alyssa was inviting him back into her life. Now all he had to do was mount that big behemoth in front of him.

"You'll never know how much I've been looking forward to this," he said and swallowed hard.

As June ended and July began, things were as they had been, and more. In exchange for learning how to plod around the fields on top of Roy (which wasn't as terrifying as he expected), Tug helped Alyssa muck out stalls. Later, riding lessons were expanded to tractor-driving lessons, in exchange for which Tug helped Alyssa change the oil. A dinner for two was exchanged for help mulching her garden.

And the morning drawing sessions continued. Tug brought his

sketchpad each day. Each day the lines grew more confident, the figures bolder. An art critic might say one could feel the tension in the hay-bale twine, see the pulse in the horses' necks. A lover might say he was drawing with his heart.

And Alyssa? She argued with herself—It wasn't a crime. She wasn't cheating on Darryl. He had friends of the opposite sex, why couldn't she?—and she won every time. What was beyond dispute was this: She was happy.

CHAPTER 28

On July 3, the morning's sketching session was brief. Alyssa had buzzed around preparing for her annual Fourth of July party and Darryl's early-afternoon arrival. Tug halfheartedly offered to help and was glad when Alyssa turned him down. He thought of Darryl as a splotch of lime green paint on a black-and-white drawing. He knew it was unreasonable. Alyssa was no less married on July 3 than she had been on June 6 when they first met. But that didn't ease the resentment.

He was halfway back to Limespring when he realized he'd left a set of colored pencils at the farm. He'd only begun using them the day before, shading earth tones into earlier barn sketches and experimenting with exclamation points of primary reds and yellows. He looked at his watch, it was just 9:45. Plenty of time to retrieve the pencils before the husband showed up.

The husband. Tug was sure Darryl was a jerk. Of course, he'd never met him. Still, Abbi had told him plenty.

"He thinks her monitor's turned too bright," Abbi had said the other night when Tug pressed her for information about Darryl. "And once when she mentioned that his brother was a great husband, Darryl said it was because his brother's wife was organized. Organized! That's his idea of an aphrodisiac."

How could Alyssa have hooked up with someone like that? The husband. *Her* husband.

As he walked back to the farm, he saw her atop one of the two hills that backed the pond. She was on her knees, contemplating something on the ground before her. It was a surprising pose considering that just a half hour before she'd been as hyper as a mosquito.

He went into the barn and searched for his pencils. He thought he'd left them by the folding chair he'd propped against the wall. But the folding chair was gone and so were his pencils. She'd obviously been ridding the barn of his presence in preparation for Darryl's visit.

The last time her husband had come out, she'd said he was "a little bit touchy about the Limespring fellows." Apparently one Limespring fellow in particular. Him. And earlier that morning she'd said it again. "You should probably lay low tomorrow at the party. It'd be better if Darryl didn't see us together much. He's just kind of touchy."

"Touchy," he muttered, his irritation growing the more he thought about being erased from the barn. He walked down the aisle, scanning for places Alyssa might have tucked away his box of pencils. Then he tried the tack room, which is where Alyssa found him, rummaging through a shelf of jars and bottles of smelly horse unguents.

"Tug?"

His mood lightened immediately. "Hey there, cowgirl." Then he put his fingers to his nose. "Yuck, there was some black slime on the side of that jar."

"And now you smell like a road, right? Icthamal, it's made from tar. It's disgusting, but it works. I thought you went back to Limespring."

Tug explained about his pencils and Alyssa opened a drawer in the desk by the phone. "I put them here for safekeeping," she said.

He wanted to say, "*Whose* safekeeping?" but he didn't.

"By the way," he said as he was leaving, "I saw you sitting on top of that hill a few minutes ago. Were you meditating or something?"

A strange look crossed Alyssa's face, but it was gone so quickly he thought he might have imagined it.

"Me meditate? I could use it, but no, I was just looking for a spot to shoot off the fireworks tomorrow."

"Oh," Tug said. It was a lie and he knew it. She'd already told him last week that they always shot the fireworks from the front pasture. As he walked back to Limespring, Alyssa's fib puzzled him. It seemed like such a stupid thing to lie about.

Maybe Abbi had some answers. He knocked on her door and got a cheery, "It's open." Inside, he found her propped up in bed, her fingers running across the keyboard of her laptop.

"Hey, Tug," she said. "Thanks for saving me. I've been struggling with this stupid scene all morning. I'm so sick of Scheherazade, I'm ready to behead her myself. What's up?"

Tug sat in the same green corduroy chair that Alyssa had occupied a week before. He started to tell her about Alyssa kneeling on the top of the hill, but Abbi made him back up. The last she'd heard of the Alyssa-Tug saga, Alyssa was making unconvincing noises about keeping him at arm's length. So Tug had to give her the full story, everything—from the post-Follies freezeout, to the big thaw, to Alyssa's blatant lie about something so innocuous.

"I can't figure her out sometimes," he said.

"Boy, you've got it bad for her," said Abbi. "Don't bother to deny it. You guys are a great match. Unless, of course, she's secretly a wacko or a closet fundamentalist. She was *praying* up there?"

"Not praying exactly," said Tug. "She was kind of kneeling there. And then when I asked her about it she got that faraway look on her face she gets sometimes. But just for a split second. Then she told me that stupid lie. All she had to do was say she went up there for peace and quiet or solitude, or just to look out over the fields."

Abbi tapped her finger against the laptop keyboard. "You know I think Alyssa's terrific," she said. "She's smart and fun and pretty. But even you have to admit, she's a little odd about her farm. It's like she's got its dirt running through her veins. I don't know, maybe she's got a horse buried up there or maybe that's where she first fell in love with the place. Or . . ."

She burst into a laugh. "Maybe she's got Darryl buried up there. No one's seen him since the Follies."

"Well, that would solve things, wouldn't it?"

The exasperation on Tug's face told Abbi everything. She was dying to play Cupid, dying to tell him about her conversation with Alyssa. But she was stopped by the memory of Alyssa's panicky voice saying, "You can't say anything to Tug." So instead she said, "Alyssa's not the easiest person to figure out. I know exactly that faraway look you're talking about. For all her ebullience, there's a real melancholy to her. Once, in the middle of a dinner party— everybody was drinking wine and telling stories and laughing— Alyssa started looking off into space for a few seconds. I could have sworn her eyes welled up. But she's nothing if not a hell of an actress, and the next minute she was back, telling a hilarious story about Marius with a dead-on impression of his Slavic accent. She's like a dotted line; she's got these gaps and I don't know what's in them. Maybe she just has to be alone sometimes. That's not so unusual."

"I guess not," Tug muttered.

"Are you going to be okay at the party tomorrow? You going to be able to handle seeing Alyssa and Darryl together?"

"No," said Tug. "But I guess I'll have to, won't I?"

CHAPTER 29

Finally Farm looked like a flag factory after an explosion. Red, white, and blue ribbons streamed from the branches of the big mimosa tree; bows of bunting looped from porch post to porch post; miniature Old Glories lined the dirt drive; a mosaic of painted rocks formed a life-sized Uncle Sam, who waved to all from the front pasture.

"Wear red, white, and blue," Alyssa's party invitation had said, and almost everyone obliged. There were patriotic combinations of all kinds. Red-and-blue socks with white tennis shoes; blue-and-red-striped ties with white T-shirts. The tango teacher known as "the Bod" wore a red halter top with blue bikini bottoms under a sheer white sarong. Three men showed up wearing identical tricolored Hawaiian shirts. Two others had pulled out bright red gym shorts from some secret layer in their closets. Everyone was issued a plastic white boater encircled by an Old Glory hatband.

Alyssa's guest list was expansive—excessive, Darryl had said— and, as usual, almost everybody showed up. Finally Farm's July Fourth was a highlight of the summer in Markham, a town so small that it was marked only by the little yellow train station that hadn't seen a train go by in thirty-seven years. Cattle farmers mixed with composers; horse fanciers, veterinarians, and blacksmiths mixed with writers and painters; performance artists and sculptors mixed with carpenters, fence men, old-money landed gentry, and Markham's postmistress, Mary Kelly, who knew all the locals by first name and home address. A contingent from the Browns' Washington life showed up, too, sprinkling the crowd with high school teachers from Emerson and biologists from the National Institutes of Health.

Guests began arriving around six. By seven-thirty, when Odie Watkins rang the dinner triangle, nearly eighty people lined up at the barbecue wagon for chicken, baked beans, and coleslaw. As the sky turned from bronze to lilac, children carrying sparklers began darting through the scene like hyperactive fireflies leaving a fuzzy trail of embers behind them. Soon after, the number of amateur guitar players on the front porch reached critical mass and a playalong, singalong began. The music—folk songs and medium-tempo pop tunes—impelled a handful of romantic couples and a few of the pleasantly inebriated to waltz gaily through the grass under the mimosa tree, while ribbons tickled their heads.

Just above them, in the tree's lower branches, a bossy cardinal hopped around making scolding noises, possibly complaining about being upstaged by the bright colors. From his bird's-eye view, he had the same vantage point that Brueghel took for his painting *The Wedding Dance*. And if Alyssa's invitation had called for aprons and codpieces, Brueghel would have felt right at home at Finally Farm's celebration. He would have recognized the boisterous eaters and tipsy laughter; he would have delighted in the sinuous steps of the dancers.

Among the dancers that evening were Alyssa and Tug, but theirs was a negative choreography. As requested by Alyssa, they kept scrupulously apart, avoiding eye contact, each pretending the other was just a piece of the red, white, and blue kaleidoscope. This waltz of avoidance was enabled by party duties. While Alyssa played hostess, Tug and Rick, a tropical landscape artist, kept busy painting faces at a table on a side lawn.

Abbi stopped by around seven, to get an American flag painted on her right cheek. She was wearing red-and-white-striped pants and a purple tank top.

"Is it driving you crazy?"

"Is what driving me crazy?"

She put her hand on Tug's cheek and turned his face toward the front of the house. Behind a long table, stocked with bottles of sparkling cider, pitchers of lemonade, a keg of beer, and rows of plastic glasses, stood Alyssa and Darryl, smiling, laughing and serving drinks.

"That," Abbi said. "Ozzie and Harriet."

Tug looked at the host and hostess and for the first time that night caught Alyssa's eye. She half smiled and quickly turned to talk to a woman Tug didn't recognize.

"Of course it's driving me crazy, " he said, snapping at Abbi as if it were her fault. And he was in just enough of a bad mood to think it was. If Abbi hadn't suggested the horse lessons, none of this would've happened. He'd be sipping beer, having a great time.

For a moment they both watched Alyssa and Darryl.

"They look happy together," said Tug. "I thought you said they didn't get along."

"Just remember, she's an actress," Abbi said. "Look, as soon as you finish up here, come meet us in the back. We'll be eating and drinking and solving the world's problems. We'll cheer you up."

"Right," Tug said glumly as he painted red and white stripes on Abbi's cheek.

A few minutes later a short, slender woman sat down at the table. Her royal blue T-shirt was emblazoned with a white nautilus and the words "Catch your dreams at Emerson."

"You must be Tug," she said as she presented her cheek to him. "Liss says your farm drawings are amazing."

Her words lifted his mood a little. At least Alyssa had been talking about him.

The woman reached her hand out. "I'm Carol Richman. Liss and I teach at"—she pointed to her T-shirt.

"Oh. You're the Sculpey lady. So how're things with the Shrike?"

"Worse than you can imagine," she said. And as Tug painted red and white stripes on her cheek, Carol began a blow-by-blow-by-blow account of the school's woes and Justine Shriker's latest actions, then veered off into a history of her own career as artist and art teacher, eventually touching on her friendship with Alyssa. "Isn't she amazing? She's like a national treasure." And she ended it all with, "Can I join you for the fireworks show?"

Before Tug could sputter out an answer, Odie Watkins rang the triangle. Rick leaned over to Tug and whispered, "Talk about being saved by the bell."

"Food," Tug said to Carol, pointing to the barbecue line. "I'll be over in a few minutes. We just have to clean up here."

Rick and Tug hung back until Carol had safely gone through the line, then they got their food and joined the other Limeys in the grotto.

Alyssa had created it years before in a rocky outcrop between the house and barn. She'd fashioned old tree stumps and left-over boards from the barn into primitive tables and set them by the rocks, creating an elfish outdoor dining spot. A faded sign nailed to the canopying mulberry tree (which precluded tea parties in berry season) announced: "Lady Rosalind's Royal Tea Room."

Sitting on stumps and boulders were Marius, Nattie, Don, Charisse, and Rudy Thomas, a new fellow from Washington who had taken an immediate liking to Nattie when he arrived six days before. Where Roz had long ago pretended to serve tea to the Queen, the Limespring group now ate blackened chicken and potato salad from starred paper plates.

As the sky grew darker, the pop of firecrackers punctuated the proceedings, including a monologue by Marius, who, by arguing for the virtues of racial profiling, was creating some fireworks of his own among the grotto group. Rudy, a documentary filmmaker, and himself a victim of racial profiling, made an impassioned case against the idea, while a half dozen others simply shouted Marius down.

At 8:45, a switch was flipped and the mimosa tree and the

rooflines of the farmhouse were suddenly outlined by strands of tiny twinkling lights. The noisy cardinal, surprised by these fallen stars, flew off for the night. Some of the partiers oohed and ahhed, practicing for the bigger display to come. Somebody on the porch began to sing the first verse of "Slip Slidin' Away." The fireworks were scheduled to begin in less than an hour.

By then, the grotto conversation, fueled by bottles of Budweiser, had hopped from politics to love to college and landed on ex-mates. Abbi told the story of a former lover who'd asked her to donate an egg so he could fertilize it and implant it in his wife. Boos and hisses. Charisse told of her ex-husband who sued for custody of the dog. And lost. Laughter. Nattie told of her ex-husband's new wife. "He wanted frugal? He got it. She rations the towels." More laughter. Then Rudy told of his ex-wife's new living arrangement. "Her new mother-in-law just moved in with them." This brought a whoop of delight from everybody.

Everybody but Tug. He'd been stewing about that evening's Tug-and-Alyssa dance when the raucous reaction jarred him out of his daze. She said lay low, not disappear, he decided. I can say hello to her. How could her husband object to that?

He grabbed his beer and stood up.

He looked down at Abbi. "I'm going to get another beer, you want one?"

"You bet," Abbi said. Then, seeing that his bottle was three-quarters full, she added, "I think she's around front."

Just then, Charisse stood up. "Oh, I could use another beer, too," she said.

Abbi put a hand on her arm. "Charisse, wait a second. I want to hear more about this dog custody case. I've got to put it in a book sometime."

Tug stopped by the drink table, which by then was untended, and scanned the front yard. Nearby, Jackie Burke stood with a group of the monogrammed-oxford-shirt crowd, potential Limespring benefactors. Tug could see that Jackie was working the crowd, in full charm mode, probably hoping they had their checkbooks with them that evening. She caught Tug's eye and winked, then surreptitiously pointed to the fence by the side of the house. Alyssa was there amid a cluster of five other women.

Was there anyone at Limespring who didn't know who he was looking for? If Abbi had been next to him, he'd have throttled her—she had a mouth like a sieve. But he'd have to deal with that later. First he had to think of something clever to say as he approached the group of women.

Surprisingly, he was rescued by Alyssa. She saw him approaching and called out, "Just the person I was talking about." She waved him over. "Come here. They all want you to draw their horses."

The women were from the Markham area, and like Alyssa, none of them had recovered from the horse fever of their childhoods. When Tug joined them they were fussing over Roy, Theo, and Poli, who were standing on the other side of the fence.

Alyssa introduced Tug to the women, who soon introduced him to one of their favorite topics: riding injuries. Betsy Parker, a pretty woman in her mid-thirties and the horse editor of the local newspaper, had been in a coma for two weeks after a crash on her steeplechase horse. Laura Jenkins, a tall blond, was once medevaced to the emergency room after a horse kicked her in the head; Louisa Woodville's arm was in a sling after she'd separated her shoulder from a trail-riding fall.

When Nina McKee started talking about her cousin in the wheelchair, Alyssa held up her hands and said, "Enough. I'll never get Tug back on a horse if you guys don't stop."

By then the sky had turned from deep lavender to India ink. Flashlight beams cut through the darkness above a small rise in the front pasture where Darryl and two other men pulled fireworks from cardboard boxes. The horsewomen decided to make a stop at the drink table before the show started, leaving Tug and Alyssa standing by the fence alone.

"How'd the face-painting go?"

"Lots of satisfied customers," Tug said. "This could be my new career."

Suddenly he turned away and faced the pasture. "Uh-oh, it's your friend Carol. I think she wants to watch the fireworks with me. Look, no offense, she's a little, uh, chatty. Is there another place to watch them?"

"Sure. The roof," Alyssa said.

"Are you serious?"

"It's the best view at the farm."

Tug glanced back over his shoulder, scanning for Carol; Alyssa looked over the pasture, scanning for Darryl. "Follow me," she said.

She led him to the house, chirping out scheduling information to each little knot of people they passed. "The show's going to start soon," she said brightly, or, "Fireworks in five minutes."

Inside, she started up the stairs ahead of him, then stopped and reached her hand back for his. "This way," she said. Her fingers felt warm and slightly damp. He expected her to let go when they reached the top, but she didn't. They kept their tentative intimacy as they walked through Roz's room to a set of open windows.

Alyssa fiddled with one of the screens and pulled it aside. "Come on. Out here." She ducked down and stepped through to the roof.

Tug followed and found himself above the porch. The roof was made of tin, and was nearly flat; they were in no danger of sliding off to the lawn below. From that vantage point, he could see the pasture where the men were huddling around the boxes of fireworks. Behind them, lights twinkled on the roofline. Below them from the porch came the sound of a single guitar and somebody singing Dave Alvin's melancholy version of "Border Radio." In the middle of the lawn, three kids were swordfighting with sparklers. Laughter and the hubbub of conversation rose up to them like an evening mist.

"Wow," said Tug. "It's perfect."

"Roz and I used to lie here and watch the shooting stars."

Tug sat down in front of the windows and put his arms around his knees. A Roman candle shot off from the rise at a low angle and sizzled along the grass for twenty or thirty yards before it sputtered out.

"Looks like they're about to start," said Tug. "Come on, sit down."

"No—you and—no—I—" Alyssa fumbled out her answer, changing her mind three times in the same sentence. "I better go mingle," she finally said. "After all, I'm the hostess with the mostest and this is the big moment."

She turned to the window, but before she could duck back inside, Tug rose up and caught her arm. "Wait a second," he said. "Before you go, I just wanted to tell you something."

He took both of her hands in his. She pulled back. But only a little, as if she were more surprised than disturbed.

"Well, I just wanted to tell you how much your farm means to me. And your kindness. You know, letting me come here every day to draw and letting me bother you with all my questions. And your generosity." He stopped. What idiotic words, "kindness" and "generosity." He sounded like he was about to give her a Ruritan award. He looked into her face and began again.

"Alyssa—"

"Tug," she interrupted him. "What are you trying to say?"

This time he was more articulate. He pulled her to him until they were inches apart. And when she didn't shout or struggle or laugh in his face, he kissed her.

To his relief and joy, she kissed him back. Suddenly, he was encircled by her; her lips and her body were pressed against him; her heat penetrated his skin. He tasted her mouth.

Then, just as suddenly, she pulled out of his arms. Shaking her head, she took two quick steps backwards toward the open window. "This can never happen again. *Never.* Do you understand? It just can't. *We* can't. Never. No matter what I want or what you want. And if you care anything about me, you'll go back to Limespring and forget about the farm, forget about me. Find another farm to draw. Please."

She ducked into the window and disappeared.

Out at the pasture, three Roman candles blazed upward in a

shower of fire. As Tug turned, two more big red bursts exploded over the pasture. The fireworks had begun. Down on the lawn the crowd began oohing and ahhing in earnest. Atop the porch roof, Tug stood alone, lost in the star-spangled night.

CHAPTER 30

At 11:45 that night, there was a knock at Tug's cabin door. His heart jumped. For a sliver of a second he knew Alyssa had come to her senses and was standing on the other side of the door. Then reality took control. Alyssa would never leave her party; she would never come to his cabin. She had never lost her senses in the first place. It was probably Abbi, wondering what had happened to him.

He was right. He opened the door to his old friend, standing there with a bottle of beer in her right hand and a tiny flag in her left.

"Thought you might need this," she said, holding out her left hand. She looked down and saw herself handing Tug the flag, then laughed.

"Oops. I meant this." She switched hands, offering him the beer.

"Things didn't go well, I take it." She walked into his cabin, her words trailing behind her, slightly slurred from the night's partying. "First I thought you and Alyssa had gone off together, but when I saw her talking to Jackie and couldn't find you, I figured you'd be here stewing."

She moved a coffee can full of pencils from a chair and sat down. Then she noticed the walls of his cabin. The empty walls. Where sketches of horse heads, barn doors, hay bales, and the face of a pretty blond had once hung, there was now just knotty pine paneling. On the floor, near her feet, lay a pile of drawings and crumpled pieces of torn paper.

"It's over," Tug said. "Alyssa, the farm, the farm drawings. All of it. It's just over. This is the stupidest goddamned thing I've ever done in my life. I should be in New York getting ready for my show in October, instead of, instead of . . ."

"Falling in love?" Abbi said.

"Don't start, Abbi, I'm not in the mood."

He clamped his lips together, folded his arms over his chest, and sat there. All that could be heard was the metallic *chrr* of cicadas. Abbi knew Tug well enough to wait it out, because the wait was never more than a minute.

"Okay, yes," he said after twenty seconds. "Instead of falling in love, instead of thinking I should 'rediscover myself,' instead of drawing. Instead of all of it. It was fucking ridiculous to come here in the first place. I'm out of here. I'm going back to New York tomorrow."

Abbi leaned down and picked up some of the torn paper. She saw part of a nose, the side of a neck, half an eye. "She didn't know you'd drawn her," she said, trying to fit a couple of the scraps back together. She started to add something, then paused, grappling with her conscience. She'd promised Alyssa she'd never tell Tug about their conversation the day after the Follies. But it was a stupid promise about an even stupider resolution. Alyssa was fooling herself and Tug was about to give up. This called for intervention. She probably should have grappled longer, but the urge to play Cupid quickly steamrolled her vow of secrecy.

"She's in love with you, too," Abbi said. "I wasn't supposed to tell you, but since you're going back to New York tomorrow, it won't matter."

Tug stomped over to her and grabbed the scraps. "That's bullshit. If she's so in love with me, why'd she push me away when I kissed her?"

"Oh, so you kissed her? What'd she do, slap your face? Scream for help?"

Tug looked at the pieces of Alyssa in his hands. "No," he said. "In fact, she kissed me back. I mean, *really* kissed me back. But then all of a sudden she pulled away and told me to leave her alone. She told me to never come back, 'If I cared anything about her.' Well, shit, of course I care about her. I'm screwed, it's hopeless."

"Funny you should use that word," Abbi said. "That's exactly what Alyssa said the morning after the Follies."

Alyssa had talked to Abbi after the Follies? Tug made Abbi tell him everything. And she did, from Darryl's threat to sell the farm to Alyssa's vow to fight her feelings for Tug. Finally he understood the week of the Big Freeze.

"So how come she changed her mind and everything was great again?" he said.

Abbi gave him the look she usually reserved for children or slow grocery baggers. "Jeez, Tug, for someone who's been with as many women as you have, you don't seem to know anything about them. You were telling her good-bye, bonehead. That's the last thing she wanted, then or now. Of course she welcomed you back. Doesn't that tell you something about her feelings? And it's no surprise she told you to buzz off tonight. She's married; she has a kid. This is incredibly hard for her. But staying away from you seems to be harder. Not that she should, her life with Darryl stinks. She needs you, Tug. But you can't convince her if you're banished from her farm. We need a plan to get you back there."

The two fell silent. Abbi studied the carpet and started tapping her left shoe against the leg of the chair. At one point she snapped her fingers, said, "I've got it." Then a second later, "Never mind."

Meanwhile, Tug lay on his side on the bed, running ideas through his mind, each one stupider than the next. When he actually considered calling Alyssa's friend Carol, asking her to visit Limespring and bring Alyssa along, he threw a pillow against the wall.

"Forget it," he said. "There's nothing I can do."

Abbi looked up from the carpet. "Would you take that hangdog expression off your face? You look like a basset hound and it's not at all flattering. We'll think of something."

Tug stalked over to get the pillow. "You want a plan?" he said, grabbing the pillow so hard a little puff of feathers escaped. "How's this: I start slapping paint on one side of her house in the middle of the night. That way, she has to let me stick around, at least until I finish the other side. There, there's your plan."

Abbi was silent for a few moments, then she started nodding her head. "That's brilliant, Tug. You're a genius."

"I am?"

"You are. You just came up with a twenty-first-century update of Scheherazade. Well, not the house painting part, but the 'finish the job,' sticking around part. Remember how Scheherazade keeps the Sultan hanging each night so she can survive another day? That's what you'll do. Each night you'll slip a half-finished drawing of something at Finally Farm under her front door—a barn scene, her horses, whatever. Then each morning you show up at her doorstep and say you have to stay there in order to finish. It can't miss. She'll think it's wonderful and romantic and charming. She won't be able to resist. No woman would be able to resist." Abbi, who had clearly fallen in love with this idea, practically levitated from the chair in her excitement. Her eyes were bright with the possibilities.

Tug's eyes, on the other hand, had a look of horror. "Oh man, Abbi, you're nuts. That's the craziest thing I've ever heard. She'll think I'm an idiot."

Abbi pointed her finger at him. "As I said, you know nothing about women. It worked for Scheherazade and it will work for you."

CHAPTER 31

Tug pulled a black T-shirt from the middle of a pile on his dresser. It was the first night of Operation Scheherazade, the stealth mission in the war to win Alyssa's heart. He'd spent the day half drawing images; trying to capture half the essence of something so compelling that Alyssa would beg him to complete it. Or at the very least, tickle her curiosity. The results lay on the bed next to a flashlight.

He put on the T-shirt and picked up one of the sketches. It was an oblique view of the barn's wash stall. A horse's head, chest, and front legs protruded from it; a bucket, hose, and brushes lay on the floor. The horse's face had been carefully shaded and detailed. The head was slightly dished, a white star was stamped between the eyes. A few pencil strokes suggested the rest of the horse and the stall.

It was meant to be a portrait of Theo, Alyssa's favorite. The one that followed her around like a dog and begged to be scratched; the one whose photo was on her refrigerator. How could she resist?

He glanced down at four other half-finished sketches on the bed. Each one was quite resistible. He looked over the Theo drawing again. If not compelling, what about mildly amusing? What about pitiful? Maybe she'd feel sorry for him that, after all this time, he still couldn't draw a damn horse.

Someone knocked on the door. "It's me," said a voice. It was

Abbi, Tug's partner in stealth. She'd insisted on joining him. "In case you need a cover story," she had said. "If Alyssa spots us, I'll tell her I lost an earring at the party and didn't want to walk over in the dark by myself."

Not the most logical cover story, but Tug was glad to have Abbi along. With two of them it became a tale they could tell friends over drinks. Alone, it was just humiliation.

They set out after midnight. Tug wore dark green swimming trunks and navy Tevas to complement the black T-shirt; Abbi wore a black tank top, black jeans, and one earring of dangling stars and moons. "Wait, we should darken our faces first," she said. "Let's grind up one of your charcoal thingies."

When Tug's eyes widened, Abbi grabbed his arm. "Oh relax, would you? I was just joking. Come on, let's go."

This was the plan: They'd walk to the farm, tiptoe to the front door, and slip the half-drawn sketch under it. If Darryl's car was there or if Alyssa was still awake they'd turn back. If anything went wrong, they'd run like hell.

The plan worked, at least the stealth part. The farm was dark, there were no extra cars in the driveway, nobody screamed, the horses in the pastures didn't even nicker. The only glitch was the screen door. As Tug began to pull it open, the hinges made a screeching noise that sounded to them as loud as a car alarm. For ten seconds they stood frozen on the porch, Tug's hand on the door handle, waiting for a light to come on in Alyssa's bedroom. It didn't. He eased the screen closed and, in the exaggerated pantomime of the stealthy, the two of them slowly turned, slowly bent down, and even more slowly taped the drawing to the porch floor so it would be the first thing Alyssa saw when she walked outside the next morning.

Then in the same quiet slo-mo, they tiptoed away, leaving behind the fragrance of Abbi's Picasso perfume, Tug's half-portrait of Theo, and a message that read: "Don't you want to see how it ends up? I do. But I can't finish it at Limespring. See you in the morning as usual. I'll be good." It was signed "Tug Palifax, The Sorry Sultan of Sketches."

The minute they got to Limespring Hollow Road, they started giggling. The giggling quickly turned to the loud laughter of relief.

"I hope to hell this works," Abbi said.

That stopped Tug's laughter dead. "What do you mean, you hope to hell this works? Yesterday you said it was foolproof."

"Wellll," Abbi said, "I'd love it if somebody did it for me. But that's me. You never know about Alyssa."

"You never know? You never know!"

"Calm down for Godsakes. What's the worst that could happen?"

"She could shoot me for trespassing."

CHAPTER 32

Alyssa didn't shoot him. When Tug showed up the next morning, he found her sitting, unarmed, on the red porch glider by the front door, holding the sketch of Theo and a cup of coffee.

There was a moment of awkward silence as they looked at each other then glanced away. Tug steeled himself for her response: Leave and don't come back. But, as the moment stretched to the breaking point, Alyssa said nothing, and Tug, for one of the rare times in his life, didn't either. Finally, Alyssa got up and stepped to the front wall of the house. She tacked Tug's drawing to the yellow clapboard and stepped back. She examined the drawing, then said, "Needs work. Theo's in the barn, I'll put him in the wash stall for you. But you have to stay five feet away from me at all times. Agreed?"

She was using her drama teacher we've-got-three-days-to-make-this-work voice. He couldn't tell if she was serious or teasing him. But when she turned to face him she was smiling. It wasn't a big smile, but big enough. Operation Scheherazade had not failed yet.

He took the sketch and walked to the barn. Everything he needed was there: his folding chair in front of the wash stall, a cup of coffee, and hope. Alyssa soon followed, leading Theo.

"If he fidgets, just talk to him," she said. "But if he really starts acting up, give a yell. I'll be around the barn."

Tug worked on the sketch all morning. Theo alternated between pawing the concrete, chewing the crossties, tossing his head up and down, and dozing. Alyssa came by several times to and from chores or the pretext of chores. They didn't say much, but each exchange was less strained than the one before. On the fourth time, Alyssa went into the tack room to get a jar of Furison for a cut on Theo's leg. As she smeared on the yellow ointment, Theo nuzzled her pockets looking for carrots.

"Think it's possible for a horse to like to be drawn?" Tug asked.

"You mean Theo? With him, anything's possible. He doesn't know he's a horse."

Tug's pencil kept moving while he talked. "It's like he strikes a pose, then looks at me to make sure I'm watching. And if I'm not, he bangs the floor with his foot. I think he's showing off."

Alyssa stood up and Theo rubbed his head against her chest, knocking her off balance. "Of course he's showing off. That's what alpha horses do. That's how they get the girls. Just like alpha men."

With the sketch nearly done at noon, Tug led Theo to his stall and gave him some hay. Then he peeked around the edge of the barn to see where Alyssa was. He didn't want any awkward good-byes or questions about the sketch or future sketches or anything that could put a crimp in Operation Scheherazade. Mystery was crucial. He cut quickly across the pasture toward Limespring Hollow Road to avoid any chance of being spotted.

That afternoon in his studio he put the final touches on sketch no. 1 and started the second half-drawing. After sorting through a stack of earlier studies, he decided on a view of the farmhouse as seen from the front pasture. The job went quickly. Even though he took a long dinner break—there was a spirited argument at his table about whether painting or music was the original art form—he was done by mid-evening. For this drawing, the finished work surrounded an unfinished center. The pasture, fence, hills, and trees were nearly complete, while only a few pencil lines suggested the house itself.

The second sneak attack began at eleven-thirty that night. This time he was alone. He'd given Abbi a full report earlier in the day and she'd decided that her moral support and earring excuse were no longer needed. It was a cloudy night, raindrops spattering down occasionally; he carried the drawings in his portfolio. When he got to Alyssa's front porch, he taped the finished Theo drawing and the half-done farmhouse sketch to the floor. This time the message read: "Hope you like Theo's portrait. Hope you want to see how the farmhouse ends up. See you in the morning." It was signed simply, "Tug."

When he returned the next morning Theo's portrait was gone and the unfinished farmhouse sketch was tacked to the door frame. Next to it was a note in Alyssa's hand. "I loved the drawing of Theo. It really captured him this time. Go to the front pasture. There's a chair there and a thermos of coffee. I'm in Warrenton, be back around 10:30."

The previous night's rain had left the day muggy and the sky a smudgy gray. Tug sat on the folding chair filling in the page's central blank. The surrounding portions had been drawn with the long shadows of a late summer afternoon. Under the morning's monotone light he struggled to capture the equivalent shading for the farmhouse image. He was caught up in the problem of windows when a voice said, "Need a break?"

Alyssa stood a few yards away, carrying a bowl filled with strawberries.

"Farmers' market," she said, nodding down to the strawberries. "Might as well have bought them at Safeway, though. They're not great, but I sprinkled some sugar on them. Here, try one."

She picked a strawberry from the bowl and walked up to him, breaking the five-foot rule. Tug held up his hands, blackened from the charcoal.

"Oh," she said. "That wouldn't taste good at all. Open up."

Tug opened his mouth and she tossed the strawberry. It hit him on the chin.

"Your foul shot's worse than Shaq's," he said, wiping an arm across his face.

"Wait, wait," she said, laughing. "Let me try again."

She tossed another strawberry and hit his nose. She tossed another, then another. It got even harder to land the shot, because they were both laughing. Eventually one made it into his mouth.

"You're right," Tug said. "They're terrible. But thanks, I needed the break. Nothing's happening with this drawing. The light's worse than the strawberries."

Alyssa looked over his shoulder. "Hmmm. I like it so far. I'll be interested to see how it turns out."

"Yeah, I will, too," said Tug.

Alyssa stood behind him for a moment longer. "Well, good luck," she said. "See you later." Then she walked back toward the farmhouse.

Tug waited till she reached the front door before he pumped a fist in the air and said, "Yes!" A little before noon, he jogged back to Limespring and told Abbi that Scheherazade, the artist, could keep his head for at least another day.

He holed up in his studio all afternoon. Instead of joining the picnic table crowd, he spread his lunchbox items on the studio's daybed and ate quickly without registering the meal. Cold cuts? If you'd asked him an hour later, he wouldn't have remembered. He was deep in a world of lines and shade, deep in the world of his own creativity.

Inadvertently, Operation Scheherazade had become a watershed for the art as well as the artist. From the time Tug had arrived at Limespring he had focused on taking things apart. The drawing paper piled on the studio table or tacked on the walls was covered with fragments—horse legs, flower petals, fenceposts, the pattern of a mosaic tile, the head of a stuffed gorilla. But the game of halves had demanded completion. So Theo's portrait became his first full Limespring composition. To his surprise, it was the act of leaving some of it unfinished, even if only for a day, that had brought it together.

Because of Operation Scheherazade, the whole became more important than the pieces. For the first time that summer, Tug had to commit to the empty spaces on his sketchpad.

He struggled with the farmhouse drawing until five. Still unsatisfied with its shadows, he decided to take a nap on the daybed for a few minutes before struggling some more. Nearly three hours later, he awoke with a start. Groggy and a little disoriented, he arrived at the cafeteria just before the kitchen closed. He wolfed down some vegetable lasagna, declined Cora's invitation to join the weekly Limespring poker game ("Too bad," said Cora, "I could've used the money"), and returned to the studio, determined this time to wrestle the farmhouse drawing to the ground.

But when he faced the easel again and examined the work clipped to the drawing board, he realized it might already be done. From the perspective of a forty-minute dinner break and a plate of lasagna, the drawing seemed pretty good.

Buoyed by this triumph, Tug dove immediately into half-sketch no. 3. The image was already in his head. It involved the north side of the barn and the aged John Deere tractor that Alyssa usually parked there. He planned to crop the image ruthlessly, focusing on mechanical shapes against an architectural background. The only softening, organic elements would be the grain of the barn's wood siding and a fuzzy striped caterpillar inching across the tractor's faded, chipped engine cover.

It was well past midnight when he arrived at Alyssa's front porch carrying the half-finished tractor drawing. He had to stop himself from bounding up the steps and pounding on the door. He'd have to wait eight hours for her reaction, but that made it all the more intoxicating. Tug had no idea how long Operation Scheherazade would continue, but at the moment he taped the finished and half-finished drawings to the porch he was willing to stretch it out for a thousand and one nights.

CHAPTER 33

When Tug returned the next morning, he found another note taped to the front door. "Go to the tractor," it said. When he got there, Alyssa was sitting on the machine's seat, drinking coffee and leafing through a slender book.

"What're you reading?" he said.

Alyssa showed him the cover: "A *Midsummer Night's Dream*."

"We do a Shakespeare play every year at Emerson," she said. "I'm thinking of this one. Last year was *Richard II*." She paused a moment, then, in a dropped voice, said, "A horse, a horse. My kingdom for a horse."

She slid off the tractor. "This year, it's time for a comedy." She twirled her left hand in an Elizabethan flourish and said:

> *Fetch me that flower; the herb I shew'd thee once:*
> *The juice of it on sleeping eye-lids laid*
> *Will make or man or woman madly dote*
> *Upon the next live creature that it sees.*
> *Fetch me this herb: and be thou here again*
> *Ere the leviathan can swim a league.*

"Impressive," he said. "You do Shakespeare better than I do da Vinci."

"I've been at it longer. I'm what, four years older than you?"

"I think of it more like four years smarter."

She reached out and tapped him on the top of his head with the paperback. "Smooth, Tug, very smooth. You're one of those 'fellows of infinite tongue, that can rime themselves into ladies' favors.'"

"A *Midsummer Night's Dream?*"

"No, *Henry V.* The king's making a bid for Katherine."

"Did it work?"

Alyssa offered Tug an arch look. "When hasn't it worked?"

For the next two hours he sat by the tractor, filling in the lines and shapes and contours. The light was perfect. He could have worked faster, but he didn't want Alyssa to come back and see a drawing so completed that it would throw off the Scheherazade timing. When she stopped by around eleven, he hoped it was unfinished enough to keep the plan going.

"Looks like you need a break," she said. "Want to go for a walk?"

She carried an empty coffee can in one hand and pointed up the hill with the other. "Let's go up Mount Buck. I have to make amends for yesterday."

He started to ask what the can was for, but she shushed him. "You'll see."

The pasture behind the barn rose steeply to a fence halfway up the hill; beyond it was forest. The temperature had already reached the eighties as Tug and Alyssa walked through thigh-high grass, scattering grasshoppers and small butterflies the color of buttermilk.

From up at the fenceline, they could see miles of the northern Virginia countryside, a soft mosaic of greens, browns, golds, and distant blues. Alyssa drew in a slow breath. "No matter how many times I see this view, it still takes me back to that first day I stood here. It's like falling in love. You know how you remember everything about the first time you fell in love? The way it looked, and smelled, and how the air felt against your skin? That's how it is with this view."

She turned and started fiddling with the rusted chain on the gate. "Damn," she said. "I meant to bring some WD-40. Oh well, just climb over, but be careful, the hinges are about to go."

Tug tried to ignore the gate's metal pipes teetering under him as they climbed over. "Tell me about the first time," he said.

Alyssa jumped to the ground on the other side. "The first time I fell in love? That's easy. It was with Joe. It was freezing cold, my breath came out in clouds, my fingers were so stiff I could hardly move them, and my toes seemed like they'd shatter any second. But I didn't feel any of it. It sounds corny, but it literally took my breath away. I remember that I had to force myself to breathe."

Tug wished he hadn't asked. He was certain no one had ever remembered him that fondly or fervently.

"Joe was something, all right. Everything a first love should be: handsome, kind, beautiful, soulful eyes."

Okay, enough about Joe, thought Tug. "So what ever happened to this Joe guy? Working somewhere on Wall Street?"

Alyssa laughed and bumped her shoulder into him. "The only job Joe could get in New York would be in Central Park. Joe's a horse, Tug. The first horse I ever rode."

The path wound through sunlight; the air was heavy with the dark green smell of damp leaves and sunbaked bark; his rival in love turned out to be a horse; and the woman he was in love with had bumped his shoulder like a horse at play. Life was good.

As they walked along, the feel of Alyssa's touch remained on his shoulder, fading as slowly as the afterimage of a lightning flash. Things had changed. The five-foot rule ruled no longer. He couldn't say for certain what those changes were, and it might be a while before he found out, but he was willing to wait.

"Now it's your turn," Alyssa said. "Who's your Joe?"

"Well, she wasn't a horse, I can tell you that. Jamie McAllister. I was a goner from the first day I saw her. It was tenth grade. Mr. Beyard paired me up with her in biology lab. She had wild carrot-colored hair down to her waist. I was in my Botticelli stage then and she was my very own Venus on the half shell. She had freckles across her face and over her arms. Like Seurat had painted her. I know, I'm mixing my artists, but you get the idea."

Alyssa pressed him for details and Tug told her the whole tale, from first glance to first kiss. One day, Jamie asked him to come to her house to study after school. He spent so much time in the shower that his mother banged on the door and told him to stop using up all the hot water. He shaved, even though he didn't have much to shave, and brushed his teeth twice. By the time his mother dropped him off in front of Jamie's house—a brick rambler with tractor-tire planters in the front yard—his stomach was in knots. His voice cracked when he introduced himself to Jamie's mother, who met him at the door.

Alyssa interrupted him: "What was she wearing?"

"Jamie's mother? I don't know what she was wearing. All I remember was that she was as big as a refrigerator. I remember thinking she could crush me."

"Stop," Alyssa said. "That's really mean."

"But true. That night, while we were studying mitochondria, I kissed her. I got a D on the test, though. She got a B, she always was better in biology. But whenever I think of cellular structure I think of Jamie McAllister."

Alyssa laughed and touched her shoulder to Tug's again. Maybe it was because the path had narrowed a little, maybe not. "Did she become a doctor?"

"She should've," Tug said. "She dumped me in about two weeks and started going out with Ron Kolb. He was smooth. He smoked between classes and drove around in a blue Chevy Impala. She got pregnant right out of high school and I never saw her again."

They walked for a while, swapping high school horror stories: why Tug got kicked out of woodshop; the day Alyssa got into a fistfight with the class snitch, Beth Comroe. As they neared the top of the hill, Alyssa stopped by a dense stand of brambles.

"Here it is," she said. "My secret patch of golden raspberries. Look."

The thicket was filled with little amber caps and jumbo-jet bumblebees that looked like they were made from fuzzy pipe cleaners. Tug picked a berry and tasted it. Red raspberries had high, sharp notes of flavor. These were deeper, richer. A whole octave lower. He picked another. There was a hint of something tropical about them. Bananas?

The golden raspberries were larger than their red cousins, and their skin was smooth. One of the big bees lumbered down on a berry next to Tug's hand.

"Don't worry, they're not interested in you," said Alyssa, who was putting berries in the coffee can, ignoring the insect activity. "I've never seen one sting. They're like big workhorses, gentle giants. Abbi calls them Belushi bees—remember the *Saturday Night Live* skit?"

The can was soon full and Tug and Alyssa sat on a log by the trail, licking fingers sticky with raspberry juice.

"Tenth grade?" Alyssa said. "That was really your first kiss?"

"I was a slow starter."

"Let me guess, you've been making up for it ever since?"

"Well, let's just say that Jamie wasn't my last kiss. What about you? When and who?"

"Eighth grade. Frank something-or-other. I don't even remember his last name."

"Were you in love?"

"Hardly. I barely knew him."

"What about now? Are you in love with Darryl?" He hadn't meant to say it, though those words had been in his mind for a long time. Finally, like a broken pressure cooker, his lips lost the seal and the words just spurted out. But if the question bothered Alyssa, she didn't show it. She just leaned back and let the light warm her face.

"It's complicated. Like all marriages, it's complicated," was all she said.

On their way back down the hill they revisited the subjects of Joe and Jamie for a few minutes, then turned to art and drama. Tug described his first solo art show, an installation called "Jekyll and Hyde," which involved department store mannequins, medical devices, and models of internal organs from a medical supply house. Alyssa told him of her first Shakespeare role, Lady Macbeth in eleventh grade. She had dreamed for months afterward about sex and death and washing her hands in blood and her teeth falling out.

When they got back to the tractor side of the barn, Alyssa held up the can of raspberries. "These'll be great on cereal," she said. "Thanks for helping me pick them. I'll save you some for tomorrow." Then she added, "Sorry about Jamie McAllister. She was a fool."

Tug picked up the nearly finished sketch and sat down in front of the tractor. The lines and shadows now seemed lifeless compared to amber raspberries and Belushi bees and the touch of Alyssa's shoulder against his. He packed up and headed back to Limespring. By twelve-thirty he was at the picnic tables eating ham salad sandwiches and arguing about science-fiction movies with Marius. As he left, he raised a hand and intoned, "Klaatu Barada Nikto."

He completed the tractor drawing that afternoon and, after dinner, returned to the studio. As he shuffled through his Finally Farm studies searching for another subject for Operation Scheherazade, he found two of the pages stuck to each other. He pulled them apart to discover that the bottom one was the portrait of Alyssa he'd taped back together. Her head was slightly turned over her left shoulder, her eyes looked straight out of the page, an imitation of Vermeer's *Girl with a Pearl Earring*. It was recognizably Alyssa, but little else. He knew he could do better.

He tore off a blank page from the drawing pad and clipped it up to the easel. He stood before the white paper for three or four minutes, creating and rejecting poses in his mind. Finally, he picked up a 2B pencil and motioned across the page, dividing it into imaginary quadrants. Then he drew two curved shapes near the middle of the page. The beginning of eyebrows.

CHAPTER 34

He was early tonight. Alyssa watched the green numbers on the clock by her bed turn from 11:07 to 11:08 as she listened to the sounds of Tug trying to be quiet: careful steps on the front porch, muffled scratchings of tape pulled from a roll (was he putting it under his shirt to soften the sound?), the light rustling of paper being positioned on the floor, the tiptoeing back across the porch, the diminishing crunch of gravel.

When the only sound left was the clicking of crickets, she threw the sheet aside, bolted down the stairs two at a time and out onto the porch. For the fourth night in a row, the dark gray planks of the floor had become an art gallery. She untaped the pages and scurried to the little bathroom under the stairs. Quickly, she closed the door and flipped the light switch, wondering what part of Finally Farm would be on the new unfinished drawing he'd left behind.

She guessed it would be the round hay bales in the front field. The day before, she'd seen Tug studying them, turning his head one way and then the other, looking at them through a square made by his index fingers and thumbs. The bales dotted the surrounding farms like giant green gumdrops and were a dramatic sight even to her. To an artist, especially an urban artist unused to seeing such extravagant shapes in the country, she knew they would be nearly irresistible. Three summers before, a painter from

Los Angeles had spent her entire Limespring fellowship painting them in every light and with every color scheme. A hay-bale version of Monet's *Rouen Cathedral* series. Alyssa thought that the mammoth bales, with their perfect curves and endless lines swirling round and round, would beckon Tug as *A Midsummer Night's Dream* had been beckoning her.

She was wrong.

A tiny gasp of air caught in her throat as she saw the drawing. She felt dislocated, like she'd just woken from a vivid dream and wasn't sure which world was real. There in front of her was—her. Or a half-finished her. Her eyes were detailed down to the dark spot on the lower left of her right iris. There was part of her nose and the beginning of her lips. The rest of the page was blank.

She flipped down the lid on the toilet and sat, looking at the drawing of herself. She examined it, following the lines of the half-formed face as if they were clues to a mystery. Who was this person? The expression in the eyes was indecipherable; the lips were unfinished and held no clue.

She knew that these half-drawings were just part of a game; Tug's way of getting back to the farm and back to her. She had been charmed by his ingenuity, even grateful for it. The drawings of Theo or the farmhouse had made her smile. Not this picture, this half of a face. Something about it was eerie, unsettling. She wanted to shake it hard, like she used to shake her Etch-A-Sketch when she was a kid. But instead of erasing the lines, she wanted to shake them together, make them join each other. Make her whole.

She held the drawing out at arm's length. And it came to her with the sickening lurch of an elevator dropping: Tug's half-drawing wasn't incomplete. It was, in fact, exactly as she was. Half there. Unknowingly, Tug Palifax had captured the essence of Alyssa Brown.

Or had it been unknowing? Had he seen what she thought no one could see? That only part of her existed and the rest had been lost; that what she presented to the world was simply the starring roles she'd mastered—Alyssa the Accomplished Drama Teacher, Alyssa the Devoted Mother, Alyssa the Emotionally Reserved

Wife—and that the real Alyssa had faded into this half-woman she held in her hand?

She stood up, put her portrait down on the toilet lid, and covered up the accusing eyes with the finished drawing of the tractor. A half of a woman, that's what she'd become. It'd taken a few lines on a piece of paper for her to finally see it.

She turned on the cold water in the sink and splashed her face. A complete face reflected back at her from the mirror over the basin. She examined it as she had examined Tug's half-portrait. It was a desperately, achingly unhappy face.

She'd fooled herself for a long time. Duped herself by her own acting ability into believing those other Alyssa roles were enough. But they weren't. And she knew it now. She'd known it for the past month, but every time the notion started creeping to the forefront of her thoughts, she had pushed it aside, distracting herself with Limespring activities or mind-numbing chores. Even Darryl had noticed the farm's clean cupboards and alphabetized spices.

A small smile appeared on the face in the mirror. The irony was not lost on her, even in her state of misery. In order to avoid the real Alyssa, she was turning into the woman Darryl wanted her to be, organized and compulsive.

It was all Tug's fault. Damn him and his horse drawings and his da Vinci dreams. If he hadn't made her so happy she wouldn't have known how unhappy she was.

Damn him for being so much fun on solstice night. She remembered the walk back to the farm, how she'd deliberately bumped into him several times in the darkness and held on to him as if to stop herself from falling, how they'd sung James Brown and danced a mock waltz across Limespring Hollow Road.

Damn Tug Palifax and his smile and his words and his curiosity and his interest in her. Damn him for kissing her. Damn him for coming back after she'd told him not to.

She picked up the unfinished drawing. That was who she was; who she'd become until she—Alyssa forced herself to complete the thought this time: until she'd met Tug.

In the time she'd known him, she'd felt her outlines becoming more distinct; she could feel her soul spreading out to meet those new lines. She no longer felt shriveled. Tug Palifax was filling her up.

Damn him.

CHAPTER 35

A breeze pressed the thin cotton of Alyssa's dress between the inverted V of her legs as she walked down the middle of Limespring Hollow Road. It stirred the roadside oaks, adding extra notes to the usual score of crickets and cicadas, frogs and beetles, cows and horses, foxes and field mice. Alyssa listened to the night's music backed by the percussion of her own heartbeat and the quick scuffing of her clogs against the road.

The thin moon illuminated the fields with pale phosphorescence; beyond them, lights from a scattering of farms glimmered like a far constellation. The road ahead, draped with the deeper night of tree shadow, was familiar to Alyssa. A quarter mile on, around a curve, would be the welcome sign for Limespring.

She picked up her pace. She wanted to get there before she convinced herself to turn around. Soon, a white sign materialized out of the gloom by the side of the road: "Limespring Art Center, Markham, Virginia." A yellow bulb burned over the office door. Two streetlights shone down over the parking lot. On her right, a series of low fixtures illuminated a gravel path that wound to the dining hall, ahead of her other lights showed the way to the living quarters.

Alyssa followed the path past the giant boxwoods and the dorm building to the cabins. She saw Abbi inside No. 7, leaning against the headboard, reading. The next four were dark. She walked to the last one, opened the screen, and knocked on the door. Inside, a light went on almost immediately. It was 11:57, less than an hour since she had heard Tug tiptoeing around Finally Farm.

The bedsprings creaked and there were some scuffling noises. Finally the door opened and Tug appeared, backlit by a bedside lamp. He was wearing a pair of running shorts and a black T-shirt.

His hair was tousled. The look in his eyes didn't seem to be surprise. He and Alyssa stood there for a moment, just five feet apart, silent. Then, just as Tug was about to speak, Alyssa handed him the portrait.

"Finish me," she said.

CHAPTER 36

"Turn just a little to the right."

Alyssa shifted her weight on the stool.

"That's it, just like that," Tug said. "Don't move." He adjusted a table lamp on top of a nearby bookshelf. The lampshade had been removed; the bare bulb bathed the left side of Alyssa's face in light and turned the right side into a land of shadow and contour. "That's perfect."

He walked back to the easel. For a moment he studied the drawing clipped there, then glanced at his subject.

"Perfect," he said again. "Now you can't move for the next twenty-seven hours or however long this takes."

Alyssa started to laugh and Tug gave her a mock stern look. "What did I say about not moving? Do you think Mona Lisa moved when she was sitting for Leonardo?"

Alyssa settled back, letting her laugh become an enigmatic smile. She wondered if the same kind of scene had unfolded between artist and model five hundred years before. Was the subtext the same? So that's what Mona's smile was about.

The dairy barn complex was dark that night except for studio C4 and a music room, assigned to a Chilean composer, a few doors away. Tug had propped open the window with some books and a coffee can. Every so often, a cross-breeze stirred Alyssa's hair; she let the strands blow across her face. From time to time, the tinkling of piano keys drifted in.

The lamp bulb was the only light. Behind Tug's easel, the white walls of the studio were overlapped with shades of gray. On them were taped dozens of pen, pencil, and charcoal sketches. Many were of horses or parts of horses. The charcoals were rough and gestural, done quickly to seize the essence of movement and mass. From Alyssa's perch, the most distant images looked like little Rorschach tests.

The easel was set up only a few feet from the stool, and Alyssa watched Tug as he concentrated on her, then on the drawing paper, and then back on her. Sometimes he peered around the edge of the drawing board so that she could see only half of his face, as she had seen her own half-face earlier that evening.

Once, she asked him if she could scratch her nose. He quickly replied, "No." When her eyes widened in surprise, he smiled and said, "You stay still. I'll do it." Following her directions, he leaned over her and, using two fingers, lightly scratched the very tip. About ten minutes after they'd begun, the smattering of piano notes suddenly became a strident boogie-woogie, heavy on the left hand, and then, just as suddenly, stopped completely. "Sounds like Neftali's done for the night," said Tug.

Otherwise they didn't speak. With the piano silent, the only sounds were the night noises brought in on the breeze and the soft scratchings of Tug at work. He used a combination of 2B and ebony pencils. Alyssa could see his right arm rising and falling. She let her eyelids droop and through her half-closed eyes the studio became a small, dim cave and Tug's movements became caressing strokes. It felt as if the tip of the pencil wasn't only touching the paper, but lightly skimming her skin.

"Something's not right."

She started out of her trance to discover that Tug had stepped from behind the easel and was examining her, hands on hips, a pencil stuck behind each ear.

"Did I move?" she asked.

"No, you're fine," he said, pausing a moment before adding, "You're perfect."

He walked up to her.

"It's me," he said. "I'm not getting the shadows right." He cupped the palm of his left hand against the right side of her face. He started to adjust her pose, but stopped, holding his hand motionless.

Alyssa put her hand on top of his and held it to her cheek. Then she looked up, knowing exactly what would happen. Instantly his lips were on hers and the pose was gone forever.

CHAPTER 37

When Alyssa awoke, the studio was washed in the light, milky gray of predawn. The open window above the daybed let in a cool infusion of damp air mixed with birdcalls and other early-warning sounds of approaching day.

Soon she'd have to get back to the farm before Limespring began to stir as well. Slowly, so as not to shake the bed, she eased herself up on her elbow and looked around the room.

The sketches on the walls were beginning to materialize out of the shadows. In one of them, she could see a horse rearing up like a circus animal; in another, she recognized the swirls of round hay bales. She knew he wouldn't be able to resist them.

Alyssa wondered what time it was. Maybe five. She didn't feel tired at all, though they'd fallen asleep only a couple hours before. She looked at the man sleeping next to her, Tug Palifax, the second man to share a bed with her in twenty years. He was on his back; one arm rested above his head, the other lay atop the sheet that was their only cover. He'd pulled it over them just before spooning up behind her and collapsing into exhausted sleep.

She thought of faces as parts of the country. Her daughter, Roz, with her fine bones and intricate lines, was the Northeast. Looking at Tug, she saw the West, with its wide expanses and geologic landmarks. He had strong brows, prominent cheeks, and a small bump just below the bridge of his nose. A slight fuzz of beard was beginning to stubble his jaw, and a tiny crescent scar, nearly invisible from a distance, bracketed one corner of his mouth. During the night she'd kissed his cheeks and eyebrows and traced his moon-scar with her fingertips and tongue.

She remembered how it felt when they first kissed, the molten glitter rushing down inside her. She remembered making so much noise through the night that afterward, slumped over on his chest, she'd asked, "Do you think anybody heard me?" "Only people in the surrounding counties," he'd replied. She remembered laughing, their chests vibrating together.

So many things to remember. Things she'd forgotten for years. Like the delicious slipperiness of sweaty lovers; the exploration of fingers; the taste of skin; the sweet achy feeling of a new mouth on her; how lovers talked to each other in voices deepened by tenderness; how they wrapped their legs around each other to hold on through the night.

The light coming in through the windows was turning from gray to gold. Alyssa slid out of bed, careful to keep Tug covered with the sheet, and walked to the pile of clothes in the middle of the floor. She stepped into the sundress, slipping it up past her hips and chest, but didn't put on the underwear. Something else she wanted to remember: what it felt like to walk around naked under her dress just because of the possibilities.

She stepped over to the easel. Another unfinished portrait of Alyssa Brown was taped there to the drawing board, but this one didn't look at her with recriminating eyes or make her feel incomplete. For the first time in years, she felt whole, as whole as she ever could.

"What are you doing over there?" Tug was sitting up on the daybed. "Come back. I need you. I need you right now."

"Last night you said your batteries had all run down."

"I've recharged. Come back, please." He held out his arms to her.

"I can't," she said. "If I come over there, I'll never leave, and I've got to get going before anybody sees me."

"No one will be up for hours," Tug said. "We've got plenty of time to make our escape."

"*Our* escape?"

"You didn't think I'd let you get away that easily, did you? But first, come here. We have time. I promise."

Alyssa walked over, the panties still in her hand. Tug grabbed them, and Alyssa, refusing to let go, toppled onto him.

He rolled her onto her back and straddled her. She started to speak, but Tug put a finger on her lips. "You can't know how many times I've pictured you here, in this light," he said. "It's the truest light there is. There are no—"

He stopped in midsentence. "Oh, Christ," he said. "I've been practicing for weeks what I'd say if this ever happened. And that's the best I could come up with. It's completely lame."

He looked at her for a moment, then said, "How about this: You're beautiful."

Alyssa leaned up, brushed her lips against his, and said, "Better."

He pressed her back on the pillow with his lips hard on hers. She felt him push the sundress up past her waist and wriggle one of his knees between her thighs, separating her legs. Then he brought his other knee there, separating them even more. She expected to feel his body sliding down on hers, feel him blanketing her with his weight, but instead he sat back up on his knees.

"You are so beautiful," he said. Then he bent over, skimming his lips up her belly to her breasts.

It made her shiver. She closed her eyes. "That's much better."

Later they lay on their sides facing each other just a breath apart. By then rays of sunlight were making bright shapes on the floor, as if someone had peeled bits of gloom from the concrete.

"I've been daydreaming about doing that, doing everything we did last night, for weeks," said Tug. "Ever since I first saw you. And the funny thing is, my daydreams don't even come close. What happened last night was astronomically better."

Alyssa gently stroked his face with her fingers. "You know, now that we're making confessions, I have one to make, too." She pushed Tug over on his back, and this time she straddled him. She leaned over, looking into his eyes with an expression of soulful melancholy, and said, "Last night wasn't nearly as good as I had hoped."

Before Tug's shock could register, Alyssa covered his face and neck with kisses.

"So it's going to be like that, is it?" he said.

"You bet," she said and hopped off the bed. She found his running shorts and tossed them to him. "Time to go."

She started for the door, but turned abruptly. Then she said, "I'm glad you're coming with me. I'm not ready for this night to end."

CHAPTER 38

Soon the brand-new lovers were walking hand in hand through the July morning. The leftover clouds of evening, trapped in the scoop of Limespring Hollow, still clung to the road and stubbly grass.

As the mist began to brighten from dusky plum to light periwinkle, it looked to Alyssa like a crazy dream sequence from a musical. Gene Kelly in Paris; Jud Fry dancing with a frontier vixen in *Oklahoma!* She half expected to see smoke machines lining the road.

"Poor Jud is dead, poor Jud Fry is dead," she sang with outstretched hands, trying and failing to reach a deep baritone.

"Who's Jud?"

Alyssa launched into a detailed explanation of dream sequences, smoke machines, and Poor Jud until Tug stopped her with a kiss. "I love your voice. Keep talking. I could listen to you forever."

Alyssa took him at his word and talked all the way back to the farm about musicals and dancing and *A Midsummer Night's Dream* and staging Stephen Sondheim. When they turned onto the drive to the farm and found Roy and Theo hanging their heads over the fences, nickering for attention, she changed course from theater to horses. "See these two swirls of hair in the middle of Roy's forehead?" she said, rubbing the red horse's white blaze. "That supposedly means he's a rogue. One swirl is good, two are bad. So much for old wives' tales. They don't come more even-keeled than this one." She kissed the soft part of Roy's nose and turned to the subjects of "wolves' teeth" and "chestnuts" and "coronary bands" and "ringbone"—a whole glossary of equine terms that Tug gave up trying to keep straight.

In the middle of an exposition on the fragility of a horse's stomach, Alyssa stopped. "Oh God! You got me started, now I can't shut up." Then she started laughing. "I can't even shut up about shutting up."

That made Tug laugh, which in turn escalated Alyssa's laughter, a laughter fed as much by relief as by the comedy of the moment. She only stopped when Tug kissed her laughing mouth and they found themselves in a frantic embrace by the side of the road with the two horses watching.

When they reached the house, Alyssa led Tug to the upstairs bathroom. The floor was laid in worn red linoleum tiles. Wrapped around the aquamarine walls was a giant purple dragon, painted by a Limespring muralist for Alyssa's fortieth birthday. The dragon's scaly tail circled the mirror over the sink; her voluptuous body (the artist painted her with breasts and called her "Marilyn") curved around the walls; her arched neck ended at the shower fixture, which sprouted a ceramic dragon's head whose mouth was the spout.

"I'm ready for a shower, how about you?" Alyssa asked. Tug answered by kicking off his sandals. As he started to pull up his T-shirt, she stopped him. "No," she said. "I want to."

She slid the shirt over his head, then moved her hands down his torso, descending the ladder of his ribs one rung at time. Tug watched her fingers reach his running shorts and slip under the elastic of his waistband.

He closed his eyes and felt his shorts pulled over his hips and down to the floor. He felt her lips press against the skin just below his belly button. When he opened his eyes again she was leaning into the shower, her dress a little heap of dusty sunlight on the red linoleum.

She turned on the faucets, felt the water for a few seconds, testing the heat, then stepped into the tub. Facing the rear wall, she leaned back into the spray. The water raced down her shoulders, around her breasts, and past her belly to darken the blond triangle between her legs.

"Come in," she said. Tug stepped into the stream of water and immersed his hands in the warm rivulets that braided Alyssa's thighs. She wrapped her arms around his neck, kissed him hard, and whispered into his watery ear, "You wash me first, then I'll wash you."

Tug took a pink bar of soap from the tile holder and rubbed until his hands were covered with a thick pink lather. He made small soapy circles down her back. He washed each leg, starting at the swell of her inner thigh. Then he reached around to her front, his soapy hands sliding up and down her curves like a car on a country road.

Alyssa cupped her hands over his and rode them to her breasts. She stopped him there. Then she pushed back into him. Soon they began to move together, slowly at first, as the water showered over them, spattering the tile and filling the bathroom with steam.

CHAPTER 39

They got out of bed that day for the last time at 5 P.M. Tug hadn't wanted to leave and Alyssa hadn't wanted him to leave. Still, she took his hand and led him to the front door.

"Go," she said, as he dragged along behind her like a reluctant child. "If you don't show up for dinner at Limespring, the gossip will start flying."

"Who cares?" he said, kissing her hand and starting to work up her arm.

"You can come back later," she said as he reached her neck. "Now, shoo." She pushed him out the door and lightly kicked him on his rear end.

"Expect a night visitor," Tug said.

She leaned against the front door and watched him walk down the road until he became a dot at the end of the drive. A vanishing point, where all lines converge.

She made a pot of coffee, the third that day, and sat on the sofa, sipping from a heavy green mug. One by one, as if taking cookies from a plate, she began to savor the images of the day. Their morning shower, their breakfast in bed, their sleepless nap in the soft heat of the afternoon.

She was wearing only a T-shirt, and the nubby red fabric of the sofa pressed against her bare skin like the tips of a thousand tiny fingers. Without thinking, she began to move her legs back and forth across the cushions, slowly and methodically like a swimmer treading water. She closed her eyes and let the sensation mix with a vision of Tug's body arched above hers.

Over the past few weeks, she'd sidetracked her brain from these kinds of thoughts by making mental lists. Things Roz would need in her dorm room, props for *A Midsummer Night's Dream*, veterinary products for the farm, seeds she wanted to order for next year's garden. It hadn't worked. The moment she wasn't vigilant, the moment she hesitated between basil and cantaloupe, her mind bolted free and raced back to Tug. She'd force her attention to another list, only to repeat the futile process time and again.

She didn't bother fighting it now. With the warm mug pressed against her chest, she leaned back, rubbed her legs against the fabric, and let her mind wander to where it wanted to be.

Who knows how long she might have sat there, luxuriating in the freedom of delicious thoughts, if the phone hadn't rung. She wanted to ignore it, but it could have been Darryl or Roz.

"Liss, you're not going to believe what she's done now."

It took a moment for Alyssa to attach a name to the voice. It was Carol, with her weekly update on the Shrike's latest atrocity: She'd called a student "a piece of work," then defended it by saying, "Everyone is a piece of God's work." Carol slipped into an alarmingly accurate imitation of the Shrike's Texas accent: "'You know I studied thee-*ahhhhl*-ogee in graduate school . . .'"

Alyssa held the phone to her ear, not really registering the rest of Carol's rant. She didn't want to talk about the Shrike. She wanted to talk about Tug; about how the yellow sundress skimmed her nipples as it fell to the floor; about how every cell in her body felt like it was shimmering.

She couldn't, certainly not to Carol, who had the biggest mouth at Emerson. Telling her would be like posting a notice on the school bulletin board: Mrs. Brown is in love with an artist.

"In love with." Alyssa weighed the words, measured them on her tongue, tried them out with her lips. *"In love with."*

"What's that?" Carol asked. "Who's in love with?"

Alyssa recovered quickly: "The Shrike, she's in love with her own voice."

"Boy you're not kidding, the last meeting she . . ."

Carol started off on another tirade. But Alyssa told her it was time to feed the horses. She made polite good-bye noises and hung up.

She didn't want to think about Emerson and her future. Up until the Shrike, she used to think she'd be there forever. Emerson and the farm were the two anchors in her life. Now Emerson seemed to be slipping away. That left just the farm.

Or did it? "You go, the farm goes," Darryl had said. She saw his face, twisted in anger; his fingers, clamped around her wrist. She stood up from the sofa and shook her arm. She refused to think about that now.

Instead she walked outside and looked up the drive to where the vanishing point had vanished an hour before. She turned to the barn, thinking about yellow sundresses and shimmering cells.

Part 2

There was a crazy bloom of flowers at Limespring that summer. Daisies ran rampant, daylilies crowded the roadsides, black-eyed Susans sprang up by the hundreds along fencelines. The coned blossoms of the butterfly bushes, which were fuller than anyone could remember, were so heavy they could barely lift their heads to the sun. The air was practically syrupy. Its hazy confection of honeysuckle mixed with the sugared incense of summersweet drove the honeybees to a frenzied dance.

But it was the colors that everyone talked about. The pastels of spring, a woodwind concerto of light green baby maple leaves and creamy dogwood blossoms, had exploded into a big brass symphony of bold color, with purple playing lead horns. Its swoopy, sexy notes were everywhere—in the violet balloon flowers that had taken over Cora Beeson's garden, in the butterfly bushes, in the phlox, the chicory, the lavender. On the edges of the fields, thistles raised their periwinkle cups to toast the sky. And the pastures were dotted by thousands of tiny amethyst flowers the farmers called knotweed and swore made the cows more fertile.

The local newspaper even carried stories about the unusual season of flowers in Fauquier County. A hot, wet spring was considered the culprit, though a county extension agent noted a record number of bees and speculated on a connection. An astrologer in

Warrenton claimed it was because Aquarius, the water bearer, was in conjunction with Taurus, a sign of the fixed Earth.

At Limespring, it wasn't only the flowers that blossomed wildly. The normally drowsy summer had become a season of infatuation. Flirtations sprang up like dandelions.

Jackie Burke took Talbot Rice, a Limespring donor who'd been widowed three years before, to dinner at Four and Twenty Blackbirds in Flint Hill. She'd intended to talk to him about increasing his donation. But something happened over the appetizers, an architectural construction of scallops and red peppers. Maybe it was the heartbreak red of the peppers or the lonely look in Talbot's eyes, but Jackie found herself taking his hand to comfort him, then saying she'd always found him to be a very attractive man. He accompanied her back to Limespring that night. The next day, Nattie saw a couple walk hand in hand toward the boxwood maze. Could the woman have been Jackie? Nattie thought so, but then it was dusk and she was in a hurry to get to Rudy's cabin where he was freshly showered and waiting for her with a bouquet of Queen Anne's lace and a bottle of cold Pouilly-Fuissé.

Charisse stopped flirting with Tug and turned her attentions to the son of a local gentleman farmer she'd met at Alyssa's Fourth of July party. A week later she began to miss dinners at the lodge, and a week after that, nights in her room.

Don said he was writing a poetry cycle about painting and began spending evenings in the dairy barn studio of a New York artist, helping her mix colors. The bald tintypes photographer from Richmond and a calligrapher from Florida became inseparable. Abbi started calling William every night.

Cora, who'd been at Limespring for eight years, had never seen so many pairings, so many shadowy couples walking hand in hand on the night-lit gravel paths that connected the buildings. She even started to look at her husband with new eyes.

What was to blame? A tipsy Puck dripping his magic purple liqueur onto sleeping eyelids? Or was it a chain reaction from the fusion of Tug and Alyssa just up the road at Finally Farm? Maybe an unwitting breeze carried particles, charged by their passion, down Limespring Hollow Road and covered Limespring with a radioactive glow of desire.

If the Limeys had asked them, Tug and Alyssa would have denied that anything out of the ordinary was happening. Tug would have said the summer drawing project had rekindled his artistic drive. And why did Alyssa seem more vibrant than ever? Just the summer diet of tomatoes and olive oil, she would have said.

CHAPTER 41

"If you do to me what you did on poker night, I'll tape your feet together."

"You seemed to be enjoying it at the time."

"That's not the point. We've got to be discreet, remember?"

"So you didn't like it?"

Alyssa bopped Tug with a bent plastic fairy wand, temporarily sprinkling his hair with a ragged spray of silver streamers. "I'll turn you into a monkey if you don't behave."

They were rummaging for props and costumes at an estate auction in the hills just outside the tiny town of Orlean. The fairy wand had come from a box of old toys that contained board games, armless dolls, and a sad tiara, its once dazzling smile of baubles now a toothless grin of empty circles.

"Here, my queen," Tug said, crowning her with the skeletal remains of the tiara. "Have mercy on your poor servant who can't keep his hands or feet off you."

To Alyssa's embarrassment and delight, he knelt down and kissed the tip of her right foot. She was wearing sandals and could feel his lips brush against her toes.

"Get up, you idiot," she said. When he ignored her and started kissing her left toes, she bopped him again with the silver streamers. "I dub thee Sir Foot-alot. Arise, sire, and be my champion."

Two middle-aged women, who had been rummaging through a

nearby box of kitchen things, witnessed this little performance and elbowed each other.

"Wish I were in love," one of them said.

"The hell with love," said the other, who was holding a set of chipped mixing bowls. "I wish I had someone who looked like that kissing my feet."

They hung around for a second act, and Tug and Alyssa unwittingly obliged. He stood up and whispered something into her ear. She in turn whispered something back, and soon they were kissing.

"Let's go before I'm tempted to put another ad in the personals," the woman with the bowls said. The two women walked away laughing, but Tug and Alyssa didn't notice.

This was their second Saturday together. Tug had told the Limespring crowd he was exploring the Shenandoahs that weekend. Alyssa had slipped out of bed at six, taken a shower, and brought him a cup of coffee in a travel mug.

"Come on, lazybones," she said, pulling at his limp arm, "here's your wake-up juice. Time to get up."

Tug, whose pre-Limespring idea of crack of dawn was 11 A.M., moaned and pulled the sheet over his head with his free hand. "Go away, you wretched woman. You almost killed me last night. I can't do any more."

Alyssa pulled his arm harder. "I don't need you for that. This is a field trip. If we don't leave now, all the good stuff'll be gone."

As much as he asked, she refused to tell Tug where they were going. They drove for thirty-five minutes on narrow back roads, past country stores that marked the towns of Hume and Orlean, then onto an even smaller road that twisted up into the hills. Even if she'd wanted to go faster than twenty-five miles an hour, she couldn't; a long line of cars snaked ahead of her.

"What's with all the traffic?" Tug asked. "And where'd you say we were going, anyway?"

They were holding hands and Alyssa squeezed his. "I didn't. For the fifteenth time, stop asking. It's a surprise. God, I bet you were the kind of kid who shook his Christmas presents to find out what was inside."

Tug denied it vehemently, though he had in fact been a Christmas-present shaker and worse. Sometimes he'd steam the Scotch tape off the packages when his mother was out of the house.

Finally they pulled up to an old white clapboard house. A sea of people milled about in the front yard, and a field to one side was full of parked cars.

"Damn, I knew we should've left earlier," Alyssa said as she saw the crowd. "Oh well, here we are. Rawley's auction. Everything goes. The lady who lived here moved into a nursing home and the family's getting rid of everything. I've been to tons of these auctions and they're the best way to find props and costumes. Remember that big orange thing you wore on your head for the Follies? Estate sale. Come on, let's get a number."

The sale included everything from dining room furniture to beds to dishes to garden tools to an unopened but yellowing set of pillowcases embroidered "King" and "Queen." Miscellaneous items like toys, books, and pairs of roller skates had been dumped indiscriminately into boxes. Interested buyers had to bid on a whole box, regardless of the mix of contents.

A couple of burly men with tattooed arms brought out the big items, like the furniture and appliances, to the front yard for bidding. The auctioneer, a white-haired man wearing jeans and a brown plaid shirt that strained at the buttons, stood on the porch and unleashed into the microphone an indecipherable torrent of words marked every so often by dollar amounts. Periodically someone in the crowd would hold up an index card with a black number on it, changing the dollar amount in the auctioneer's rolling rap.

There was a whole houseful of furniture to sell, giving Tug and Alyssa plenty of time to prowl through the boxes. When Tug started to talk excitedly about having found a near-new set of wrenches buried underneath an old shower curtain, Alyssa shushed him quickly.

"Don't say another word," she said. "Someone'll hear you and then we'll pay three times as much for this box."

The estate sale game was all about being nonchalant, Alyssa explained, not alerting anyone to the treasure you've found. If they were lucky, they'd walk away with that box of tools, a shower curtain, and an old eggbeater for $3.

"And by the way, keep an eye out for contraptions like that eggbeater."

"You're calling an eggbeater a contraption?"

"It is when I use it in a play. I just thought of it. I'm going to put it on Puck's head—that's how he takes off to fly."

She reached down and, grabbing the eggbeater, held it against her hair and started cranking the handle.

"See, it'll be perfect," she said. "Now I need to find other gizmos for the rest of the characters."

As they searched for other contraptions, Alyssa told Tug about Becky, her roommate in New York. They'd both been fledgling actors trying to make it on the stage. Not long after Alyssa left the City, Becky moved to Chicago and later founded an avant-garde theater troupe that incorporated puppets, masks, and Rube Goldberg–like devices into its productions of the classics.

"You'd love her. She's your spiritual doppelganger," Alyssa said. "She can't walk down the street without bringing home something someone threw out. She's finally put all that stuff to good use: the Red Moon Theater Company, ever hear of it?"

Tug shook his head.

"They're small, but critically acclaimed." Alyssa then dropped her voice to sound official: "'Verges on the near miraculous,' according to the *Chicago Sun-Times*. But that reviewer got it wrong. They don't verge on anything. Their production of *The Seagull* was out-and-out miraculous. Transformational. It made me laugh and cry and think. The props moved, they made weird noises and did all kinds of crazy things. All that wacky stuff made the satire more satiric and somehow made the tragedy even more tragic. I'm going to do that with *Midsummer*. Becky's going to help me plan it when I see her later this summer."

"This summer?" said Tug, who had picked up two ceramic book-ends shaped liked elephants.

"I told you, remember? I'm flying to Chicago in August to see Roz. She wants to take me on site to see the project. I'm going to see Becky, too. She might even give me some of her old thinga-majigs."

"You're leaving in August?" He slowly put down the elephants.

"Only for five or six days."

"But I'll miss you."

"It'll be at the end of August," Alyssa said, pretending to exam-ine the intricacies of a nutcracker. "You'll be in New York by then."

They fell silent, the auctioneer's words hanging between them.

"Hey, look at those," Alyssa finally said, pointing to a jumble of crates stacked up against the porch screen. "We're bound to find contraptions here."

Soon they were rummaging again, Alyssa shaking her head over the junk people save, Tug reminding her of what an estate sale at Finally Farm would uncover. If the two middle-aged women had hung around they would have seen Tug balance a sewing basket on his head and Alyssa hug Tug's face with a blue teddy bear. They would have seen them bump up against each other far more often than accident or chance would expect. And they might have overheard this conversation:

Alyssa: "I'm serious about this canoe trip with the Limeys to-morrow. You can't act like I'm anything special to you."

Tug: "Who said you were?"

Alyssa: "Okay, smart-ass. Perhaps you'd like to start sleeping in your cabin again."

Tug: "No. No. Not that lumpy bed. Please, I was just kidding. I'll be good. Nobody will suspect that we're anything but friends."

Alyssa: "I'm sure they already suspect. But, please, please, we have to be careful tomorrow."

Tug: "I promise. Besides, how could I do anything bad in a canoe in the middle of the Shenandoah River?"

Alyssa: "That's what you said about poker night. And suddenly I felt your foot between my legs."

Tug: "Nobody saw. And if you didn't like it why did you press up against me?"

CHAPTER 42

The white van pulled onto Limespring Hollow Road at 7 A.M. the next morning with twelve Limeys and friends, all grumbling about the early wake-up. Tug, who was sitting in the last row next to Abbi and her boyfriend, William, was the most vociferous, saying a little too loudly and a little too often how he couldn't remember the last time he'd been up before eight o'clock. Alyssa, next to Marius in the second row, faked a yawn and said, "Summer vacation was meant for sleeping in."

In fact, Tug and Alyssa were used to getting up early. It was all part of their charade. Each morning at six, the alarm would ring, sending Tug home to Limespring, where he would slip into his cabin unseen and, around eight, appear in the lodge for breakfast. He was even starting to enjoy the world of dawn, with its birdsong and mists.

That morning, they'd greeted the sunrise with mugs of coffee on Alyssa's front porch. Then, as usual, Tug jogged down Limespring Hollow Road unnoticed. Twenty minutes later he walked out of his cabin with a loud slam of the screen door. Meanwhile, Alyssa timed it to arrive at the van just a few minutes before the scheduled departure, so everyone could see that she'd walked to Limespring alone.

"Sorry," she said to Jackie, who'd organized the Shenandoah canoe trip and had been checking her watch nervously, "I slept through the alarm. Didn't even have time for coffee, so if I seem foggy, that's why."

Alyssa seemed suspiciously unfoggy. She was buoyant, smiling, and unnaturally alert for seven in the morning. Even her hair was bouncier than normal. Under other circumstances, Abbi might have asked if she'd won the lottery or something. But she was certain she knew what the "or something" was and she'd promised Tug she wouldn't say a word.

Abbi wasn't the only Limey who had noticed. Alyssa and Tug's just-friends act was about as convincing as a politician's promise. Tug didn't have the acting chops to pull it off. He sounded like Dustin Hoffman around Mrs. Robinson.

"So, Alyssa," he said woodenly as the van pulled out. "What do you think the next year's Follies show will be?"

Alyssa, who did have the acting chops, artfully shifted the question to the rest of the group. "What do you guys think? *Death of a Salesman? Streetcar Named Desire? Madame Butterfly?*" She knew her crowd. For the rest of the ride, suggestions, from the outrageous to the practical, bounced around the van like errant tennis balls.

By the time they'd gotten to River Bend Outfitters, a few miles outside of Front Royal, the choices had narrowed to another version of *Hamlet*, this one redubbed *Spamlet*, that involved the indecisive son of a computer magnate, or *Twelve Angry Men*, where the case involved a parking ticket instead of murder.

At the outfitters, which was just a plywood shack next to a huge rack of canoes, Alyssa and Tug avoided each other like sixth-graders with a secret crush. They stood on opposite sides as the group listened to the safety talk, was urged to wear sunblock, and was fitted for life vests.

"Just grab a paddle from that bin over there," said the canoe guy, a thin, ropy blond with a diamond stud in his top left eyetooth, "and choose your canoe mates."

That was easy. Limespring couples fever was running high. Jackie had brought her new beau; so had Charisse; Nattie and Rudy were glued together; and Abbi had William, who'd come down to Virginia for the weekend. That left only Tug, Alyssa, Marius, and Don, whose New York artist friend had refused to come because she was afraid of water snakes and leeches, even though Jackie assured her she'd never seen a water snake on the Shenandoah River and was certain no leeches lived in Virginia.

Alyssa quickly turned to Marius and said, "Bow or stern?"

"I like it when women are in charge, especially beautiful ones," he said. "I'll take the bow."

That left Tug and Don, who rock-paper-scissored for the stern. Tug won.

With water bottles, sunscreen, sack lunches, and vests in hand, the Limespring group climbed into the shuttle for the twelve-mile ride upriver to the put-in spot.

Runoff from the heavy spring rains had kept the Shenandoah deep, giving the amateur canoeists long stretches of calm water. At first they practiced the strokes the outfitters had taught them, but after a while the hot sun, the slow current, and the love plague began to take their toll. A languid ease settled over most of the canoeists, who stowed their paddles and drifted lazily down the river. The little flotilla looked like an Impressionist painting come to life.

Alyssa and Marius, bored with the sedate scene, snuck up on Charisse and Alex, a tall forty-year-old man with a soul patch. While they were busy murmuring to each other, Marius angled his paddle in the water for maximum splash. "Attack!" he screamed, letting loose a spray of water. Alyssa joined in and they drenched the lovebirds.

Shaking off their stupor, Abbi and William rushed to Charisse's rescue, splashing Alyssa and Marius. Attracted by the mayhem, Nattie and Rudy joined in. Nattie, who was a strong swimmer, dove over the side and attacked from the water.

"They're boarding us, Captain!" Marius yelled to Alyssa as he tried to push Nattie under. But it was like throwing Brer Rabbit into the briar patch; Nattie just swam to the other side.

Marius, who handled a paddle like a three-year-old learning to use a fork, tried to move the canoe away. "Full throttle ahead!" he shouted to Alyssa. But it was too late. Nattie shimmied up the side and pushed down hard. The canoe spit Marius and Alyssa into the water.

In less than two minutes, the entire contingent was splashing and screaming and dunking each other in the Shenandoah. Alliances formed and disbanded in rapid succession. Marius and Alyssa versus Nattie and Rudy morphed into Alyssa and Nattie versus Marius and Rudy, which quickly shifted to boys against girls, then artists against writers, then Klingons against the *Enterprise*.

Somewhere in the watery melee, Alyssa hurled herself against Tug. "Take that, pointy ears," she said.

Tug caught her in his arms, and for a moment they forgot themselves. If it hadn't have been for a sneak attack by Nattie—or Captain Kirk, as she insisted she be called— he might have kissed her.

"Mr. Spock," Nattie shouted to Tug, "take the Klingon to the brig."

"That is illogical, sir," Tug said. "But I will comply."

He threw an arm over Alyssa's chest and swam her to shore. The others followed, bringing their canoes with them. Soon all were on the grassy bank, drying in the hot sun and eating soggy sandwiches.

CHAPTER 43

Five hours later, the Limespring fellows and friends sat down to a second meal together, this time at El Camino Real, a popular restaurant on the outskirts of Front Royal.

They'd arrived a little after six and were ushered to a long table on the outdoor patio. The seats quickly filled up, and, after spending the day trying to keep apart, Alyssa and Tug found themselves, like partners in a game of musical chairs, standing by the only two spaces left.

For the rest of the evening, while the other couples kissed occasionally and let their fingers entwine, Tug and Alyssa kept their secret below the table, rubbing their legs and touching toes.

As platters of food came and went, so did the pitchers of margaritas. There were loud toasts to canoes and Vulcans and Rudy challenged everybody at the table to tell a joke that began, "A priest, a minister, and a rabbi . . ."

Of all the rowdies, Alyssa was the rowdiest. At one point she proposed they all go to the tattoo parlor down the street and get smiley faces on their butts. After she was shouted down, she tried to talk Don into dancing the *zembekiko* with a margarita glass on his head.

It made Abbi smile to see Alyssa so loose and unguarded. And made her a little smug; she knew the reason why, and it had nothing to do with margaritas or canoeing.

About the time the pitchers hit empty for the second time, Marius yelled down the table, in an accusing voice, "Lissy, you're drunk as a skunk."

Alyssa assumed an exaggerated expression of hurt dignity. "I beg to differ, my Czechoslovakian friend. I can hold my margaritas as well as anybody in this room."

"Not as good as me. I'm as sober as a judge," said Marius. He was wearing a ragged T-shirt and dirty shorts and his eccentric tufts of yellow and white hair stuck out from a newly sunburned scalp. He looked like someone who should be standing in front of a judge.

"Oh?" she said. "All right then, do this." She cleared her throat and said, so quickly that no one could be sure exactly what they'd heard, "Rubber baby buggy bumpers. Rubber baby buggy bumpers. Rubber baby buggy bumpers."

That silenced the group for a second. "Wow," Nattie finally said, "I've never seen anyone's mouth move so fast. Okay, big talker, it's your turn." She pointed to Marius.

He waved his hand in dismissal. "What is this? What is this, 'Rubby bumper buggy bumpies'?" he asked, mangling the phrase.

"Calisthenics for actors," said Alyssa. "It loosens up your jaw and mouth. All my kids at school can do it, even the sixth-graders. Go ahead, three times fast. The sixth-graders do it five times, but I'll compensate for age."

Marius took a drink from his margarita. "I need fuel first." He swallowed, then started: "Bubber babies—" He stopped again and took another sip. "Rubber bubbers baby booper. I mean rubber-bububub— Roooberbaby—" He threw his hands up in surrender and the group whooped in appreciation.

Marius clinked his fork on the edge of a margarita glass for attention. "You have vanquished me, fair and square, my blond goddess. I will never be able to say, 'Bubber rabies bugger . . .' three times fast or slow or anything."

He picked up his glass. "But this I can say. Here's to the finest canoeists ever to row the Shenandoah. Here's to an exceptional group of artists and friends."

Then he raised the glass higher and looked down the table at

Alyssa. "To borrow from the Irish: May the road always rise to meet you, may the wind be always at your back. May the sun shine upon your face. And may you find peace in the arms of your true love, my fair friend."

CHAPTER 44

For the rest of July and into August, Alyssa did find peace in the arms of Tug Palifax. Though she would admit to no one, especially herself, that Tug was her true love.

Tug spent his days at the farm, his nights in Alyssa's bed, and his early mornings sneaking back to Limespring. A two-hour afternoon nap in his studio kept him from total collapse. Despite the distractions, his drawing regime intensified. Partly inspired by Degas's horse-racing pastels, he concentrated on the connection between horse and rider. Alyssa took him to the Middleburg Horse Show, where he watched riders taking horses over a series of large, colorful jumps.

Meanwhile, Alyssa had a farm to run, animals to tend to, and a new school year to prepare for. Sometimes while Tug drew, she sat next to him, marking up a dog-eared copy of *A Midsummer Night's Dream*, absentmindedly running her fingers against his leg.

They only altered the routine for weekends. On the pretext of exploring the surrounding area, Tug, day bag over his shoulder, would get in his Chrysler station wagon on Saturday morning and roar off from Limespring. Three minutes later he'd turn into the Finally Farm drive, park the Chrysler behind the barn, and spend the weekend exploring Alyssa.

The other Limeys weren't buying it. Tug was gone too much and engaged too little. He didn't even argue with Marius at lunch anymore. He'd just sit by, listening to the banter, letting his thoughts drift down Limespring Hollow Road. He was clearly preoccupied, and when he wasn't around, the Limeys gossiped about what, or who, was preoccupying him.

Abbi asked him point-blank after Operation Scheherazade, when Tug had resumed his drawing sessions at Alyssa's place.

"I stopped by your cabin at eleven last night," she said, cornering him at breakfast one morning. "You weren't there. Does this mean what I think it means?"

"It means I was at the studio," Tug said, putting on a bland expression.

"No, it doesn't," she said. "I checked there, too."

"Well, then, I was out for a walk. It's too hot to walk in the day. So I go out at night."

Abbi gave this excuse the derisive snort it deserved. "All right, you don't have to tell me," she said, starting to walk away. "I guess I'll just ask Alyssa."

He seized her arm and pulled her back. "There's nothing to tell. Operation Scheherazade worked. That's all there is to it. Nothing more, nothing less. And if you say anything to her, I'll break your arms."

"Oh, relax," said Abbi. "Your secret's safe with me."

Alyssa had no one to convince but Darryl, whose weekly phone calls from California were short and businesslike. She could set her clock by him. Every Thursday night at ten the phone would ring; she'd take it to another room and reappear shortly thereafter. "Darryl," she'd say matter-of-factly to Tug. He'd nod, then the two of them would go back to pretending Darryl didn't exist.

And while Roz called frequently, her conversations were filled with chatter about the structural beauty of Chicago. "This city is eye candy for architects, Mom. Everywhere you go there's a building more beautiful than the next. And now Uncle Ron's letting me actually design! Oh my God, you wouldn't believe . . ."

Alyssa missed Roz terribly, but between her daughter's explosive happiness and her own exhilaration, there wasn't any room for moping. She'd read once that people who fall in love think about each other more than five hundred times a day. She thought about Tug at least that many times. But "in love"? She couldn't let herself think that.

Alyssa's official version to herself was that it was just a summer fling. What else could it be? Tug was four years younger, a successful artist with a name and a following, and probably not just a professional following. Tug clearly loved women; she just happened to be the one he was with now.

It was ridiculous to think he'd give up New York and the adoring legions of young, beautiful, and thin females for a forty-three-year-old, ten-pounds-overweight married drama teacher. Nor would she ever move back to New York. It made her suffocate to even think of it. And she'd never give up the farm.

In a few weeks she'd tell him good-bye and tuck away the memory of this summer like she'd tucked away Roz's starbug earrings. From time to time she'd pull it out and let herself be overwhelmed by the past.

CHAPTER 45

Tug was ducking out earlier and earlier from Limespring. When he and Alyssa first started their charade, she had insisted he not only eat dinner every night with the fellows, but also hang out with them afterward for walks, chats, showings, and poker games.

"Finally Farm's off-limits till ten," she'd said the first week.

But by the second week, he was showing up at nine. And by the middle of the third week, Tug and Alyssa found themselves eating dinner together on her front porch.

"Up for some dessert?" Alyssa said. "We've got that Ben and Jerry's from last night."

"Later," he said. "I've got other ideas."

It wasn't long before they were upstairs in her bedroom.

"You look like you've been dipped in gold," Tug said. Alyssa was standing by the window that looked out onto the side pasture. The late evening sun hung low in the sky, gilding everything, including her naked body.

He'd taken off her clothes, leaving them in a little pile by her feet. He knelt down and slipped off her sandals. As he lifted her right foot, he pressed his lips against her toes, lightly running his tongue across her skin. Then he moved to her foot, her ankle, her shin, the inside of her knee, the smooth skin of her inner thigh. As he ascended her body, his hand traced the same path on her other leg, until his mouth and fingers came together between her legs.

She leaned back against the window screen, into the stream of sunlight, and closed her eyes. Putting her hands on Tug's head, she pulled him close. She swayed her hips into his mouth, rhythmically, pressing him harder and harder against her. The sun slipped below the mountains and the golden light deepened to dusk. Finally she grabbed his hair in her hands and pulled him to his feet.

"I want you in me," she said.

Tug wrapped her in his arms; they kissed. She could taste herself in his mouth. Then he pulled back. "Turn around," he said. She turned to the window. He pushed against her hard; her face and chest pressed into the window screen.

And then the phone rang.

"Shit," Alyssa said.

"Don't answer it," Tug said.

"It's Thursday."

Tug looked at the bedstand clock. "It's only eight-fifteen. He doesn't call till ten."

"I have to get it. It could be him."

She pulled away, a grid of little squares imprinted on her breasts and the left side of her face. She sat on the edge of the bed and reached for the phone.

"Hello," she said, trying to hide the breathlessness in her voice. She mouthed at Tug, "It's Darryl," then turned back to the phone.

"You're calling early. How's everything in San Diego?"

The upstairs phone wasn't cordless; she couldn't leave the room as she usually did when Darryl called. She motioned for Tug to leave, but he ignored her, flinging himself facedown on the bed instead and putting a pillow over his head.

Though the sound was muffled, he could still make out some of the one-sided conversation going on next to him. The phrase "the Amerigas guy finally fixed it" came through, so did "Yeah, she called me last night." When he heard her say, "Things are fine. Terrific," the temptation was too great. He moved the pillow slightly aside.

"Of course. Right after the Chicago trip," she was saying. Then, after a pause, "August twenty-fifth or twenty-sixth." Another pause. "No, that weekend I'll be in D.C. There's a faculty meeting Monday."

It was the very ordinariness of the conversation that made it so maddening. It was as if the summer hadn't happened, as if he never existed. Tug listened, horrified, fascinated, unable to pull the pillow back over his ears.

"So you haven't gone surfing yet?" she said into the phone and chuckled at her own insignificant joke.

Jesus, he thought, they're chatting together and laughing together like an old married couple. Which is exactly what they are. What did I expect? When Darryl calls I become invisible.

"Okay, that's great. I'll talk to you next week."

The phone clicked down. The next thing Tug knew, the pillow was pulled from atop his head and he was back in the darkening glow of her bedroom.

"Now, where were we?" She was standing next to the bed, the pillow in one hand, an anticipatory look on her face.

"You were married."

CHAPTER 46

At five in the morning, there was no going back to sleep for Alyssa. She lay in bed, kneading the satiny edge of the cotton blanket between her toes. It's what she did when she was upset. Her mother used to joke that she'd given birth to a kitten instead of a little girl.

She and Tug had gone to sleep angry at each other, breaking Dear Abby's cardinal rule for a successful relationship. She and Darryl had obliterated the rule years ago. For a while, she'd even stopped sleeping in the same room with him. She'd read Roz a story at night and pretend to fall asleep next to her. Then Roz got too old for bedtime stories.

"You were married," Tug had said, with an unfamiliar edge to his voice.

"You knew that going into this," she'd answered, her voice mirroring his. When the lights were out, she'd lain on her side, offering her back to him. He'd done the same.

He was still turned away from her as she waited for him to wake. When he finally stirred, she ran the tips of her fingernails down the shallow valley in the middle of his back.

"That feels good." The edge in his voice was gone. "More."

She added the other hand, running them in waterfall succession.

"I know this is hard for you," she said quietly. "It's hard for me, too."

Tug turned onto his back. "Come here." He pulled her to him.

Forty minutes later, they were interrupted by a bell for the second time in less than twelve hours. But this time it was an alarm clock, not a telephone.

Tug left Finally Farm even more bedraggled than usual, with dark circles and puffy little sacks under his eyes. "I'll be back after breakfast," he said. But he didn't return. After a big plate of pancakes and sausage, he went to his cabin and, while sorting through some pencils, decided to lie down for a few minutes. The next thing he knew, Abbi was knocking on his door, holding both their lunchboxes.

He bolted through the meal, sidestepped a discussion about the "outsider art" at Baltimore's Visionary Art Museum, and got to Finally Farm at one-thirty. There he found Alyssa, trowel in hand, in the garden amid basil plants.

"You look better," she said. "I figured you'd collapsed and taken a nap." Her understanding smile hid the fact that she'd worried all day about how much Darryl's call had hurt Tug, or worse, if he were beginning to pull back, knowing that they had only the final days of August left together.

She pinched off some shiny basil leaves and crushed them between her fingers. "Smell this." She held her hand under Tug's nose. "This is proof there's a God."

Tug cupped his hand against hers and inhaled deeply. The air was filled with the strong, unmistakable scent of basil.

Objectively, he could say the smell carried overtones of mint, citrus, licorice, and cloves. But he could no more think of basil as a catalog of overtones than he could think of a Matisse as a collection of pretty colors.

When he pressed his nose against the crushed leaves, the whole summer flooded in. Along with the smell came the image of Alyssa, sitting next to him on the porch, sharing a lunch of tomatoes, basil, olive oil, and French bread. When he inhaled the smell of basil, he inhaled the feeling of her back pressed against his chest as they drifted in and out of sleep, he heard the little humming noise she made in the shower, he tasted her skin.

He took another breath and held it. He knew that smell would always bring him back to Virginia and to Alyssa. Basil, summer, Alyssa, inextricably linked. He also knew that this would be one of those indelible moments. Alyssa bending over him, the soft-turned earth of her garden under him, the insistent whine of the mosquitoes, the thick, damp air—all of it would be etched forever in his mind.

He pulled her hand, bringing her closer to him. "I think *you're* proof there's a God."

Alyssa was wrong about the call from Darryl and summer's end. They didn't give Tug a reason to pull back, they were powerful forces pushing him on. He refused to be invisible.

"Alyssa," he said, "I don't want the summer to end. I don't want us to end."

Alyssa froze. She didn't want it to end either. But it had to.

"Tug," she said, pushing away the panic, "we're months, years, eons from the end of summer. Look, even the dogwoods haven't started turning yet and they're the first to let you know when fall's closing in. There'll be plenty of time for talk later. Maybe in bed, afterward." She gave him a lascivious look. "But now, we work. I'll finish around the basil, you tackle the tomatoes."

Tug let her evasiveness slide by. Along with draftsmanship, he was also learning patience that summer. He'd wait. But he didn't have eons, and he wasn't going to give up.

CHAPTER 47

"Don't stop. Show me more."

Alyssa was stretched out on the bed, eyes closed, arms resting on the pillows behind her head. Tug was on his knees facing her. He cleared his throat with a pedantic "ahem" and touched her face.

"Note the zygomaticus muscle," he said as he ran an index finger down her cheekbone to her mouth. "Artists often call this the 'smiling muscle.'"

Alyssa stretched her zygomaticus.

It had begun to pour an hour before. She and Tug had rushed around the kitchen putting pots and pans under the leaky spots. And it was still pelting down hard on the tin roof, sounding like a concert of snare drums. But they'd kept the French doors to the balcony open, letting in cool air and the occasional ricocheting raindrop. The only light came from the living room, which diffused up the stairwell and into the bedroom, creating a kind of twilight. Illumination enough for an anatomy lesson.

"Further note," Tug continued, "that when the zygomaticus is used, it tends to create wrinkles at a right angle to the pull of the muscle."

Alyssa's zygomaticus contracted. "Wrinkles?"

"I mean, theoretically. It creates them, theoretically," said Tug.

"Move on to other parts, please," she said.

"Certainly." He ran his fingers down her bare breastbone. "This, of course, is your sternum. And these are your clavicles." He traced the long bones below her neck that connect the chest and shoulders. "You have excellent clavicles, Miss Brown. I would venture to say they are world-class clavicles." He stroked them slowly, back and forth.

"How come you know all this?"

He moved his fingers lower. "Professor Reifman's drawing class," he said, circling the small mound of her stomach. "The bald anatomy nut I told you about. One day he came to class with the names of the head bones written in Sharpie all over his skull. I don't know how he ever got it off.

"According to him, we'd never be any good at drawing the human body unless we knew our bones. 'Take a lesson from Leonardo,' Reifman used to say. 'In fact, take a hundred lessons from him,' and then he'd laugh at his own bad joke. Leonardo had his own set of human bones that he studied, and Reifman wanted us to do the same. His syllabus even included a list of places to buy them."

"Did you?"

He shook his head. "But I still did pretty well in his class."

"Oh yeah? Then tell me what this is." She pushed his hand down below her belly.

"Ah. That, of course, is Poupart's ligament. Let me demonstrate how it attaches."

"I was hoping you would," said Alyssa.

An hour later, Tug resumed his anatomy lecture. They were lying on their sides, facing each other. He skimmed the tip of his forefinger through her pubic hair to the crease of her inner thigh. "I love your symphisis pubis," Tug said. Then, after a moment's hesitation he added, "I love you, Alyssa."

Alyssa abruptly rolled over and got out of bed. "No you don't," she said. She faced away from him; her voice sounded thin and distant. "And don't say it again. I don't want to hear it."

She walked out to the balcony. By then the storm had passed;

the moon shone through a few dawdling clouds, highlighting her hair and shoulders and intensifying the shadows below.

Tug followed her outside. Both of them stood for a moment facing the rain-washed, moon-washed hills.

"Alyssa, I love you," Tug said again. "And I'm going to keep saying it because it's true. You know it is."

"Stop it. Everything's fine just the way it is right now. Why do you have to complicate things?"

"I'm not complicating things. I'm just telling you I love you. I love you."

He faced the fields and flung his arms wide. "I love Alyssa Brown, I love Alyssa Brown, I love Alyssa Brown!" he shouted to the cows, the horses, and the man in the moon.

Alyssa threw her arms around him and tried to drag him back inside. "Shhh—you'll wake Dr. Holland." She put a hand over his mouth. His lips moved under her fingers as he continued yelling his declaration of love.

"No. Not until you say you love me back." He broke free from her grasp and leaned over the balcony shouting even louder, "I love Alyssa Brown!"

"Okay, okay, stop. We'll talk about it, just stop shouting, okay?"

Tug was going to keep shouting, but he saw something in her face. Panic? Sadness? Whatever it was, it made him stop. "Alyssa, it's not like I said you had three months to live. I told you I loved you. Most people like to hear someone loves them."

Alyssa walked inside and Tug followed her. "I'm not most people," she said as she sat on the bed.

"I know, and that's what I love about you." Tug put up his hands in surrender. "Oops, I did it again. I just can't seem to help myself."

Alyssa gave him a half-smile. "You goofball."

"Okay, I've stopped yelling. Now, admit it. You love me." He'd never worked so hard in his life to get a woman to say those three words to him.

She examined the blanket. "It's complicated."

"No it's not. Just say the first one-syllable word beginning with 'y' that comes to your mind when I ask you the following question: Do you love me?"

"Yes."

"Aha," he said. "I knew it. Say it again."

"I love you, Tug. But that doesn't solve anything. We can't just ride off into the sunset together. I have a husband. You have a life in New York. You have a career there."

"Fuck my career. Fuck your husband," Tug said. "I want to be with you. Alyssa, *I want to be with you.* Doesn't that count for something?"

"It counts for a lot. But not everything. We're not kids who declare their love and set up housekeeping. I wish we were. I'd be the first one on the time machine to take us back. Like I said, it's complicated."

Alyssa got up and wrapped a white terry robe around her. "I'm making some tea, want some?"

"Alyssa? I'm talking about a life together and you're talking about tea? What's so complicated? I love you, you love me, your life sucks with Darryl. I don't see a lot of complications here."

"I never said my life with Darryl sucks. And that's beside the point. Life's like buying a house—not every room is perfect. If you're lucky, most of them are. Most of mine are, Tug. I have a wonderful daughter, the farm of my dreams, good friends, a fulfilling career—"

Tug filled in the rest of the sentence: "An unhappy marriage."

Alyssa sat back down on the bed next to him. "Maybe. But we've reached a kind of peace over the years. We each have what makes us happy. Darryl has his work, I've got the farm."

"The farm, the farm, the farm," Tug said, wagging his head from side to side, his voice rising. "I know you love it. And, yeah, it's great. But you can't be held hostage by fifty acres, Alyssa. Let Darryl sell the fucking place if he wants to."

Alyssa stared at him in surprise.

"I know all about the threat," Tug said. "Abbi told me. You can't choose the farm over happiness, Alyssa. In the end, it's just dirt and grass."

"No. It's not."

She leaned down and put her head in his lap. Tug could feel the heat of her breath on his skin and tears sliding down his thigh.

CHAPTER 48

Alyssa awoke, sunlight jabbing her face. Disoriented, she propped herself up and looked around. Tug was sprawled to her left; facedown on the bed. To her right, the clock read 8:30.

Damn, they'd slept through the Limespring breakfast. She'd fallen asleep with her head in Tug's lap and had forgotten to set the alarm. Marius and Nattie were probably speculating right now about Tug's whereabouts.

Well, we weren't fooling anyone anyhow, she thought, and fell back against the pillows, jarring Tug. He turned over and said groggily, "Hey, sweetheart." Then he put his head back down and closed his eyes.

She watched him settle back into sleep and tried to do the same, but the morning's sharp yellow light and the memory of the words "just sell the fucking place" kept her awake.

Tug couldn't understand her attachment to the farm unless she told him everything. And she couldn't. Or was it wouldn't? She didn't know, she just knew it hurt too much to talk about it.

Alyssa flipped the pillow to the cool side, hoping that would lull her back to sleep. It didn't.

Just as she started to slip out of bed, a hand wrapped itself around her wrist. "Come here, gorgeous," Tug said. He took her other wrist in his hand and pushed her back down against the pillow, pinning her there. He kissed her, then moved his mouth to her ear.

"I'm sorry I raised my voice," he whispered. "No more talk about the farm, I promise."

That morning they sat on the porch rockers drinking coffee and eating cherries from a ceramic bowl. Soothed by birdsong and a brightening day, the previous night's drama didn't seem so ominous. Alyssa found herself talking about her marriage and Darryl and how they met.

"He was everything I thought I was looking for," she said. "He's smart, responsible, conscientious . . ."

"Those are the qualities for a dog, not a mate," Tug said.

"There were other good things about him, too. But we were just a bad match. And by the time we had Roz, it was easier to stay together."

In the middle of explaining how she and Darryl first went searching for a farm, Alyssa suddenly stopped. "Wait a minute: I'm telling you everything and you've told me nothing. It's your turn now, Palifax. Do you have any girlfriends? Who are they and how many? I want a complete list."

"Just one, sort of," Tug said. He squirmed a bit in the rocking chair. He didn't mind talking about his life, as long as relationships weren't involved. "It's kind of over."

"'Kind of over.' What does that mean?"

"I told her I thought we should take a few steps back and see how we felt when I got back."

Alyssa threw a cherry pit at him. "You mean you wanted to break up with her but didn't have the guts?"

"It could be interpreted that way."

Alyssa threw another cherry pit at him.

"But I'd left a little sculpture by her door before I left. That was a nice gesture, don't you think?"

"Maybe. How long had you been together?"

"A few months. Ten or eleven."

Alyssa rolled her eyes. Tug held up his hands. "No more pits.

She liked the sculpture. Believe me, in a few months she'll be much happier having it than me."

"She's an artist?"

"Painter."

"What's her name? What's she look like?"

"Margaux. Margaux Cuberta. She looks like . . . I don't know, she looks like anybody. She's tall, nearly my height, dark hair. That kind of thing. "

Under further cross-examination, Alyssa got Tug to admit to a series of bungled "let's take a few steps back" breakups with other women. His confessions brought him another hail of cherry pits and little sympathy. But he seemed so crestfallen that, eventually, she relented. She walked over to his chair and leaned down. "The women of New York owe me a big favor, taking you off the streets." Then she kissed him and said, "I love you."

The rest of the day, Tug drew, Alyssa did chores. They ate dinner on the porch—pasta tossed with basil and garlic and olive oil—and moved to the bedroom before the sky turned dark. They made love as the sky went from gray to black. Alyssa didn't bother to set the alarm. They slept till nine and stayed in bed till noon.

The subject of their future wasn't brought up again.

CHAPTER 49

A few days later, Alyssa was cleaning stalls when she heard tires crunching on gravel. The car coming down the driveway was black, which eliminated all the usual unexpected visitors. Betsy Parker, the horse editor of the local paper, drove a big blue truck; Nancy, the wife of her neighbor, Dr. Holland, drove a silver sedan; Jackie, a white compact; and Reedy Collins, the blacksmith, a red van.

This was a station wagon. Tug? Driving to the farm? He'd just left an hour before to have lunch at Limespring; she hadn't expected him back until after dinner.

She wiped her hands on her jeans and tried to smooth her hair. It ignored her efforts and bounced back out in all directions.

"Something wrong?" she asked as he got out of the car.

"Yes and no," he said. He put a hand on each side of her face. "God, I love looking at you. Especially when you do that twisty thing with your mouth. Oh man, talk about bad timing. I've gotta go back to the City. Now. Of all damn times. Shit."

Back to the City. The words felt like four kicks to the stomach. Instantly, Alyssa regretted every day of the past month. She'd told herself it was all too good to be true and she'd been right.

"Really?" she said. "Are you coming back?"

Tug looked at her as if she were speaking a foreign language. "Are you nuts? Alyssa, how can I make this any clearer? *I love you.*

I'm just going for four or five days, that's all. 'Am I coming back?' How can you ask that so calmly?"

She reached down to pick a weed so he couldn't see her face. "You forget I'm an actor."

He knelt down and put his face next to hers. "Yeah, well, stop acting. I want to know you'll miss me. Look, I'll say it first: 'I'm gonna miss you.' Now it's your turn."

She smiled. "All right, maybe I'll miss you a little."

He nudged his shoulder against hers. "'A little'? Bullshit. You'll be lighting a candle by my drawings. Don't you want to know why I'm going?"

Alyssa pushed him back with her shoulder, hard enough to topple him onto his butt. "Sorry, I'm all out of candles. So tell me, what could possibly draw you away from my infinite charms?"

It was a long story and Tug told it with flourishes and asides. It had to do with his best friend, Joel Feinblom. Joel, a video artist who'd been trying for years to get his work shown at an important gallery, had finally got a shot at it, *if* Tug came back to New York right away.

Joel had called Limespring not more than thirty minutes before. Tug had been eating lunch with Marius and Don when they saw Jackie running up to the picnic tables.

"Tug, quick," she'd yelled out, "there's someone on the phone for you. Joel, from New York. He says it's urgent. Better hurry, it sounds like something's wrong."

Tug had run to the office with images of dead friends rushing through his mind. He expected to hear the worst when he picked up the phone. Instead he heard Joel singing, "Happy Days are here again . . . ," followed by an excited explanation of why Tug had to get in his car that instant and leave for New York

Scott Ungstead, owner of the Scott Ungstead Gallery, one of the edgiest galleries in SoHo, had just called, asking if Joel's show, "Clean Up Your Room," could be ready for the next weekend. The gallery's scheduled exhibit, "Inchworm"—a video sculpture involving cardboard boxes and seven TVs playing a tape of the artist's tongue licking the floor—had had to be canceled. The artist had totaled his car on the way to the gallery, destroying the televisions and landing himself in the hospital.

"It's like *Rosemary's Baby*," Tug said to Alyssa. "If I didn't know better, I'd say Joel joined a satanic cult and put the hex on the poor guy."

Ungstead wanted "Clean Up Your Room" as a replacement. The problem was that the show involved fifteen artists and a complicated setup, so they'd have to act fast. It was also a problem that none of the participants were well-known, and Ungstead would only give them the space if at least one contributor was a name artist. That's where Tug came in.

"You've gotta do it, Tug," Joel had said on the phone. "Ungstead gets reviewed by everyone. I've been waiting for something like this for years."

The show re-created a teenager's bedroom, except that everything in it was artwork from Joel and his friends. The wall posters were paintings and erotic drawings by Tari Smolens, a hot young graphic novelist; the computer screen saver was a series of photos; one of Joel's video works played on the room's TV screen; the teenager himself—a lifelike nude sculpture made from polyester resin and fiberglass by a Brooklyn artist—sat on a bed covered by a textile artist's handmade quilt. Other artists, including a guy who had made a skateboard out of fried pork rinds, supplied teen stuff scattered about. Tug contributed a work called *Wash Day*, a hamper overflowing with dirty clothes made from melted plastic and street junk. Everything in the installation was for sale, making "Clean Up Your Room" a work of art, a group show, and a gallery all at the same time.

Tug was explaining what was involved in putting the show together, when he slapped his palm against his head.

"Duuuuh!" he said. "How could I be so stupid! Come with me! You can see it all for yourself. You can even help us. Consider it Limespring Follies North. It'll be great to have you there. Besides, I want to show you where I live. Just throw some sexy underwear in a bag and let's go. We've gotta go now, though. Joel made me swear I'd get there tonight so we could get started."

He grabbed her hand and started to pull her toward the house.

"Whoa, Tug," Alyssa said. "Hold on. I'd love to go to New York, but you know I can't. I've got horses to feed."

"Get your friend Betsy to do it, she won't mind."

He started pulling her again.

"I can't, Tug. I just can't pick up and leave."

"Why not? What's holding you here?"

"Roz."

"Roz? She's in Chicago."

"She might call."

"Well, call her first. They have phones in New York. She doesn't have to know where you're calling from."

She looked away. "I can't go, Tug. I want to, but I can't. Remember Darryl calls every Thursday. What am I supposed to do, call *him* first and tell him I'm going to New York with the Limespring guy he thought I was having an affair with?"

Tug dropped her hand and started to walk away. "Jesus H. Christ, Alyssa, what are you going to do, sit by the phone forever waiting for Darryl to call?" He kicked a foot full of gravel down the driveway. "You don't even love the guy. At least that's what you tell me."

She walked after him. "Don't be jealous of Darryl," she said as she tried to take his hand.

He shook free of her. "Why not? You share a bed with him, don't you?"

His words hit her hard. "Stop it. Stop it, please. You're not being fair."

"Fair? You want to talk about fair? Tell me what's fair about this whole fucking thing? How do you think I feel knowing you'll be sleeping with him when he gets back from California? How'd you like it if I slept with someone in New York? You want fair? *That's* fair."

Alyssa took a few steps back. "Fine," she said, spitting out the word. "Just go to New York and do what you want. I'm married, you knew that all along."

"Okay, fine, I'm going to New York. I'll be back sometime."

He got in the car and slammed the door closed. Caught between anger and misery, Alyssa watched him spin the car around and gun down the drive like an angry teenager.

CHAPTER 50

The station wagon's rear end fishtailed as Tug sped through the curves of Alyssa's drive and onto Limespring Hollow Road. The Dixie Chicks blasted from his car radio, but they weren't loud enough to drive away the memory of: "I'm married, you knew that all along." Tug turned from Limespring Hollow Road onto Route 688, tires squealing, all the frustrations of the summer boiling over. He was sick and tired of getting jerked around. "Remember Darryl calls every Thursday." He pounded the steering wheel with the heel of his right hand. Jesus H. Christ.

But when he reached I-66, he began to calm down. She was married. He had known it all along. He backed off the gas and slowed to under sixty-five, a good thing, considering the age of the station wagon and the number of state troopers on patrol. And maybe he hadn't been fair.

By the time he passed the Delaplane exit, he was deep into regret. He recalled the time when, on one of their prop-hunting trips, he and Alyssa had stopped by the old Delaplane train depot that had been turned into an antiques store. The owner, a blond woman everybody called Popcorn, let them rummage through a storeroom of newly acquired stuff. Two hours later, Alyssa's truck was piled with a stack of rusted street signs, a cast-iron playground horse missing one leg, an assortment of bottles, and a bucket of cast-off tiles she'd bought for Nattie's mosaics.

Farther east on I-66, every exit seemed to lead to a memory of Alyssa. After Delaplane, Tug passed a sign for Marshall, where they'd once gone to the co-op to buy grain and bug spray. Then came The Plains, the little town where they'd eaten at the Rail Stop restaurant and seen Robert Duvall. He used to own the place and was sitting at a table with two men wearing wraparound sunglasses and a young, dark-haired woman so beautiful Tug pretended he didn't notice her. "Oh, go ahead and look," Alyssa had said. "I can barely take my eyes off her either."

That was followed by Haymarket, where late one night they'd turned off for gas, two Mountain Dew Slurpees, and an animated debate about which Brady kid was the most irritating.

As the Gainesville exit receded in his rearview mirror, so had his anger. The frustration remained, but he knew he wasn't going to do anything stupid like sleep with someone else out of spite or not come back. He couldn't. He loved her.

Around Manassas, he decided that an e-mail apology would be a good idea. He started concocting one before he realized he had no idea what her e-mail address was. A call, then. He wasn't great on the phone. Margaux used to complain that he sounded "like a deer caught in the headlights" when she called. It might have been a mixed metaphor, but it was true. Still, a phone call would have to do. He'd wait a couple of days, let things cool down, then, no matter how frantic the gallery show got, he'd call.

As Tug composed phone conversations in his mind, Alyssa speared piles of manure and heaved sawdust into a wheelbarrow. She hadn't planned on stripping the stalls that day, but it felt good to kick something, even if it was just a pitchfork.

She slammed her foot down on the metal shoulder, digging the tines deep into a crusty layer of sawdust turned red from a horse's urine. As she lifted a wedge of it, the stinging smell of ammonia rushed up at her. She tossed the chunk into the wheelbarrow, where it lay like a piece of ancient crumbling pottery.

What a spoiled brat Tug was, Alyssa thought as she attacked more of the red sawdust. A woman says no to him and he throws a tantrum and runs off.

She continued digging until all that remained was the clean brown floor of tamped earth. Then she tackled the piles of manure in the back of the stall. When the wheelbarrow was heaped to overflowing, she started to roll it out. But she pushed harder than she meant and it toppled over sideways, spilling everything.

"Shit," she said, glaring at the mound of manure and dirty sawdust. Then she realized what she had said, and started laughing.

"Shit! Shit! Shit!"

She righted the wheelbarrow and began to fill it up again. So Tug had acted like a baby—could she blame him? He had every reason to be angry. The fact was, when Darryl came back in three weeks, she would share his bed again. She couldn't imagine making love to Darryl, but she couldn't imagine asking for a divorce either. How would she feel if Tug were sleeping with someone else? How would she feel if he were married to someone else?

She walked to the tack room to get some lime to sprinkle on the stall floor. But she was thinking more about Tug's words than the job at hand. When she dug the plastic cup into the sack, she shoved her fingers against the caustic white powder.

"Shit," she said again, as the lime ate into a cut on her hand. She dropped the cup in the sack and rushed to the hose.

The next time she reached into the lime bag, she was more careful, but she kept thinking about Tug's words. Four stalls later, she was still thinking about them.

CHAPTER 51

The only thing Alyssa liked better at her Washington, D.C., house was the high-speed Internet connection. Googling at the farm could take hours, literally. Two tin cans and some string would have been more reliable than her phone connection with America Online.

She sat down at the keyboard at seven-thirty that night. By eight-thirty, she'd located Tug's e-mail address. It took four searches and two computer crashes before she finally found it on a site for the Martin Oppenheimer Gallery, where Tug had last exhibited.

"I bought candles in Marshall," she wrote to junkman@hotmail.com. "Come back before I run out. I miss you."

Alyssa had decided to write Tug an e-mail somewhere between piling sawdust into the second stall and stripping the third. She preferred the emotional distance of cyberspace to a phone call. She didn't exactly want to apologize—after all, he'd been the baby, not her. But his words—"How would you feel if I slept with someone in New York?"—made her realize how hurt he was.

Visions of Tug making love with another woman kept tumbling around in her mind. But who was she to even think about fidelity? As happy as she'd been the past month, there'd been times she'd felt such acute shame that she wanted to draw a big red A on her forehead as an act of penance.

Still, she wished she could have gone to New York. Being there with Tug would have been wonderful. The show sounded exciting and she wanted to see his world. But the only way she'd be traveling to New York tonight would be through cyberspace.

She typed the words "Clean Up Your Room" into the Google box. Five minutes later, the first thirty responses of more than 2.2 million appeared. She'd forgotten to narrow the search. What was the last name of Tug's friend? She searched her mind, but her connection was even slower than Google's. Nothing came up. So she typed "Palifax" next to "Clean Up Your Room" and chewed at her top lip and tapped the table, waiting for the response.

This time she got only one result. It was a new site; it hadn't been there that night she'd first Googled Tug's name. She clicked on it and eventually it came, unfolding slowly to a black screen with miniscule white letters that read "The Scott Ungstead Gallery." The black dissolved to a white screen with text boxes about upcoming shows. She clicked on "Clean Up Your Room" and waited. Finally a picture started to appear. It was of Tug's friend. Now she remembered: Joel Feinblom.

She watched his face begin to fill the screen, starting at the top and working down, from curly brown hair to a high forehead, to thick eyebrows, to a straight but prominent nose that looked like something stamped on a Greek coin, then to thin lips in a half-smile, chin and neck. A clip from his video work followed—a ripening banana, its skin turning from green to yellow to speckled black to black—then a statement about the idea behind "Clean Up Your Room," explaining that it was a collaborative effort featuring the following artists.

Tug's picture came next. It was a sophisticated, moody photo. Only half of his face was lighted, though the photographer had managed to illuminate the eye on the shadowed side. It made Tug seem distant, cool. Below his photo, a picture of his artwork began to materialize. Unlike the portrait, it was a simple snapshot of what looked to be a garish basketful of dirty laundry.

Curious about the other artists in the show, Alyssa let the page unfold completely. Along with photos of their work, some artists had included blurbs from gallery press releases and critical commentaries. The artworks were so silly or whimsical or wacky and the blurbs so lugubrious that at first Alyssa thought it was a joke, additional hijinks from the "Clean Up Your Room" team.

But as she clicked onto a second page and read more, she realized the comments were meant to be taken seriously. A series of dime-store photos of a severe-looking woman wearing an assortment of baseball caps was "a meditative observation of herself because the body is a source of knowledge and the union of the abstract and the solid." A sculptural collage of dried caterpillars, barnacles, a stuffed snake with a rat in its throat, and two of the artist's front teeth was hailed by an art critic as "the unironic observation of an optimistic smile that degrades into a painful grimace of uncontrollable salivation."

She found it nearly impossible to picture Tug in this pseudo-sophisticated, art-babble world. Torn between amusement and horror, she read through the site, shaking her head at the pretentious and impenetrable prose.

As page three unfolded, the photo of a woman artist emerged line by line. Its lighting contrasts were similar to Tug's, as if the portrait had been taken at the same photo session. The woman had long glossy black hair and exotic features; her mouth was full and sensual, her eyes half-lidded. She looked like a Hollywood casting agent's idea of a gypsy. She was startlingly beautiful.

Below her picture was a photo of one of her works, an intricate painting in serious, somber colors, and another inane blurb. But Alyssa never got that far. She stopped at the artist's name: Margaux Cuberta.

Tug's girlfriend. The woman he'd described as "nothing special," someone who looked like anyone else. This was the woman he needed to take a few steps back from, to "see how we felt when I got back." And now he was back.

She hadn't felt this kind of jealousy in more than twenty years. She'd forgotten this flip side of being in love. She stared at the picture. All she could think of were his parting words. "How would you feel if I slept with someone in New York. That would be fair, wouldn't it?"

CHAPTER 52

Alyssa was on the phone with Roz when she heard a knock on the door. Roz usually called in the evening, but her news couldn't wait seven hours. Her cabinet detail was being used in the $4 million, 12,000-square-foot summer house her uncle was designing for the pop novelist James Brighton.

"Just think, every time James Brighton opens his kitchen cabinet, he'll be looking at my work!" Roz practically shrieked. "And, oh my God, Uncle Ron says *Architectural Digest* wants first dibs on the house when it's finished! My cabinets in *Architectural Digest*! Oh my God!"

"I'm so proud of you, sweetie," Alyssa said as she walked to the door and saw Abbi, Marius, and Nattie standing there. She motioned them inside as Roz chattered away. Alyssa loved to hear Roz talk. The words hardly mattered, just the sound of her voice was enough. As the three guests plunked down on the couch, Alyssa nodded and squeezed in "Uh-huh" and "That's great" whenever there was a break in the sentences, which wasn't often. For the next few minutes, Roz described the rest of James Brighton's house in such technical detail that Alyssa was both overwhelmed by her daughter's knowledge and saddened by her maturity. There was no denying that her little girl was no longer a little girl.

"Hi, guys. That was Roz," said Alyssa when she hung up. "What's going on?"

"We came to rescue you," Marius said.

"From what?" Alyssa said.

Nattie glanced at one of Tug's horse drawings taped to the kitchen wall and wanted to say "loneliness," but Abbi had made her promise to keep her mouth shut about Tug, even though the romance and Tug's trip to New York were hot topics at Limespring.

Instead she said, "Boredom. We're going crazy over at Limespring. It's too peaceful. We need drama. We're going for a hike. If we're lucky we'll find a rattlesnake."

"More likely a copperhead," said Alyssa.

"Rattlesnake, copperhead, whatever. We need a diversion," said Nattie. She stared ostentatiously at the drawing and added, "Don't you?"

Abbi shot Nattie a poisonous look. "Come on Liss, join us. We've haven't seen you in ages. Besides, we don't know the trails, even though Marius says he does. If we listen to him, they'll have to send the bloodhounds for us."

Alyssa thought about all the mindless chores she was supposed to do that day and all the time it would give her to think about Tug. She'd been obsessing over Margaux Cuberta and the fact that Tug hadn't responded to her e-mail yet. She'd sent it two days before. Nattie wasn't the only one who needed a diversion. "Count me in," she said.

She started to put on her hiking boots. "Wait, I've got a better idea. Let's take the horses up Mount Buck instead of a walk. One of the refugees is going to his new home tomorrow and I'd love him to get one last trail ride in. The other horses could use some work, too. What do you say?"

"That's a lot more dramatic than a walk," said Marius. "I'm game."

Abbi and Nattie agreed, and soon the four were riding up Mount Buck, retracing the path Alyssa had taken Tug on the raspberry walk, the same path the real estate agent's car had started up so many years before.

Alyssa unlatched the newly oiled gate and the horses followed through. On the other side, the trail was narrow and overgrown from the heavy spring rain. But a few hundred yards on, it opened up wide enough for two horses to walk side by side.

Alyssa found herself next to Marius. She was riding Theo, the smallest horse in the bunch. But he had a big, energetic walk, and the only horse that could keep up with him was Poli, the huge gray gelding. Marius was riding him.

When Marius began talking about world climate and the desertification of sub-Saharan Africa, Alyssa decided she didn't need to be that diverted. On the pretext of checking out the other riders, she held Theo up and pulled alongside Abbi, hoping for some news of Tug.

After polite questions about the progress of Abbi's book, she asked innocently, "Is Tug back from New York yet?"

Abbi squinted suspiciously. "Didn't he tell you how long he was going to be gone?"

"Not really," Alyssa said in a blithe tone. "Just that it might take a few days or more, depending on how fast things went. That show he's helping put together sounded, well . . . inventive."

Abbi rolled her eyes. "Inventive? How about preposterous? But that's Joel for you. You should see some of his so-called video art."

"I did," said Alyssa. "I saw a clip of his stuff the other night when I was surfing the Web. It showed a banana ripening and rotting."

Abbi groaned. "Typical Joel." She glanced over at her riding partner. "What site was it on?"

"Oh, I can't remember, some site about the show. They had a list of the artists involved. There're so many of them, it's like a herd." Alyssa hesitated, then asked, "Do you know them? Are they all friends of Tug's from Pratt?"

"Well, Joel is," said Abbi. "And the guy who made a skateboard out of chitlins—he was once Joel's roommate at Pratt. I don't know about the others."

"Oh yeah, the chitlin skateboard, how could I forget," Alyssa said. "Well, what about those intense mandala paintings? They're pretty riveting, know anything about that artist?"

Abbi ducked under some tree branches before she replied. She knew exactly who Alyssa was asking about and figured that Alyssa had seen a photo of Margaux on the same site. She wondered how much Alyssa knew about Tug's almost-former girlfriend. Maybe just seeing the photo was all she needed to know.

"You mean Margaux Cuberta?" Abbi said.

"I don't remember her name exactly, but that sounds close. Know her?"

"Not well," Abbi lied. "I've met her a couple of times, but that's it."

"Is she one of Joel's friends from Pratt?"

"I don't think so," Abbi said, trying to sound neutral.

"There's a picture of her on the site," said Alyssa, finally getting to the point. "She gorgeous. What's she like?"

"Lethal."

Alyssa was about to ask what that meant, when they came up to Nattie and Marius, who'd stopped at the crest of the hill. Below them, the trail descended for a short way and then opened to a wide meadow that bordered a large pond.

"Beautiful, huh?" said Alyssa. "That's Cove Lake down there. It was supposed to be the centerpiece for some fancy vacation home development. But it got tied up in a nasty divorce, then sold to a former CIA spook who unloaded it to the Nature Conservancy. It's a long story, but the upshot is this." Alyssa waved her arm in front of her. "My own private Lake Placid. I'm usually the only one up here. Sometimes the kids come up on their ATVs, but I can't really complain too much, they cut these trails. And they pretty much stay on the south side where the trails are bumpier. Let's go down to the lake to give the horses something to drink."

Marius and Nattie rode ahead while Alyssa and Abbi followed. When the others were out of earshot, Alyssa resurrected the Margaux conversation. "So," she said, "you were saying 'lethal.' That's an odd way to describe someone."

"Well, she's tall, thin, gorgeous, smart, brooding, and completely devoid of a sense of humor," said Abbi. "And she eats men for breakfast. They love it. They all want to crack the mystery of Margaux."

That stopped the conversation cold. They continued down toward the lake in silence, Alyssa mulling over the words "lethal" and "thin," until Abbi leaned over and tapped her shoulder.

"Liss?" she said. "You hear what I hear?"

It was the whine of an engine. The ATVs weren't on the south side of Mount Buck this time.

The sound grew louder and Alyssa began to worry. Theo was starting to jig. Up ahead, she could see Poli's tail swishing back and forth—a sign of agitation. She wasn't concerned about Abbi, who was riding Roy. As a thoroughbred, he was an aberration; you could light a stick of dynamite next to him and he wouldn't flinch. Nattie would be safe, too. She was on Lane, a twenty-three-year-old gelding who could still be a little fractious. But Nattie was an experienced rider and could handle most things.

Not Marius, however. He claimed he'd ridden as a young boy in Bohemia, but many days had passed since then, and his riding skills were rudimentary at best. While Poli was normally calm, he had a thoroughbred's heightened sensitivity. Alyssa had taken Poli on trail rides before, but never with ATVs whizzing by. She had no idea how he'd react.

She glanced back up the trail.

"They must be heading for the lake, same as us," she said to Abbi. "Don't worry, you'll be fine. Roy won't even notice. But I'm going to ride next to Marius and have Nattie ride back here with you."

Alyssa pressed her legs against Theo's sides and he half jigged, half cantered up to Nattie. "If the ATVs come close or want to pass, Lane may jump around a bit but he won't do anything stupid. You'll be fine. Just let Abbi catch up with you and keep an eye on her."

"Maybe I shouldn't have made that crack about wanting some drama," said Nattie.

"At least we haven't seen any rattlesnakes," Alyssa said, forcing a laugh.

Alyssa then edged Theo next to Poli. The engine noise had turned into two distinct, and louder, roars. Theo began to prance and blow short, hard puffs of air through his nose. Poli's ears flicked back and forth and his eyes widened, the whites shining like headlights in the trailside shade.

"Easy, boy," Alyssa said to Theo, and in the same measured voice said to Marius, who appeared as nervous as his mount, "All you have to do is sit still and talk to him. Just like I'm doing."

Behind them, the roars grew louder. Poli started jigging in step with Theo, bouncing Marius around in the saddle.

"Grip with your legs, Marius, and try not to pull back so much on his reins," Alyssa said.

Then she stroked her hand down Theo's sweaty neck and swung around again to look up the hill. Just as she did, a red ATV barreled up over the ridge, slammed into a bump at the crest, and launched into the air. It thudded down on the trail and headed straight toward the four horses, a plume of dust rising behind it like a mini-tornado.

Alyssa grabbed both reins in one hand and pumped the air furiously with the other. "Slow down! Slow down! Slow down!" she yelled.

The kid at the wheel waved back and nodded, bringing his mud-caked vehicle to a sudden stop about twenty yards behind Lane. But just as he did, another ATV hurtled over the ridge even faster, jumping even higher. When it hit the trail, the driver jammed on his brakes. But it was too late. He plowed into the back of the first ATV with a loud *Whoomp!*

The horses exploded. Even Roy. He bolted to the side, throwing Abbi into a patch of raspberries. Lane leapt to the left, much like a flying Lipizzaner, though Nattie managed to stay mounted. Poli reared straight up and Marius, panicking, grabbed Theo's bridle as he was catapulted backwards.

The sudden jerk sent Theo into a frenzy. He whipped his head hard to the right to free himself. As he tried to spin out from what must have seemed like an attack, his hind legs slipped under him and he toppled to the ground, throwing Alyssa back-first into a tree stump.

Then, struggling to stand, Theo flailed out with his legs to gain traction and, before she could move out of the way, kicked Alyssa in the stomach.

"I can't breathe," she gasped.

CHAPTER 53

It took the medevac helicopter twenty-five minutes to reach the field by Cove Lake. The 911 operator had told Abbi not to move Alyssa, just to sit tight and keep her talking.

"Don't let her fall asleep," the operator said.

As the two boys on the ATVs watched nervously by their vehicles, Marius held Alyssa's hand and Nattie pressed her shirt, which she'd dipped in the cool lake water, against Alyssa's forehead.

"She's still having a hard time breathing," Abbi said to the emergency operator, her voice rising. "How much longer before they get here?"

"Any minute," said the operator. "But you have to stay calm. If you get excited, she will, too."

"Listen, here it comes," Nattie said. She pointed to ridgeline in back of them. The distinctive *whacka-whacka-whacka* sound of the approaching helicopter got stronger and stronger. Then from over Mount Buck it appeared. It landed in the meadow and two EMTs jumped from the open doors and ran up the trail toward them, carrying a folded stretcher.

"Anyone else hurt?" one of them shouted over the roar of the helicopter as the other started examining Alyssa.

The three of them shook their heads, as did the ATVers. Abbi had only suffered some scrapes. Marius, who'd stopped his fall by grabbing on to Theo's bridle, had miraculously landed on his feet.

And Nattie had never come off. One of the ATV drivers had been thrown onto the trail, but hadn't been hurt.

Alyssa was scared. She'd gotten the breath knocked out of her plenty of times from falling off horses. It was always shocking at first, feeling like the front and back of her body had been vacuum-sealed together. But then her lungs would unstick and expand, allowing her to breathe again.

Not this time. When she hit the tree stump it felt like someone had taken a baseball bat to her back. And then, when Theo's hoof caught her in the stomach, it felt like her insides exploded. By the time Nattie had run over to her and Alyssa had pointed to the cell phone on her belt loop, she could barely say, "Call 911." Now, a half hour later, each breath was still shallow and excruciating.

"Something's really wrong," Alyssa said to the EMT. "Am I going to die?"

The EMT, a thirtyish woman with short red hair, took Alyssa's hand as the other tightened a blood pressure cuff on her arm. "You'll be fine. We're going to get you to the hospital. I know it's hard, but try not to worry."

They lifted her onto the stretcher and carried her to the helicopter. Over the deafening roar, the red-haired EMT yelled, "I'm going to cover your face with the sheet." She motioned to the whirling blades. "It'll kick up dirt and hit you in the face otherwise."

Abbi, Nattie, and Marius watched as they loaded Alyssa feet first into the helicopter and twirled up into the sky.

"We've gotta call Darryl," Marius said.

"And Tug," said Abbi.

CHAPTER 54

The young woman with the cap of spiky brown hair sat by the bed in room 813 of Fairfax Hospital. She'd spent the night in the recliner chair, reading and dozing. She had dark, deep-set eyes that turned down slightly, and an aquiline nose. She was slight, small-chested, and narrow-hipped; her skin had the translucent quality of someone who spent more time under fluorescent lights than the sun.

She was the first person Alyssa woke to that morning.

"Roz?" Alyssa said. She could barely get her mouth to form the word. When she blinked, her eyes moved in slow motion. Everything was confused. She felt as if she were at the bottom of a cave looking up at her daughter. But Roz was in Chicago.

"Roz?" she said again.

The young woman squeezed her mother's hand. She'd been holding it on and off through the night.

"Mom, it's me. I'm here," Roz said.

Alyssa closed her eyes and was overcome by a swirl of confused images: A white sheet pulled over her head, a whirring roar, a red-headed woman she didn't recognize, bright lights, people in green masks. She fluttered her eyelids open.

"You're in the hospital," Roz said. "You had an accident. They had to operate, but you're going to be okay."

Roz leaned down and kissed her mother's cheek. "You're going to be okay," she repeated. She was crying.

Alyssa reached up and wiped away Roz's tears, as if she were a little girl again. "What happened?" she asked.

Roz told her about the accident, the helicopter ride, and the operation. "You lacerated your liver, Mom," she said. "Could you try to cut back on the drama a little? You scared the you-know-what out of Daddy and me."

Alyssa started to laugh and a jolt of pain jabbed through her insides.

"But the cool thing is they didn't have to cut you open or anything like that. They went in through a vein in your leg and blew foam around the liver to stop the bleeding. Just like you'd insulate a house."

Afraid to laugh again, Alyssa smiled. "I love you, Noodles," she said. "You can't know how good it is to see you."

Normally, the use of her old nickname would have warranted at least an eye roll, but Roz let it pass. "Daddy's downstairs getting coffee," she said. "I'm gonna run down and get him. He's been a basket case."

But Alyssa held on to her hand. "No, can you wait a few minutes, please? Just sit with me for a little bit. It all seems like a dream, I'm so tired and I don't even know if I'm dreaming now . . ." Alyssa closed her eyes and drifted off to sleep.

When she awoke, everything was mixed up again. Darryl was sitting in the chair Roz had been in. Roz was in another chair next to him. Why were they there? Where was she? Alyssa opened and closed her eyes, trying to make sense of the images.

"It's all the drugs, Liss," Darryl said, taking her hand. "The doctors told me you'd be a little out of it until the anesthesia works its way out of your system."

Alyssa nodded, but it was like standing up too quickly. As she waited for the dizziness to pass, she slowly began to remember: Riding accident. Operation. Liver insulation.

"Sorry," she said. "I'm having a hard time keeping things straight."

Darryl leaned back. "Understandable," he said. "Your body's suffered a major shock. How do you feel?"

"I hurt. My stomach feels like it was used for batting practice."

"It was. Or more accurately, kicking practice. Those damn horses."

Roz nudged her father's shoulder. "Daaad," she said. "Now's not the time to start in on the horses."

"Well, I'm just glad you're okay." He leaned forward and kissed Alyssa on the forehead. "The doctors say you'll be fine. They think you'll be up and around in a few days."

A nurse came in to check on medicines and offer some orange juice. By the time she left, Alyssa was alert enough to sit up and hear the story of urgent phone calls and plane flights and how Darryl and Roz came to be at her side.

"Daddy didn't want me to fly out at night. God, sometimes he's worse than you." Roz stood up and wrapped her arms around her father's neck and put her cheek against his. Alyssa looked at the two faces. They bore a startling resemblance to one another, down to their nostrils, which curved like perfect little question marks.

"Don't stop talking," Alyssa mumbled, "even if I drift off again."

Roz continued her travelogue. Darryl added a few comments, but mostly Roz talked.

"Don't stop," Alyssa mumbled again, struggling to keep her eyes open. "Don't leave."

Roz squeezed her mother's hand. "Mom, we're here, we're not going anywhere."

The sound of their chatter soothed her. She felt buffered by their words and their presence. She closed her eyes. An image came to her of a camping trip they'd made to the Poconos a million years ago. It was as clear as a photograph: Darryl and Roz trying to start a campfire; Roz wearing a Girl Scout hat.

She felt Roz's hand on hers. She sank deep into the pillow and her dreams.

"Hi. Can I came in and see the patient?" Abbi stuck her head in the door. "Hey, Rozzie. Hello, Darryl."

Abbi entered with a flourish of flowers, then saw Alyssa asleep.

"Oops," she said and tiptoed over to the sill, where she put a big spray of purple wildflowers from Limespring.

Alyssa stirred and saw Abbi. Things were getting clearer, faster. She remembered where she was and how'd she gotten there.

"Hi Abbi," she said weakly. "Thanks for calling Roz and Darryl."

Abbi leaned over to kiss Alyssa on the cheek. "You scared the holy crap out of us," she said. "I made so many deals with God, I can't swear, drink, or talk poorly about successful writers for the next three years."

Alyssa started to laugh, then groaned. "Damn, I forgot. It hurts to laugh."

Abbi stood by the bedside and filled in the details of the trail ride Alyssa had forgotten.

"Marius landed on his feet?" Alyssa said. "Unbelievable. I thought he was a goner. It's a miracle none of you were hurt."

"Some miracle," said Darryl. "More like a cosmic joke."

"Daddy!" said Roz.

"Darryl," Alyssa snapped at him.

Abbi said nothing.

"Sorry. That was stupid. I'm just upset. It's no fun getting an emergency call in the middle of a meeting saying your wife's just been medevaced to the hospital. It was a long night and I need to get some sleep. Liss, I'll be back this afternoon. Need anything from home?"

Alyssa shook her head.

Darryl stood to leave, leaned down and kissed the top of his daughter's head. "You want to stay or come home?"

"Stay," Roz said.

After Darryl left, Abbi went to the cafeteria to get lunch. Roz had brought her drawings—the famous cabinet detail—and gave her mother a full presentation.

In the middle of it, she stopped and asked, "Is everything okay with Daddy? He seems kind of, I don't know . . . weird. This morning when we were talking about the farm and stuff, I asked him how the Follies went. All I could get out of him was, 'Fine.' He didn't even take pictures this year. Is something wrong?"

Alyssa squeezed Roz's hand. "Don't worry, sweetie. He was just worried about me. You know how men are, they can't multitask. Tell me more about Mr. Brighton's dream house."

CHAPTER 55

By the time Tug got to Fairfax Hospital it was five-thirty and he'd been on the road for seven and a half hours. The drive down from New York had been a nightmare, thanks to a pileup on I-95 north of Baltimore and the usual rush-hour parking lot clotting the American Legion Bridge between Maryland and Virginia.

He felt trapped inside his car as his foot tap-danced between accelerator and brake, inching his way through the northern Virginia bottleneck. "Don't kill yourself on the way down," Jackie had said on the phone, assuring him that Alyssa had come through surgery successfully and everything looked good. But once he heard the words "lacerated liver," her assurances flew out the window.

He had visions of her in a hospital bed, tubes running in and out of her arms, her liver shredded to coleslaw. He wanted to jam the pedal to the floor and blast his way to Alyssa.

It didn't help that he was half-dead from lack of sleep. The previous four days in New York had been as manic as a Marx Brothers movie. When he arrived at the gallery, the show was in disarray. It turned out that half the works wouldn't arrive for days and others didn't fit the teenage theme. The first hour he was there, three artists delivered ultimatums and Joel nearly punched out one of them.

Tug and Joel were in the middle of negotiating with graphic

artist Tari Smolens—she wanted her drawings on the bedroom
door, Joel had promised that position to someone else—when
Margaux walked in.

"Uh-oh," said Joel, "more trouble. And this one's all yours,
Tug."

They watched the tall brunette approach. Every straight guy in
the room watched her approach. She wore tight blue jeans and a
black T-shirt, no bra. She was shorter than Tug by an inch, but her
legs were longer than his by two. Her hair was pulled straight back
in a ponytail, exaggerating the upward sweep of her cheeks. She
looked like a Modigliani portrait come to life. Tug had forgotten
how she parted a room when she walked in. He'd also forgotten
the thrill he felt each time he knew she was walking toward him.

Joel leaned over and out of the side of his mouth said, "Tell me
again why you want to take a step back from her?"

"Right now I'm not sure," said Tug.

Joel turned to the irate artist next to them and said, "Tari, let's
figure it all out tomorrow. We'll get you a great display. I promise."
Then he folded his arms and waited for the fireworks to begin.

Margaux stopped in front of them, looking straight at Tug but
addressing his friend. "Are you really going to be able to pull this
show together, Joel?" she asked. Without waiting for an answer,
she said to Tug, "So, how's Limespring? Have you found what
you're looking for?" Her mouth wore the slightest of smiles; her
voice gave away nothing.

With her hair pulled back, Tug couldn't help but notice her earrings. They were dangling gears from an old watch that he'd
twisted together with some gold wire and given to her as a Christmas gift. A week later, she had worn them to a New Year's Eve
party. Right before midnight, she'd pulled him into a bedroom and
they'd made love in the host's walk-in closet.

"Yeah, Tug," Joel chimed in, "I'd like to hear about it, too. Anyway, I'm starving and I need a break before I kill someone. Tell us
about the country muses over pizza."

When they left the gallery, Tug held the door open for Margaux, and as she passed by him, she brushed his ear with her lips and whispered, "You still have a key to my place, don't you?"

Over dinner, Tug gave Margaux and Joel an expurgated version of his summer. He told them elaborate details about Limespring, his drawing project, and his progress. Finally Farm got a couple of mentions, Alyssa Brown did not. They walked back together afterward, but before Tug could enter the gallery, Margaux held him back.

"Will I see you when you're finished tonight? I think we need to talk, don't you?" Her eyes were hooded by the night glare of the street; her lips were slightly parted.

"Did you see the mess in there? We'll be lucky if—" Tug began. Before he could finish the sentence, Margaux leaned over and kissed him.

"Later," she said. "Wake me."

But Tug never left the gallery that night. He and Joel split the twin bed that was part of the exhibit. Tug got the mattress ("I drove five hours to get here," he reminded his friend); Joel got the box springs.

Over coffee the next morning, Joel, who'd been suspicious about the previous night's story, interrogated him about his real Limespring summer. In less than five minutes, Tug confessed that he'd lied, and he told Joel the whole Alyssa story.

"I'm crazy in love with this woman, Joel," he said, summing up. "And I don't know what to do. She's there; I'm here. She's got a farm; I've got a city. She's married. I'm . . . I don't know what."

Joel shook his head. "I wish I had some wise words, my friend. Just be careful is all I can say. This husband isn't going to come after you with a shotgun, is he?"

"I doubt it. He studies bacteria or something."

"Would she really divorce him for you? Where would you two live? And what about her kid?"

"I don't know, I don't know, and I don't know." Tug rubbed his face with his hands. "And meanwhile I've got Margaux on my tail."

"You can't just leave her hanging."

"I know, I know. But all I can think about right now is Alyssa. And for all I know, this whole thing is a ridiculous pipe dream. She's never promised me anything. Not once has she said anything about us after this summer."

"Tug, you gotta tell Margaux something. Just call her. Tell her we were up half the night and you couldn't come by. Tell her it's going to be that way for the next few days because the show's a fucking shambles. At least that part's the truth. And it'll give you time to figure out what to do."

Tug, eager to put off the Margaux confrontation as long as possible, agreed. And it turned out that his excuses were true. The logistics for "Clean Up Your Room" were even more formidable than Joel and Tug had anticipated. At night, they got less than four hours' sleep. During the day, they were so busy that they barely had time to think. They survived on take-out food and lattes.

The frenetic pace of preparations and negotiations was only temporarily jarring to Tug. By the second day he felt plugged back into the art world's energy grid. He was surprised to find that, if his two months in the quiet of the country had done anything, it was to sharpen his dull edges. "Clean Up Your Room" was creating a buzz. A reporter from *Artworld* magazine called asking for details, and there was excited speculation about a piece in the *New York Times Magazine*. Tug was buzzing right along with it. It wasn't until 2 A.M. on his fourth night back, when gallery owner Scott Ungstead started suggesting changes in the show's layout, that he finally left Joel to handle things and dragged himself off to his own apartment.

Six hours later the doorbell rang. Tug was so groggy that at first he thought it was the apartment's fire alarm. He staggered out of his bedroom to answer it.

"Why isn't your phone working?" Joel walked in carrying take-out coffee and a breakfast croissant filled with scrambled eggs and mushrooms.

"What?" said Tug, still dazed. "Oh, I had it turned off while I was away. What's up? I told you I'd be back at the gallery around eleven."

"Here, I brought this for you." Joel handed Tug the food. "You're going to need it for the drive."

"What? What drive?"

"I went back to my place early this morning and there was a message on my phone for you. From Abbi. There's some kind of emergency down at Limespring. It's that married woman you're in love with. Alicia? She's been in an accident. You're supposed to call."

One call and forty-five minutes later, Tug was heading south on the New Jersey Turnpike.

CHAPTER 56

The hospital ward was bustling when Tug arrived. Patients, leaning on walkers, made tentative laps around the nurses' station; friends and relatives spilled out of the rooms; doctors banged in and out of swinging double doors.

Tug carried gift-shop flowers and a large packet. He walked around the central station looking for No. 813, which turned out to be a corner room. Its door was ajar and its curtains partly open. Tug saw that Alyssa had company. Standing around her bed were Abbi, Marius, and a pale young woman with short hair. For a second he thought the young woman was a new Limey he hadn't met. But when she leaned over and kissed Alyssa on the cheek, he realized it must be Roz.

He backed up a few steps. He didn't want to meet her. Not this way. It seemed unsavory, even cruel. He was hesitating by the nurses' station, trying to decide if he should come back later, when Abbi glanced up and caught his eye. He put a finger to his lips and motioned for her to meet him outside the room.

"What's the matter? Why don't you go in?" Abbi asked as Tug pulled her around a corner out of view.

"That's Roz, isn't it? I don't know. It just doesn't feel right," said Tug.

"Yeah, you're probably right," Abbi said. She looked at her watch. "Just as well. Darryl's due back at six and that would be awkward. But he's not staying for long—he told Liss he's got a dinner meeting. And Marius is just about to take Roz to get something to eat. So just hang out awhile in the coffee shop, I'll come get you when the coast is clear." She pointed to the packet sandwiched under his arm. "What's that?"

"A present, some drawings," he said.

"Great, Alyssa could use some cheering up. How about if I bring it to her now? That way you don't have to schlep it all over the hospital. Besides, she could use a nice surprise. Believe me, she needs it. It's been hell."

Tug handed Abbi the packet. "But she's okay, right? Jackie said everything went fine."

"Fine, as far as lacerating your liver goes," Abbi said. "It could've been worse, believe me. I thought she was dying. She thought so, too. Anyhow, vamoose. I don't think it'd be a great idea if Darryl saw you here. That's all Alyssa needs. I'll be down in the coffee shop in a little while."

When Abbi returned to Alyssa's room, Marius and Roz were thumbing through the Yellow Pages for a restaurant, a nurse had just come in to draw blood, and the phone rang. No one noticed as she slid Tug's packet under a stack of magazines on the windowsill.

"So Red, Hot and Blue it will be," Marius said, escorting his young charge out the door. To Alyssa he said, "Your daughter has a hankering for barbecue. And as you know," he said, slipping into his genie accent, "her wish is my command."

The nurse finally left, but Alyssa was still on the phone. "A friend from D.C.," she mouthed. Abbi sat by the bed flipping through that week's *People* magazine. Just when she got to the part about Jennifer Anniston hating her jawline, Darryl walked in.

"Thank God," Abbi said to him, who looked at her like she was crazy. She pointed to the magazine. "You spared me from reading more about Jennifer's body flaws. Anyway, Liss just had her blood drawn and I'm off for coffee."

As she left the room she said to Alyssa, "I'll be back in about thirty minutes."

CHAPTER 57

Alyssa hung up the phone. "That was Carol," she said to Darryl. "The Shrike just fired the girls' soccer coach, three weeks before school starts, and enrollment's so far down the board's thinking about closing the high school."

He sat on the chair where Abbi had just been sitting. "In other words, business as usual at Emerson. I told you to start sending out résumés the minute I met that woman."

"I know, I know. I should have. Anyway, how's everything at home?"

"Just like you'd imagine. Musty. I opened all the windows but I closed them before I left. Supposed to pour. It was already drizzling on the way over."

"That'll be good for the azaleas," Alyssa said. "How're they doing? Is Woody watering them enough?"

"They're fine. They look great, so does the lawn. He's been doing a good job."

Alyssa and Darryl spent a few more sentences on Woody Fuller, a neighbor kid, and his college plans. Dartmouth, possibly Yale. Then they fell silent. They'd run out of conversation. Earlier that day, they'd already gone through the checklist of topics for two people who hadn't seen each other in a month: things at the farm (the roof still leaked); things in California (the resistant bacteria were more resistant than expected); things about their Washington home (they'd definitely need a new furnace); and things about Roz. Their conversation had been most animated when they'd talked about their daughter, who'd regaled them with stories of her summer and showed off the architectural drawings of James Brighton's now-famous cabinets.

Darryl picked up the *People* magazine Abbi had tossed on the table, but Alyssa wanted to fill the empty space with talk. She'd woken up this morning with Roz by her side, so soothed by her presence that she hadn't thought about Tug. It was in the disconnected hours that followed—a haze of fitful sleep, visitors, nurses, the first tentative meals—that she started thinking about him. She missed his touch and their long, meandering conversations. She missed hearing his pencil scratching against the drawing paper; she missed falling asleep nudged up against him.

She'd thought they have the rest of August together and then say their good-byes. But the doctors told her she couldn't go back to the farm alone. She'd need help getting around for at least the next three weeks.

And now Tug was in New York. She wouldn't even get a chance to say good-bye. Maybe it was just as well.

"Boy," she said, trying to sound perkier than she felt. "I've never seen Roz so excited about anything. You were right about letting her go to Chicago this summer."

Darryl looked up from the pages. "Ron told me she's the best intern he's ever had. Of course, he's somewhat prejudiced. She is his niece, after all. But still, she's accomplished quite a bit for someone her age. Where'd she go, anyway? Out with friends?"

"No, Marius took her to dinner."

"Oh, great," Darryl said. "He'll be salivating all over her."

"Don't be ridiculous. He wouldn't do that with her. Plus it's just an act, anyway." She switched the topic back to Roz's work.

"That cabinet design is really interesting. Where'd she come up with an idea like that, suspending them from the ceiling with high-tensile aluminum?"

"I don't think they were suspended. I think they were mounted to look that way. Hold on a second, let's look at her drawings. I think that's them, on the windowsill."

Darryl walked over to the pile of magazines. There was the sound of rustling and then a long pause. Alyssa looked over. Darryl was standing, back to her, studying something on the windowsill.

"Darryl?"

"'*Shenandoah Summer*. For Alyssa,'" Darryl read aloud.

"What?" Alyssa said.

Darryl repeated it louder. "'*Shenandoah Summer*. For Alyssa.' Well, I see somebody's been busy. Let me guess, more drawings from your *co-star* in the Follies?" He exaggerated the word "co-star," making it sound lascivious. "Tug, right? Did he bring them by last night while I was on the plane rushing to get here?"

Alyssa was confused. Could Tug have been here last night? She closed her eyes and tried to remember the images from the night before. All she could remember was the red-haired woman and people in green masks.

She opened her eyes. Darryl was now standing in front of her. "I have no idea what you're talking about," she said. "Did he bring *what* by last night? You're not making any sense."

"I'm not making any sense? Then what's this?" Darryl shoved the packet in front of Alyssa. She saw a book of sketches sandwiched by two pieces of white posterboard tied together on one side with orange baling twine. She recognized Tug's handwriting.

"I . . . I . . . I've never seen that before," Alyssa started. "I don't know how it got here. Maybe someone brought it."

But Darryl wasn't listening. He was pulling the sketches out of the book and tossing them, one by one, on Alyssa's bed, each toss accompanied by a sarcastic description.

"Ah, the beautiful barn. The quaint manure spreader. The lovely fields."

"Darryl, stop it now," Alyssa said. She reached for the packet, but he pulled it away.

He continued his diatribe, blanketing Alyssa with Tug's drawings. "Oh, your favorite horse in the morning sun. The herb garden. The hill out back. Roz's tea room. The babbling creek. What's he been doing, living at the farm?"

Alyssa tried to sit up and gather the drawings in a pile, but she was too tired. She slumped back against the pillows. "He's just an artist looking for things to draw, that's all. Just stop it, okay?"

Suddenly Darryl did stop. He held up one of the sketches, then turned it around so Alyssa could see. It was her own portrait. In it, a slight smile teased the corners of her mouth, her expression lay somewhere between welcoming and hopeful. She seemed vulnerable, wanting. It was an expression Darryl had never seen before on his wife's face.

"It's just a drawing," Alyssa said.

"Right, 'just a drawing.' Well, I'll tell you what, I've had it with the drawings. I've had it with Limespring."

"Darryl, I can't fight about this now."

"Fine," he said, slamming his hand against the door as he left.

CHAPTER 58

"Does Margaux have any idea why you left New York?" Abbi asked Tug.

They were sitting at a table in the coffee shop. He'd been telling her about the "Clean Up Your Room" debacle and the Margaux situation.

"Doubt it," Tug said, sipping some lukewarm coffee. "Joel's the only one who knows, and he's probably avoiding her."

"That's not so easy with Margaux. She's not the kind of person who likes—" She stopped in midsentence and stared over Tug's shoulder.

"Who likes what? Abbi?" Tug waved his hand in front of her face. "Hey. You still there?"

Abbi lowered her eyes and her voice. "Uh-oh," she said.

Before Tug could ask what she meant, Darryl was standing by the table.

He hunched down between them, propping himself on the brown Formica with his fists. The knuckles on his hands were white. The zipper of his jacket clinked against the salt shaker. His face, just a couple feet away, looked as big as a billboard to Tug.

"Stay away from my wife," he said, squeezing the words through clenched jaws. His voice had a strangled, high-pitched tone. "Do you understand what that means or do I need to draw you a picture?"

The blood rushed to Tug's face. He didn't know what to say. "Who are you?" he finally blurted out, though he knew exactly who it was. "What are you talking about?"

"I'll tell you who I am," Darryl said, louder. People at nearby tables looked over at them. "I'm Alyssa Brown's husband. You do remember Alyssa, don't you? The woman you've been drawing, or should I use another word besides 'drawing'?"

Darryl moved his face closer to Tug's. "And I'll tell you what I'm talking about. I'm talking about wanting to beat your fucking head in."

Tug glanced down for a second, forcing himself to stay expressionless. "It's Darryl, right?" he said, pretending he hadn't heard the man's last words. "I know you're upset about the accident and all, but you're making a mistake. I'm just one of the Limespring fellows, that's all. Sure I've been drawing your farm and I've drawn Alyssa. But I've been drawing a lot of things. That's why I'm at Limespring—to practice drawing. That's all there is to it. Really." Tug made a half-shrug, putting his palms up, as if to show he was unarmed.

Darryl continued to glare at Tug. Then he straightened up; his fists no longer rested on the tabletop. "Well, practice on something else and stay the hell away from my farm."

He turned and started to walk away, but stopped. "You know, she'll never leave me for you, or anyone else," he said. "She'll never leave the farm. As far as she's concerned our daughter's still there."

"Roz?" said Tug, completely confused. "I thought Roz was in Chicago this summer."

A mean smile turned the corners of Darryl's mouth. "You mean she hasn't told you about Julie? Well maybe I was wrong. Maybe you *are* just another pretentious Limespring asshole."

CHAPTER 59

Julie? Who the hell was Julie? Tug rushed up to Alyssa's room, Darryl's words looping through his mind like a stuck song. The door to room 813 was closed. He knocked softly. When there was no answer, he opened it and peered in.

He wasn't prepared for what he saw. Alyssa looked small and pale, swallowed up by the hospital bed's mechanical arms and nearby gadgetry. Her head was to the side, her eyes were closed; tubes ran in and out of her. Her arms lay loosely on top of a thin blanket; one rested on a pile of his drawings.

He remembered his father lying in a hospital bed just a year ago. He'd had to hold himself back from running up, pulling out all the tubes, and cradling his father in his arms. He felt the same way now. But, as he had done with his father, he just walked to the chair by the bed and sat down. For a while he watched her breathe and listened to the rhythmic beeping of the monitors. Eventually he put his hand lightly on top of hers.

Her eyelids fluttered and then opened halfway. "Dar—" she started, then she opened her eyes fully and saw Tug. Still fogged by sleep and painkillers, she tried to make sense of the man sitting by her bed.

"Alyssa, are you okay? I was so worried about you." Tug leaned close and tried to kiss her but she turned her head away and pulled her hand back.

"Don't," she said. "The nurses will see."

"So?" The sting of her rejection caught him off guard and the word came out louder than he'd intended.

"Tug, I'm Mrs. Brown here, and Darryl's around someplace." She pressed a button on the bed, raising the back until she was in a half-sitting position.

"Not anymore," Tug said. "He left, after he threatened to punch my fucking head in. "

"Oh God," she groaned. "How . . . I mean, where? Where were you?"

"In the coffee shop, with Abbi. Did he see my drawings? Is that what set him off?"

Alyssa rolled her head slowly back and forth, her hands cradling her face. "Oh no," she kept saying.

"Damn, I should never have given those drawings to Abbi. But she said you could use the cheering up." It seemed to Tug that everything he'd done in the hospital had been wrong.

Alyssa let her hands fall to the bed. "Ha, that's a good one. Darryl went ballistic when he saw them."

"I'm sorry," Tug said again. "I'm sorry about what happened to you and I'm sorry how we left things. I was a jerk."

She ignored his apology. It didn't matter now. It seemed like another lifetime ago when Tug had peeled out of her driveway and her biggest worry was what he was doing in New York with the gorgeous woman she'd seen on a Web site.

"Tug, what did Darryl say to you?"

"He accused me of—well, you can imagine what. I told him I was just an artist looking for things to draw, and that was all there was to it. At first he wasn't buying any of it. He just kept getting madder and madder. I really thought he was going to punch me. Then he said something strange. He told me you'd never leave him or the farm because of Julie. Alyssa, who's Julie?"

Alyssa didn't respond.

Tug took her hand again and held it tightly when she tried to pull away. "Alyssa, who's Julie?"

She yanked against his grip. "I thought I asked you not to do that here."

"Alyssa, I asked you who Julie is."

"And I asked you not to hold my hand," Alyssa snapped back. "Just leave me alone. I'm tired."

"I'm not going anywhere until you tell me who Julie is."

Alyssa closed her eyes. Tug was horrified to see tears falling down her cheeks. He let go of her, realizing how bullying he'd been. This was not at all how he'd imagined their reunion.

"I'm sorry," he said, for the third time that night. "You don't need this from me. Go to sleep. Just rest, okay?"

He pulled the blanket up around her and took the pile of drawings from under her hand. "Go to sleep," he said. He kissed her salty cheek and slumped back in the chair.

Once again, the only sounds were of Alyssa's shallow breaths and the vigilant beeping of the monitor. He thought she'd fallen back to sleep.

"Julie is my other daughter." Alyssa's eyes were still closed when she said it, and her voice was so quiet that at first Tug wasn't sure if she'd spoken or he'd imagined it.

"Juliette Mercer Brown. She died eleven years ago."

CHAPTER 60

Alyssa felt a profound sense of relief, and release, when she spoke Julie's name out loud. It had been a long time since she'd said it to anyone but herself. She'd stopped going to grief support meetings a couple of years after her death. Friends, acquaintances, and co-workers who knew about it carefully avoided the subject. Darryl had told her early on that he didn't want to talk about it anymore; that was his way of dealing with the grief. "She's gone," he'd said. "There's nothing we can do about it. It just makes us feel worse when we talk about her." And at Limespring, no one even knew Alyssa Brown once had two children.

"She was five when she died," Alyssa said. "A car accident. She'd gone to the movies with her best friend, Megan." Her breath began coming in short bursts; her cheeks were wet again with tears.

Tug went to the bed and put his arms around her. He could feel her chest heaving against his.

"*Beauty and the Beast,*" she said between sobs.

It was difficult to understand everything, but Tug got the gist of it. Icy roads; Megan's mother was driving; a truck lost control and crossed lanes; Megan was in the hospital for two weeks; her mother was burned by the air bag; Julie died at the scene.

"And I wasn't even there," Alyssa cried.

Tug held her as tightly as he could without dislodging the

tubes in her arm. Her skin felt hot to his touch. They sat there, rocking slightly, with Tug whispering, "I'm so sorry; so, so sorry." After a while her chest stopped heaving; her breathing became more regular. Tug drew back a little and wiped her face with his fingers.

"I love you," he said.

She stiffened and abruptly pulled away after glancing at the door. "Tug, if someone comes in and finds us. I . . . I can't deal with anything more today, just please sit over there, okay?"

Tug shrugged and moved to the chair.

Alyssa saw the hurt on his face and she felt a catch in her chest. He'd just said he loved her. A week ago, she'd been telling him the same thing.

"I'm sorry," she started. "I didn't tell you about Julie because . . ."

She stopped and looked over at the window. She could see the other wing, the lights in the other rooms. "Because . . . I don't know, because we stopped talking about her. Darryl wouldn't and after a while I couldn't. It just hurt too much. I almost told you that day you saw me on top of the hill. I said I was looking for a place to set off fireworks. I lied."

"I know," Tug said.

"I knew you knew," she said, her eyes still turned to the window. "But I couldn't make the words come out. I wanted to, but I couldn't."

They sat there silently for a few moments. Then Alyssa turned back to Tug. "I named the two hills at the farm the first day I saw the place. Mount Roz and Mount Julie. I was on Mount Julie when you saw me."

"Is that where she's buried?"

Alyssa nodded. She was crying again. It was difficult for her to get the words out. "Her ashes," was all she could say.

She wiped her fingers across her cheeks. Tug started to get up, to be next to her, but she held up her hand to stop him.

"Please," she said and shook her head. Then she took a few deep breaths and started talking again. "I couldn't do it. Darryl had to. I had the cardboard box in my hand and it was so small. Half the size of a shoebox. And so light. It didn't seem fair. I wanted her to have more weight. I wanted the box to be so heavy I could barely pick it up. But I could hardly feel it. I couldn't let her go. Darryl took the box from me. He took off the lid."

Tug was silent for a while. Any response seemed inconsequential after what he'd just heard. Finally, he said, "I wish you'd told me sooner."

"It wouldn't have changed anything," she said flatly. "Darryl's right, I'll never leave the farm. It's the only place I'm still Julie's mother."

So it had come down to the farm again. And Tug finally knew the reason why.

"Alyssa," he said, "you can't change what happened. I wish to hell you could. I wish to hell I could. I know what it's like to lose someone. But Julie's not on top of that hill, any more than my father's in his grave. He's here." He took her hand and put it on his chest. "He's inside me."

"Stop it!" she said, her voice rising, raspy and strained. "I don't want to hear it. It's different. You can't understand. You could never understand. You've never had a child."

The words hit Tug hard, and before he could stop himself, he struck back. "I understand plenty. I understand that you've turned that farm into some kind of ghoulish shrine to your dead daughter. Well let me tell you something, it's not going to keep Julie alive or bring her back. That farm is your prison, Alyssa, and you've got to let it go. Otherwise you're going to wake up one day, alone with your memories, trapped in a house that leaks every time it rains. You're not afraid of losing Julie, you're just afraid of moving on."

He put his hands up to his face. "Jesus Christ, Alyssa, I shouldn't have said that. I just don't want to lose you. I love you."

"Well, I don't love you." She turned away and knocked the call button from the arm of the bed. Tug started to pick it up, but she stopped him.

"Just get out," she said. "I can manage on my own. I always have."

CHAPTER 61

A storm front was expected to blow in later, but it was mostly sunny when Alyssa drove down Limespring Hollow Road. The air was lighter and crisper than the last time she'd been in Markham.

So much had changed in six weeks, including the landscape. As much as she loved the early fall colors—the slight blush on the dogwoods, the reddening edges of the maples, and the deep gold of the autumn wildflowers—they always made her sad. It meant winter was coming.

She drove straight to the barn. Though Betsy had assured her that Roy and Theo were fine, she wanted to see for herself. Besides, she missed them. Missed their smell, missed the way Theo nudged her pockets looking for carrots, missed Roy's kind eye. Tug once told her that Roy would have been a priest—"the good kind"—had he been human, while Theo would have been a cad. "I know these things," he'd said.

She walked through the pasture toward the distant red and brown dots by the fence. Roy and Theo were as far away as they could get and still be on her property. She put her fingers in her mouth and whistled. Theo lifted his head. She whistled again. They came cantering to her and she pulled some carrots out of a coat pocket. Betsy was right, they were fine. No cuts or scrapes, just pig fat from all that grass and standing idle.

She stood there for a long time, running her hands down their necks and rubbing their faces, breathing in their horsy smell. She forced herself not to think about the summer. Instead she thought about Roz.

She pictured her in her dorm room, meeting her roommate for the first time. Prentice Walters was a Valkyrie from a prep school in Baltimore. It wasn't a match she would have made for her daughter, but sometimes opposites attract. When she first met Darryl twenty years ago, their differences had drawn them to each other and, for a while, kept them together. Roz didn't need a long-term relationship with Prentice, just a year.

She and Darryl were getting counseling. She'd agreed to it the day after he stormed out of her hospital room. Neither had said the name "Tug" again, but he was always there, always the subtext of Darryl's discontent. Even in the sessions, they skirted the issue of what had happened that summer.

"What's past is past," Judith, the counselor, would say. She was a gray-haired woman who wore hand-painted glasses. "Let's figure out a way to move forward."

They'd tried, but their differences were no longer attractive. Darryl complained that Alyssa was overly dramatic; twenty years ago he'd called it "delightful exuberance." Alyssa accused Darryl of being emotionless and judgmental; twenty years ago she'd found his steadiness and discerning eye reassuring.

Judith said they needed to drop the labels. Each had to relearn to appreciate the other. She'd even given them exercises to do at home: Write ten things you like about your mate. Both she and Darryl made excuses the next week that they'd been too busy to complete the assignment. So Judith gave them in-session exercises. "Sometimes it helps to just sit and look at the other person, the way you did when you were first in love."

They sat and looked at each other, Alyssa trying not to think about Tug. She had no idea what was on Darryl's mind, but she was fairly certain it wasn't her.

Still Judith was hopeful. "It took a long time for things to unravel, it'll take some time to reweave it back together."

Darryl hadn't wanted her to go to the farm. He said she wasn't ready for the drive. "Liss," he'd said that morning, "you can barely walk around the block without getting tired."

"I have to go. The blacksmith's coming and I can't find anyone to hold the horses." Then she added, halfheartedly, "Come with me. The leaves are starting to turn. It'll be a beautiful drive."

Darryl shook his head and said something about a tennis lesson. "Just call as soon as you get in, okay?"

She started back to the barn, holding carrots to Roy and Theo so they'd follow her. She wanted them in stalls when the blacksmith came at three. Darryl had been right about her stamina. Walking through the pasture, she had to stop three times to catch her breath.

On the last stop, she stood and surveyed the farm. Odie Watkins's cows had kept the grass down in the front pasture and his son had just mowed the lawn; the centaur whirligig kicked out in the light breeze and a tangle of hoses still lay by the back door waiting to be straightened out.

The familiarity was disconcerting. It seemed odd that the farm appeared just as it had the morning she'd ridden up Mount Buck with Abbi, Marius, and Nattie. She wanted there to be a difference, something to mark the change in her life.

She led the horses to their stalls. Roy and Theo were the only ones left. Betsy had picked up the rest of the herd after the accident and taken them to their adoptive families.

Alyssa gave each horse some hay and filled their water buckets. The mundane regularity of this chore tricked her—for a split second it was summer and she expected to see Tug's folding chair in the aisle.

Of course it wasn't there, but his presence was palpable. When she closed the door to the tack room, she saw the photo, the faded ribbon, and the hanging bridles that he'd drawn his first week at the farm. When she walked under the loft, she was up there again, wedged between hay bales, spying on him. When she walked past the tractor, the manure spreader, the piles of sawdust, she saw him sitting there, drawing.

But she'd made her decision and sealed it with: "Well, I don't love you. Just get out." During the next few days in the hospital she wondered if he'd come back. When he didn't, she told herself she was grateful.

Alyssa left the horses to their eating and walked down to the house, deliberately avoiding the herb garden. She wasn't ready for memories of basil and tomatoes. Inside, she phoned Darryl and left a message. "It's me, I'm here. Everything's fine. I'll be back tomorrow afternoon in time for the barbecue with the Fullers."

The doctors had told her it would take months to fully recover. They urged her not to push herself and to nap when she got tired. She was beat from the walk in the pasture, so she lay down on the red sofa and quickly fell asleep.

A knock at the door woke her up. It was Reedy Collins, the blacksmith. She walked him to the barn and held Roy, then Theo, as he trimmed their feet, hammered on new shoes, and filled her in on Fauquier County gossip. The tango teacher who'd worn the red, white, and blue bikini to Alyssa's July Fourth party was sleeping with the house painter; the dressage lady in Hume liked girls; the gazillionaire banker who'd been building the mansion across Route 688 was leaving his wife and selling the property. Some things never changed.

The storm front rolled in just as Reedy drove off. By five, there were rumblings and lightning flashes on the horizon. Alyssa was cleaning out the refrigerator when the rain came. She got out the usual array of pots and placed them under the known leaks, hoping there wouldn't be any surprises.

She was tired again. So she walked upstairs to the bedroom, opened the French doors, and lay down. The comforting sound of rain drummed on the tin roof. She began to drift off.

Zygomaticus.

She and Tug were in bed together. Her arms were flung back on the pillow. He was giving her an anatomy lesson, telling her about Mr. Reifman. The rain drummed harder; they made love.

She slept fitfully for a couple of hours; she'd wake, feeling woozy, fall back asleep, then wake again. She wished the rain would stop. It was impossible to escape her memories with the soundtrack of summer playing overhead and the thick summer smell of fresh-cut grass riding in with the storm. She got up, closed the doors to the balcony, and lay back down. The rain pounded harder against the roof. She covered her head with a pillow to block out the sound.

In the breezeless cell of her room, in the muffled darkness under the pillow, she thought about what Tug had said to her in the hospital. He'd called the farm her prison. "You're going to wake up one day, alone with your memories, trapped in a house that leaks every time it rains." She could picture the anger in his face when he'd said it. She remembered the anger in her when she'd heard it.

He could never understand.

She threw the pillow off her head and walked over to the balcony. The hard rain had become a drizzle. She opened the doors. Off in the darkness were the faint outlines of the two hills she'd named twelve years ago. Tug was wrong. The farm was not her prison, it was the place that still connected her to Julie.

She went downstairs, put on a raincoat, and went outside. The storm was moving on. Through breaks in the clouds, Alyssa could see pieces of the sharp night sky. She walked through the pasture by the side of the house, past the little pond, and up Julie's hill. She had to stop several times to catch her breath. By the time she got to the top, she was so lightheaded she had to sit on the wet ground.

Next to her, half buried, was a small green-glazed flower vase. Julie's kindergarten class had made it in her memory. Alyssa kept it filled in the summer, usually with black-eyed Susans. The day Tug had seen her up there, she'd been telling Julie about the Limespring artist who was spending every day drawing the farm.

She often talked to Julie up there. Mostly about family news: how Roz was doing in school or a trip Darryl had made. She wanted to talk to her now, but what was her news? That she was miserable? That she couldn't stop thinking about that artist?

"I miss you, sweetheart," she said out loud to the darkness.

There was no reply. There never had been. But for the first

time, she felt no closer to her daughter on the top of that hill than if she were in the supermarket picking apples.

She stood up and steadied herself.

"I'm Julie's mother!" she yelled.

Who was she trying to convince? She was the one who had relegated Julie's memory to the farm. She looked down at the little vase at her feet. The words echoed inside her: "I'm Julie's mother."

Alyssa said it again, this time quietly. She *was* Julie's mother and always would be, regardless of where she stood. She'd gotten lost in the dream of Finally Farm and of being near Julie. But that wasn't the only tether holding her. She knew she'd stayed married to Darryl because it was safe, not just because he held title to the farm.

It scared her to love Roz and Julie as much as she did. That exquisite vulnerability was the double-edged sword of love. She'd barely made it through Julie's death. If something happened to Roz, she knew that would be the end of her. She wouldn't allow herself to be any more vulnerable than she already was. But then Tug had come along.

She looked over to the farm. The windows made a bright pattern of squares in the night. Tug had been right. It was her prison.

She pressed a button on her watch. The dial glowed for a few seconds. It was 8:30. It was time to leave.

It was time to leave.

CHAPTER 62

Alyssa walked in just before ten that evening and dropped her umbrella into the ceramic stand by the front door. The stand was shaped like an elephant's foot. It was one of the few touches of whimsy in the Browns' small brick colonial. "Home simple, farm extravagant," had been Darryl's motto, and Alyssa had agreed.

"Hey, is that you?" Darryl's voice and TV sounds bounced out from the den.

"Yes," she answered back.

She found him lying on the couch watching a rerun of *Law and Order*. He hit the remote's mute button when she entered the room.

"I thought you were staying at the farm. What happened? You okay?"

"No."

He sat up with a grimace. "Oh, man, I knew you were going to overdo it. You always do. Should I call the doctor?"

"No, it's not that. I feel fine, just tired."

"So what's wrong?"

She had no idea how to answer. On the drive back from Markham, her mind had spun crazily. How were they going to tell Roz? How were they going to tell their friends? Where was she going to live? How would she move? How would they divide up twenty years of life? A hundred scenarios and questions. But she had never thought about how she was going to tell Darryl.

She looked at her husband, wondering how to begin. Already he seemed different, older, as if her decision had somehow aged him.

"Did something happen at the farm?" he asked.

"Yes." She said it hesitantly, but it was the right question. All she needed was to answer it honestly and twenty years were done.

"What?"

"It's over, Darryl. I'm sorry." And she was. Sorry for not trying harder, for not being more honest, for not honoring Julie's death with a better life. And, most of all, sorry for not having had the courage to leave sooner.

"What's over?" he said, but he looked away when he said it. And she knew that he knew.

"Us. We're over. The marriage counseling is a joke. You know it, I know it. There's nothing left between us, except your hold on the farm. And that's just not enough anymore. I got Julie's death and the farm all tangled up. I should have cut free a long time ago. She's dead. There's nothing I can do to change that. You can have the farm. I don't care anymore. It's over. It's just over."

Darryl stood up from the couch. "You're leaving me?" It was more an accusation than a question.

"We don't even like each other anymore, Darryl."

"Oh, I get it. Your boyfriend called you at the farm, didn't he?"

Alyssa shook her head. "It's never been about Tug, it's always been about us. Don't you see? Even before Julie died, there wasn't enough. And then when she died . . . Yeah, I fell apart. I wanted to die and all you could do was tell me my big emotions scared you. Well, they scared me, too. Darryl, there's no us anymore. There hasn't been for years."

He walked toward her. The color had drained from his face, his muscles were coiled. Alyssa thought he might strike her. But he stopped a few feet away and she saw the fight leave his body. His shoulders slumped, his hands unfurled. He stood that way for a while.

"I know," he finally said.

"I'm so, so sorry," said Alyssa, fighting back tears.

Darryl reached out to hug her, twenty years of habit, but Alyssa pulled back slightly, and instead he caught one of her hands and held it as she cried.

CHAPTER 63

There are four things Alyssa Brown knows for sure:

She'd kill to protect her daughter, Roz. On the eighth day God created Shakespeare. No matter how little she ate, she'd never get below 137 pounds. And she could love something but let it go.

She didn't really know the last one until an October morning when she stood at the top of the gravel driveway that led to the little yellow farmhouse in the distance. It was the first time she'd been back to Finally Farm since the rainy night she'd stuffed a pillow over her head. It would be the last time.

B.J. Goode, the same tweeded real estate agent who'd shown them the property twelve years before, would be putting up a for sale sign in a few hours. Alyssa had driven out not just to make her farewells but to comply with B.J.'s request to "thin the place out."

"It'll show better if it's just a little less cluttered," she'd told Alyssa on the phone. Darryl hadn't had the guts to ask her to clear out her stuff, so he'd asked B.J. to do it.

"You know, just tidy it up a little. I'd start with that large gorilla thing in the living room and then the hanging swords. I also think the lines of the house would show better if you took out the . . ."

The list went on. After a while, Alyssa stopped listening. She knew what to take. Anything that made the house hers. If she could have, she'd have piled the mosaic floors in the back of her truck next to Mr. Monkeysocks. She'd store the costumes and set leftovers at Emerson. The rest she'd put in her new apartment.

She stood for a while, remembering. One evening, during their second summer at the farm, she, Darryl, Roz, and Julie had invented a game that was half baseball, half dress-up. If you hit the ball you had to put on a mask or a funny hat before you ran to first base. The masks and hats were too big for the girls, flopping over their faces. They ran around trying to keep them on, shrieking with laughter. The four of them played until it was so dark nobody could see the bases anymore.

Costume-ball. Alyssa hadn't thought about it in years.

She blew out a deep breath and climbed into her truck. She'd been dreading this day since she'd told Darryl she was leaving and he could have the farm. But she knew she could get through this; she'd been through worse.

As she approached the farmhouse she saw a car parked in the drive. She banged her hand against the steering wheel. "God damn it," she said. She'd argued with B.J. about their timing. B.J. had wanted to get there early to prepare for the next day's open house. Alyssa wanted to spend her last hours there alone. B.J. had reluctantly agreed—at least that's what Alyssa had thought.

"God damn it," she said again. She slowed down and stopped by a gate in the fence. Later there would be time for a confrontation; first, she had to say good-bye to someone.

She got out and began walking up the slope of Mount Julie. It was clear and mild, an Indian summer morning. The autumn reds and golds brightly confettied the surrounding landscape.

At the summit, she knelt down by the little vase half buried there. She jostled it back and forth until it broke free. She filled it with a handful of soil and put it in her jacket pocket. Then she laid a small bouquet of black-eyed Susans over the tiny hole that remained.

The day they'd scattered her ashes had been clear, too, but bitterly cold. The three of them had bundled up and walked to the top of Julie's hill for the little ceremony. They took turns telling Julie stories. Alyssa told about the time Julie had said, "Hi, clown!" to the bank teller who was wearing too much makeup; Roz told one about Julie thinking she'd seen Tinkerbell; Darryl talked about watching her be born.

Alyssa knelt on Mount Julie for a long time, looking out over the countryside, letting wave after wave of memory and emotion wash over her. Then she stood. "It's time for me to leave this place, my sweet, sweet baby," she said aloud, and, without looking back, walked down to the car.

In a minute, she was roaring up to the house in a cloud of dust and gravel, ready for a fight. But the car wasn't B.J.'s black Hummer. It was a black Chrysler station wagon.

Tug's station wagon.

How had he known she'd be there that day? She hadn't talked to him since that evening at the hospital. She purposefully didn't tell Abbi about her breakup with Darryl, because she knew Abbi would tell Tug instantly.

She hadn't been lying when she told her husband that their problems had nothing to do with the artist at Limespring. What happened between her and Tug this summer was like a window in an advent calendar—one perfect, contained moment.

But that was it. There were too many differences between them. It was fantasy to think they could live happily ever after. Living in a dream world had already cost her too many years of her life.

But now he was here.

"Tug?" she called out. No answer. She said it louder: "Tuuug!" Nothing but the usual farm sounds answered back.

As she approached the front door, she saw a piece of paper taped to the porch. Drawn in charcoal pencil, in Tug's unmistakable hand, was the message: "Hi, Cowgirl. Go upstairs. There's something for you in the bedroom." It was signed, "Sultan of Sketches."

The door was open, which wasn't surprising. She always kept an extra house key under the metal pig sculpture on the front porch.

"Tug," she called out again as she walked up the stairs. Still no answer.

The bedroom was nearly stripped. The bedstand was gone, the

walls were bare, the old shoe-drying rack where she used to store her clothes was already in her apartment. The bed was covered by a white sheet. In the middle of it was a drawing and a big book with a blue cover.

She picked up the book. *Gray's Anatomy*. The word "clavicles" came to mind and the image of Tug running his fingers down her torso. At first she didn't understand what the drawing was about. She tilted it up, down, and sideways before she realized it was a piece of a larger picture.

She turned it over. On the back was a yellow sticky with a note that read: "To see the next part, go to the garden." It was signed, "S of S."

The garden was a jungle of weeds, desiccated tomato vines, and basil plants with long, frizzy shoots covered in tiny blue flowers. On one of the raised beds sat a ripening pumpkin the size of a soccer ball. On top of it was one seed packet for Genoa basil and another for Brandywine tomatoes, the heirloom variety they'd eaten at the Rail Stop restaurant. There was also a second drawing. It was another part of the picture, and when she put the two pieces side by side, it looked like a country scene. There was a field and part of a barn.

On the back of it was another message: "Go to the barn."

Outside the tack room, now empty of horse gear and ribbons, stood a folding chair with a toy red barn sitting on its seat. Underneath the plastic barn was a third piece of the drawing; on the back, another yellow sticky.

"Belushi bees and raspberries. Meet me there."

Alyssa left the barn and started to climb the back pasture. A couple of hundred yards ahead, next to the iron gate, stood Tug.

Still weak from the accident, Alyssa was breathing hard as she approached the fenceline.

"How'd you know I was going to be here today?" she called out.

"Abbi heard all about the sale from Jackie. I think Jackie knows your real estate agent. And Abbi called me."

"No one at Limespring can keep their mouths shut," Alyssa said.

"Aren't you glad they can't?"

Alyssa thought of a couple of snappy answers. But the truth was in a single word. "Yes."

"Here, this is for you." Tug held out a jar. "I couldn't find golden raspberry jam, only regular raspberry. You'll have to use your imagination."

She took the little dimpled jar.

"I wanted you to have parts of the farm you could take with you," Tug said. "I knew this would be a hard day for you and I didn't want you to have to go through it alone."

They looked out over the fields Alyssa had first fallen in love with twelve years before.

"It sure is beautiful, isn't it?" she said.

"That it is." He paused. "Do you want to see the last part of the drawing?"

She nodded.

"Put the other pieces on the grass," he said.

She knelt down and laid out the three quarters. There were fields, three-board fencing, and the back half of a barn bleeding off the left side of the page. He placed the final piece of the puzzle in the empty space on the upper right and completed the drawing. On it was a small house that she didn't recognize. It had a wraparound porch with a swing hanging from the rafters. She leaned over and examined it.

"That's Mr. Monkeysocks in the swing."

"It is," Tug said. He knelt down next to her and pointed. "Look at the front door."

Alyssa did. "It's Roz's hammer knocker."

There were other pieces of Finally Farm in the drawing. Inside the front window, Alyssa could see the tips of hanging swords. Next to the front door was the centaur whirligig. At a corner of the final piece was Marius's installation, the one that looked like a cement mixer.

"As much as I like Marius, I can't stand his art," Tug said. "That's why I put it way up there."

A breeze began to rustle the drawings; Tug anchored each piece with a rock. "We could have a place like this if we tried. Or something close to it."

Alyssa looked down the slope at the lost Finally Farm.

"I love you, Alyssa. I want us to be together. I want all your crazy things mingling with all my crazy things. I know it won't be easy. You've got your life, I've got mine. But nothing's insurmountable. I've already called a few galleries in Washington and they're interested. I'm not sure what I'll be showing them, but it's a start, isn't it?"

Alyssa turned back. "I guess this is where the music swells, I run into your arms, and we get a standing ovation?"

"Hopefully."

She knelt down and traced her fingers along the lines of the drawing. "Tug, I don't know if that's our ending. Everything's changed. I'm leaving Emerson at the end of this year, Roz's in college, I'm about to be divorced, you love the city, I love the country—"

"Alyssa, shut up," Tug said, cutting her off. "I don't care about any of that. All I want to know is this: Do you love me?"

She didn't answer directly. Instead, she moved her fingers to the two small figures near a fence in the corner of the drawing. "What are these?"

"Horses. Roy and Theo."

Alyssa looked at the drawing. She touched the images of Roy and Theo again then turned to him.

"You're going to need more horse lessons." She was smiling. "They still look like dogs."